Disclaimer & Copyright

Bag of Bones Press

STEP INTO THE LIGHT

An anthology of daylight horror

By various contributors

A collection of original, bone-chilling, sunshine-drenched tales from some of planet Earth's best new dark fiction writers.

Content Warnings:

This book is recommended for adults only.

Themes of murder, violence, assault, death, infant death, sexual assault, incest, gore, blasphemy, mutilation, and abuse may be dotted throughout. Please be aware, this book may shock.

British and American spellings are found within this book.

About the Editor:

SJ Townend lives in Bristol, UK with her family. She has had several pieces of horror and speculative fiction published through a variety of presses. Her first horror collection, SICK GIRL SCREAMS, is set to be published this year (Brigids Gate Press), along with her debut contemporary romance novel, PICK-UP LINES (Champagne Book Group Press). When not reading, writing, or editing, you might find her screaming at the moon or following the cat around the house.

Find her on Twitter: @SJTownend

About the Cover Artist:

David Bowman lives in Indiana. A software developer and illustrator, his art has been published by Undertow Press, Dread Stone Press, Gibbon Moon Books, and most recently, Grimscribe Press. He is currently working on original illustrations for a new anthology and a video game. You can see more of his work on Twitter as @dlbowman76 or Mastodon as @dlbowman76@mastodon.art.

We challenged our contributors to write a piece of horror set in daylight, and wow, for a sunshine-themed affair, they sure came up with some hideously dark material! We've collated a selection of our favourites here, in this anthology, for your entertainment. Read with caution—contents may unsettle—sleeping with the lights on won't help you this time.

If you enjoy writing, please check out our website for our current submission calls:
www.bagofbonespress.com/submission-calls

This book is dedicated to everyone who submitted a story for this project Bag of Bones Press project.

~TABLE OF CONTENTS~

The Second Sun

Maxwell Marais

When I first saw the city, I was dying.

And how radiant— resplendent, how sun-drenched and beautiful it was. Through the morphine haze and the dull buzz where I imagine there should have been searing pain, I saw the city. I looked upon its towering spires and its gossamer bridges and the golden-robed denizens that walked its shining avenues and I thought—hoped—that this was heaven, and I was dead.

When I was thrust back into the living world, in hospital and clinging to life seemingly against my own will, when the city was ripped from my outstretched fingers, I was crushed. When I saw what had become of *myself* while my mind had walked its streets, I was devastated further still.

I would never be the man I was before the war. The man who was brought into the hospital had become a thing, a near-corpse, an *it* with face torn away and torso lacerated by shrapnel shards. There were no mirrors in the convalescent ward—they did not *allow* mirrors—but I knew from the nurses' expressions when they looked at me that the damage, even with the doctors' efforts, had been irreparable.

In my time at the ward I chased the city through my dreams, scrambling for an escape from a world I was not yet ready to face. But it did not compare to when I had first seen it. I stood only on its edges, its outskirts, and never for long enough to walk further, to feel the warmth of its sun on my skin. I was an outsider, now, though I could not understand why.

I was an outsider everywhere.

When they allowed me outside the hospital grounds for the first time I was a ghost. Eyes turned quickly away from me, no one spoke. In the park there were benches painted blue, to let the ordinary passerby know that those who sat there might be 'distressing' to look at. Might be a jarring reminder of what their brothers and fathers and sons were facing out on the front.

Might look like me.

When I was sufficiently healed they sent me to London, The 3rd London General Hospital, where a man was making painted tin masks to imitate the proper faces of soldiers disfigured in the war. It took time; it was a craft in itself, I suppose, all that plaster-casting and paint-blending, all that poring over the countless photographs of men Before. Before France, before their injuries, as far before as one could manage in order to find a version of oneself that still has light in its eyes.

When it was done… it almost worked. It was, if nothing else, *close* to a real face. When I received my own finished mask I stared at it a long while before putting it on, stared into the missing pieces of my old self traced in fine metal detail. As I slid its smooth form onto my skin, I felt, just for a moment—

The sun. The warmth of the sun that shines above the city.

*

After returning to a life outside of wards and hospitals, my hiding behind paint and metal did not grant me solace for long. It could never be real enough to stand up to flesh and bone, and if I was not a ghost now I was certain not a *human* either. I could not smile, I could not speak without a lisping and metallic lilt, and only one of my eyes was still capable of crying. What an excess, what a well of indescribable emotions I had in those times, and no means to express them.

Everyday life was, if no longer a hell, something close to it. A gradual rot would be a more apt description, I suppose. I was the apples and oranges arranged on a tablecloth somewhere in a still life artist's studio, moldering—the only problem was that the artist had never made themselves seen. Maybe they were laughing.

In my dreams I walked the city and in my waking hours I desperately grasped for anything within my means to make myself dream. The opium den quickly became a second home to me. I understood my waking life would deteriorate—I knew that from the start. But I had nothing, no reason in all my mind, to preserve it.

That reason only came when I delved deep enough into the city to be *seen* by it.

*

All the denizens of the city wore masks. At first this was a sort of odd comfort, but eventually I (as waking people did when looking at *me*, I'd imagine) began to wonder what exactly was underneath them. There were no shadows in the city—just one perpetual, feverish noon—which meant there was no place to hide… except for behind the masks.

In a dream, small details, little inconsistencies, often pass us by without our second thought. It was because of this that it did not strike me as strange for so long that the masks had no eye holes.

At the center of the city was a palace. A massive, resplendent construction that glowed a searing and golden yellow beneath the sun, rippled like the air above a hot sidewalk. Staring at it long enough traced its afterimage in painful blues and greens across my eyes.

Since the first time I saw it I have never *stopped* seeing it; I saw it when I blinked, when I closed my eyes, when I slept. There was something about that golden edifice that put me on edge—something about it that gave me the prickling hot-and-cold sensation of coming down with an illness, something that made the roots of my teeth hurt a little more with each step I took towards it.

It was, of course, precisely because of this that I had to get closer. That I had to walk up the steps. That I had to lay my hand on the wavering, humming surface of its gates. Yes, the palace had a *resonance* to it, the resonance of the pulsing heart of the dream, and I needed to touch it.

The palace was empty. It had been set for some kind of ball, or festival, but the drapery and carpets lay in tatters, the tapestries had been torn away (or rather, their *faces*, specifically, had been torn away), the candelabras had left trails of crusty, oozing wax across the entry hall, and the whole place reeked of stale, spilt liquor and rot. Nothing stirred. Thrown about the velvet chaises and cracked upon the floor were a collection of masks, feathered and beaded and sequined and adorned, but the shapes were wrong—here, one with a mouth that traced a long, grinning curve up through the cheekbone, there, a face clearly designed to be worn on the *back* of the head.

And none of them, not one, had eyes.

Through the glassy yellow walls the sun was scalding and headache-bright. I had never felt so utterly alone.

*

It was after I had walked within the empty palace that I began to feel something of the city's presence in the waking world. The shivers along my skin whenever I stepped into the sun (the *wrong* sun, I felt). Traces of yellow in the corners of my vision. The faint aroma of rot. The afterimage of the palace. But most of all was a sensation that took me quite some time to identify, something that itched at the corner of my mind like an insect bite until I named it—

Something *watching me.*

Something breathing its scorching breath down the back of my neck, something waiting, silently, for me to return to its domain.

*

I walked further into the palace.

The hallways stretched into infinity. Rooms repeated. The sun beat down, searing deep and impossible colours into my aching vision. The way out quickly became as lost as whatever it was I'd come here for. Answers? Truth?

Death?

I pressed on. The floors shuddered with a low, slow rhythm, the beating of one leviathan heart, the ticking of the city's inner mechanism. I walked down a hallway and a hallway and a hallway, and when at last I felt near ready to scream from the endlessness of it all I felt my hand hit the smooth glass surface of a door.

The *burning* glass surface of a door. By the time I pulled my hand away I could already smell my own charred flesh in the air.

I had pushed the door ajar.

Radiance—the room was bathed in sunlight so glaring and effulgent I could feel my skin redden to a blistering point just from standing in the doorway. The room beyond had no floor—looking out past the doorway ledge sent a hot, agonizing rush of air into my face, and I knew by the time I could open my eyes again to see what was at the chamber's bottom, it had *seen me*.

What sounded like the grating scrape of several thousand fingernails on glass echoed down the hall as it pulled itself up. At first all I could see was the fabric—coils and coils of threadbare yellow silk, finery left to decay—and what I imagined must have been its limbs, crawling centipede-like up all sides of the chamber, one after the other, pushing out on those curving turret walls so hard they cracked.

Between the fabric tatters those limbs were blistered. Blackened. Emaciated. *Dead.*

The hum and pulse of the palace rose to a shriek as the thing heaved up its lolling, robed head.

I could feel my own skin melting like candlewax.

It wore no mask.

*

The tremors and vomiting did not take long to set in when I started refusing myself my usual poisons. I spent days in a half-dead, nauseous fog. But I could not allow myself to dream again.

I could not go back to the city.

At times I drifted off, lost consciousness, fell into a sort of half-sleep. But I awoke almost immediately afterwards, hands searching the uneven edges of my face for the places where surely it had blackened, blistered, and burned. I had stopped wearing my tin prosthetic. Its one, hollow eye stared at me mockingly from across my darkened room—it was always darkened, now. I kept the curtains pulled at all hours.

Whenever I closed my eyes I saw it. The thing—the heart of the sunlit palace—had no mask, but it had no *face* either. *It was a sun itself.* A second, a twisted mirror of the one above the city, this one sunk deep below, burning itself to its own blazing demise, grasping for the rule of its subjects even as it blinded them, scalded them, *rotted* them.

It had not spoken to me, not aloud, but when it turned to look at me it gave me an *understanding* of something:

The city was dead.

The city has *always* been dead.

The sun above, the spires and bridges, the denizens... lies, ruins, and sightless puppets, one elaborate staged play as the sun below clawed for its final hours of life—hours that would not, could not end, that left it eternally half-alive and half a corpse so long as it kept cycling out those final, radiant moments.

And it would have had no escape from its own self-constructed hell, not ever, *if it weren't for me.*

Maybe not only me. Maybe there have been others. People lost, people missing pieces, missing faces, people desperately searching for an escape, a death without dying.

But when it looked at me I understood that I did not dream in the city as a guest or a wanderer or a traveller.

I dreamt in the city as a *gateway*. My sleeping mind was a conduit, a passageway the city and its burning king could drag itself through. Could make itself real.

Could give itself life.

*

I can only stay awake for so many days. Despite myself, despite all my efforts I am so impossibly tired. I just want to rest. Just for a moment. A deep, dark, dreamless sleep.

But I know it cannot be dreamless.

I know what I will see.

I know what crawls, centipede-like, a few steps closer to the waking world every time I close my eyes.

I see the outline of the city in sun-struck afterimages dancing in the corners of my vision.

I can only stay awake for so many days.

And when, finally, I sink into that long-awaited sleep, I know, I understand—

There will be a dawning, a daybreak—

The sun will rise.

***

Maxwell Marais is an author and illustrator of all things horror. They live in Canada. When they aren't frantically scrawling down weird fiction and horror that crawls out of their brain, they can be found attempting to summon (with limited success) horrible abominations from beyond our world. Their works feature in such publications as The NoSleep Podcast, Thuggish Itch, and Dark Recesses Press.

Proliferate

Bryson Richard

Aurora, a bright girl in a dark time, sat on the porch swing and kicked her bare feet out of boredom.

She was waiting for the screaming to stop.

Her hair – thick, curly, yellow, like she wore a mop as a wig – had streaks of dirt and clumps of grime in it, like a real mop. Big, blue eyes maintained an awareness unseen in most six-year-olds. Her smile, wide and crisp like an apple slice, was newly missing a front tooth, leaving a window in the white wall of her teeth.

She couldn't say how long it had been, only that it was dark when the screaming started, and she and her cousins were roused from their single shared mattress.

It would be dark again soon.

The screaming was expected. Grandma Patty had set Aunt Emily's due-date for mid-October, and here they were a week from Halloween. Grandma was never wrong, even if the liars and sinners said she was. The liars and sinners didn't come around anymore. Neither did Aurora's dad. Grandma had seen to that.

The women were in the master bedroom downstairs, Grandma's bedroom. All the grandchildren had been born in that room.

Grandma took charge of the delivery, and Aunt Kimberly was there to help, as was Aurora's own mother, Jan.

The men were working in the fields.

The children were left to their own devices. Helga, the oldest at eleven, was supposed to be watching them all, but she'd complained of having one of her belly aches again and fell into a sweaty, restless sleep a while ago.

Aurora kicked her feet and considered checking on Helga. She wished the screaming would stop already. She didn't remember it taking so long or being so loud when Aunt Kimberly had little Josh, or when Aunt Emily gave birth to Sven.

She wondered if she'd been so difficult and painful to bring into the world.

Something thumped loudly in the house.

Thinking it finally time, Aurora dropped out of the swing and trotted inside.

Helga was still curled up on the couch, her face a grimace of sustained pain. Some of her other cousins ambled around the stuffy rooms. Nobody was doing much of anything. Sven and Josh both wore bulging, swollen diapers, weighed down by contents that smelled as ripe as the fields after the season's fertilizing.

Aurora stood before the sliding door to the master bedroom, deliberated on whether she should knock or not. Before she could make up her mind, the door slid open abruptly.

Aunt Kimberly, sweating and red faced, barreled out.

Her sons Josh and Greg both shouted, "Mommy, Mommy," and swarmed her legs.

Kimberly brushed them off and continued to the kitchen where she filled a glass with tap water and grabbed a pair of scissors.

Aurora made sure she was out of her aunt's way before she spoke, because sometimes Aunt Kimberly kicked. "What was that noise?"

Kimberly flicked a look down at her. "Nothing. The mirror fell." She turned to re-enter the master bedroom.

Before she could, Aurora spoke urgently, "Helga's sick. She says it's her belly, again."

Kimberly's back was to her, but the little girl saw the woman's shoulders sag and her head shake. She straightened up and called into the master bedroom, "Helga's sick again."

Helga's mother was currently in the throes of childbirth, so when no one replied, Kimberly closed the bedroom door without another word, and the strenuous, grunting sounds within, commenced.

The gathered children dispersed back to their various corners.

Aurora considered changing the channel. Some cartoons would help distract them, she thought. But then she knew how important it was to keep the news on. That was what she'd been taught by Grandma. Grandma insisted the television be on and stay on, so they could watch for lies, but also watch for truths. Sometimes, people like them, people who knew the truth, would signal with hand gestures or certain coded words while on television.

She meandered into the kitchen, her feet black from the scummy linoleum floor. She could go back out on the porch and pretend her dad was coming. She knew he wasn't, hadn't in a long time, but sometimes she liked to excite herself by pretending he was going to arrive any second. She would will him to manifest. She'd hear the sudden roar of him down-shifting, then the black Mustang would charge hard into the driveway. He always arrived in a spray of gravel.

Any second now, the down-shift, the swift turn, and the spray of gravel.

Any second.

She watched the silent county road at the end of the driveway, bordered by crispy yellow corn, so much corn that if you weren't familiar with the region, you would never know there was a road there. So much corn that the house, the barns, the property were like an island in an ocean of agriculture.

She squeezed her eyes shut as the screaming in the house reached a pitch yet unheard, like Aunt Emily was being ripped in half.

Any second now, Dad.

Please.

She heard the bedroom door slid open again. The sounds that poured out were animalistic, bestial.

Aurora peeked inside and saw it was her own mother who'd

stepped out this time.

"Helga? Wake up, Helga," Jan purred.

Aurora approached and watched her mother's hand pet the sleeping girl's brow. She immediately noticed the blood ringed around Jan's wrist, splashed up her forearms, and the smears on her apron.

She looked like a butcher.

Aurora had always thought her mother the most beautiful woman in the world. She'd put a lot of work into her appearance: her hair extended, her makeup painted, both arms tatted completely, her clothes ripped strategically, clinging to curves sensually. The only imperfection, if it could be called one, was a circular black ring on her neck, not a tattoo, more like a bruise that never healed, or the trace of a kiss left in black lipstick.

Helga stirred but did not open her eyes or speak.

Jan glanced at Aurora, smiled, and though she was beautiful as always, Aurora didn't like how her mother never seemed to blink anymore. Her tiny pinpoint pupils left the rest of her bulging eyes too white, too intense.

Her cousins lingered close.

"How much longer?" Aurora asked her mother.

"As long as it takes, baby. It's hard coming into the world."

Jan gave her daughter that awful, bulbous eyed smile again, then tried once more to wake Helga. When the girl finally stirred, she began to weep instantly.

"My belly," Helga sniffled. "My belly again, Aunt Jan."

Jan stroked the girl's head, made soothing, shushing sounds.

"Come now," she said to the children. "Let's help her. Let's pray it away. Pray the pain away."

Jan cradled Helga's head in her arms and began to rock back and forth. The children gathered and all placed their hands on Helga's abdomen.

"Help ease this child's suffering." Jan moaned, rocking, her eyes closed. "Oh please, we beg you to take away the pain. Take it away. Take it, take it, take it, we beg you!"

Jan thrust her eyes open and glared at the ceiling. Aurora watched as her mother's sculpted beauty morphed into ugly zeal. Her face contorted, her neck became taut, her nostrils flared, her jaw clenched so that the muscles bulged. Jan opened her mouth and what came out were not words, but guttural, spasmodic utterances, more animal noises to compete with the animal noises coming from the bedroom. She kept her head tossed back, her blonde hair hung behind her like a cape, her tongue waggled from her lips convulsively, spittle sprayed forth. Gibberish, snorts, howls poured from her.

"Let us pray to the angel! Our bejeweled angel!" Jan screamed and then wagged her tongue lasciviously. Her eyes rolled to the whites.

And the children joined her in memorized prayer.

*

Aurora knew of angels. They had an angel that visited their farm.

They were blessed, chosen.

Holy.

That was why the angel came to them. The handsome angel, the bejeweled one.

He never came from the road, like her dad. Never in a car. No, he came out of the fields, as if he were just wandering around out there, waiting to be summoned, or out of the dark interior of the barn, which smelled of animal shit and housed shadows against the day. Sometimes he came up from the basement, though how he got down there without anyone noticing was beyond Aurora's understanding. Tall, with silky blonde hair, a solid, smooth tan, and a white smile that glistened. He wore flowing white robes, jewels around his neck, gold rings on his fingers, watches, and bracelets of articulate craftsmanship. Most prominently, a single indigo sapphire the size of a kneecap was imbedded in his forehead, where what looked like liquid but could have been smoke swirled mysteriously inside.

He gave them the knowledge, worked miracles, illustrated the signs they were to watch for. He spoke words that were code for deeper meaning, revealed hand gestures that seemed innocent to the uninitiated, but were clear to those who knew. He explained how other chosen people could be identified by their dress, by their speech, by their customs.

They were uniting, he said, growing in force to do the righteous thing.

They were righteous.

Chosen.

Holy warriors.

*

The silence in the bedroom was louder than all the noise of the birth. The children remained outside the room, much as they had the last twenty-four hours, but now Jan and Aunt Kimberly were with them, freeing Aurora of the responsibility of her cousins.

She listened as the two adult sisters talked of their third sister.

"Thirty-six hours," Kimberly said, her voice low. "That's a long labor."

"But she delivered," Jan said.

"But Emily…" Kimberly sighed.

Emily was chosen early in the year, escorted by the bejeweled angel down to the basement and blessed with copulation. It took a toll on her, as had the pregnancy. She was the oldest of the three sisters, Kimberly the youngest. Emily had always been the leader, but during the pregnancy she'd begun to have misgivings. They'd found her over the summer, behind the barn, with a bottle of whiskey and Grandpa Ross's old service pistol. Since then, she'd been confined to the bedroom, and her roll among the family had been usurped by Jan, who took to it with such force and vigor that everyone wondered why she wasn't chosen in the first place.

Now it was only a matter of minutes before Emily would depart this sinful plane and ascend to her reward in paradise.

The men had come in from the fields claiming the birth had

been announced in a great voice like a thunderclap across the landscape.

The clan were all given a chance to great the babe. Mother clutched child in a towel, damp with red. The infant was slathered in blood, and a membrane that reminded Aurora of the sausage casings Grandpa kept stored in the refrigerator on the front porch.

Kimberly gathered the afterbirth to be preserved in the kitchen for later use in tonics, poultices, and rituals, and Grandpa Ross inspected Emily's birthing wounds; he had the most experience with sutures.

Aurora reluctantly stood next to the bed with her cousins and observed the newborn. They watched as Uncle Devon, Kimberly's husband, used scissors to cut the infant out of the caul, revealing a floral thing, like the petals of a flower closed against the morning frost. Two of the petals sprung open, more akin to wings, and exposed a wailing orifice, opened like a jagged wound, and inside the orifice a bulging white eye, the size of a softball, looped by a mean red iris. There were no other limbs. No torso. Not even a head, just the flower-petal wings gathered around the single blinking eye.

Aurora turned, pushed through her gathered family, and fled the room. Holding a shaking hand to her mouth, she stood at the back door, and waited for the nausea to abate.

"'Ora?" her mother said behind her. "What's the matter?"

Aurora turned to face her, a young woman in her twenties. Pretty, so pretty, but lost to something that seemed both impossibly complex and dangerously senseless to the little girl.

"What's wrong with the baby?" Aurora asked.

"There is nothing *wrong* with the baby. In fact, it's quite right, probably the most right thing in our lives." Jan bent down to her daughter, took her into her heavily tattooed arms, and gazed into the girl's glistening blue eyes. "The father is an angel, so it's not going to look like your other cousins. It's the first of the warriors, prophesied to be born unto us. Do you understand?"

Aurora nodded deliberately, not because she understood her mother, but because she realized she needed to indicate she did, or she'd be in further trouble.

A door in the kitchen crept open behind them.

The bejeweled angel came up the dark steps from the basement, the swirling jewel in his head glowing eerily. He smiled broadly, perfectly. He wore his white robes, and a red tie or scarf looped around his neck tightly, the end dangling down his chest to his groin.

Jan stood slowly, her eyes wide, her breathing suddenly labored. She gestured towards the living room.

"This – this way," she stuttered, eyes focused on the perfectly fashioned blonde pompadour, the evenly tanned flesh, the indigo gem pressed into his head.

The bejeweled one grinned and sauntered through the kitchen towards the living room. He winked at Aurora as he passed, and her mother followed him.

Aurora remained in the kitchen, and moments later she heard the combined sigh of exaltation from her gathered family.

She walked back towards the bedroom, her curiosity momentarily drowning out her revulsion.

The bejeweled angel stood on the bed, his legs spread to either side of Aunt Emily's sprawled form, looming, staring down at her and the cycloptic child. Grandma and Grandpa prostrated themselves upon the floor outside the door to the bedroom, and Grandma lifted her hands to the ceiling and began to blabber, her eyes squeezed shut in exertion. Meaningless sounds spewed from her doughy face and Jan, following in her parent's footsteps, dropped to her own knees, and motioned to the others to do so, too.

Bleating and blathering filled the house.

Aurora squirmed, ready to bolt, but the red eye captivated her. There was a clear awareness in the eye as it rolled slowly, curiously, observing the kneeling family.

It settled on her, blinked, and Aurora flinched.

Then she fled.

Running through the kitchen, a bitter, acidic sting in the pit of her belly, she burst from the screen door, out onto the porch and gazed around the barnyard helplessly. Bright afternoon sun illuminated the property, contrasting the dingy interior gloom of the house.

They were calling her name inside.

Breath ragged, tears welling in her eyes, the girl took off across the dusty barnyard, towards the barn, where she knew a select few hiding spots that even her cousins had yet to discover.

She lurched up an old, splintered ladder, into the hayloft where she carefully made her way to the far side, and, lifting a bale, dropped down into a cubby created by the uneven stacks of hay. She then pulled the hay bale back over the hole. No one knew about this spot. She'd fashioned it while playing by herself, something she did increasingly more often these days.

The interior of the cubby was large, large enough that she and five or six of her cousins could crowd into it, not necessarily comfortably, but comfort while hiding was rarely considered. There was even a little alcove she'd cleared so that she could peer out at the rest of the hayloft without being seen.

Her breathing slowed in the dust and dander of the cubby and sweat beaded on her brow immediately.

She heard them enter the barn.

"Aurora? Dear? Where did you go?" Grandma.

"'Ora? Don't be shy now." Grandpa Ross.

"Do any of you know where she is?" Her mother asked her cousins.

There was a murmur among the other children, then the clamour of them scaling the ladder up into the loft.

Suddenly Aurora was worried. Did they know her spot? She was certain she'd kept it secret. No one knew. How could they?

"Don't worry, they won't find you." A whisper on foul breath spoke into her ear. She turned from her little peek hole and gawked into the gloom of the dark cubby, at a shape on hands and knees just inches behind her. The smoky liquid within the indigo gem shone, radiating out and across the angel's face, casting its features into an ugly, inhuman ruin; moist, darkened, covered in weeping pits like a rotted apple; his true face.

She shrieked, stood with such force that she lifted the bale and knocked it aside like it was a couch cushion, and scrambled out of the hole just as her cousins appeared in the loft.

"Got her!" One of them said.

"She's up here!" Shouted another.

Aurora crossed rapidly to them and glanced behind her at the empty cubby hole.

"Get down here!" Her mother demanded.

She came down the ladder, her family there to receive her.

"I'm tired of this! Not everything is about you!" Her mother barked. She grabbed Aurora by the wrist and pulled her across the barnyard toward the house, where Emily, slack-jawed, eyes slits, a string of drool dangling from her chin, stooped next to the bejeweled angel, who held aloft the newborn. The three of them stood together, like proud parents on the porch.

"I don't want any more of these outbursts!" Jan growled, wringing Aurora's arm.

The rumble of an engine rose suddenly across the surrounding corn fields.

A black muscle car veered into the driveway, a spray of gravel behind it.

"Dad!" Aurora screamed. Her face lit up with relief and excitement. She wrenched free of her mother's grip and bolted towards the car as it tore up the drive. She ran to her savior. Her dad wouldn't put up with any of this, she knew. In fact, it was why he'd left in the first place.

She also knew what was coming: lots of shouting, curse words, and threats of violence. Her father was not an even-tempered man.

The driver's side door opened and his long, denim clad legs appeared, his work boots well worn. He stood from the car, cigarette poking from the corner of his mouth, sunglasses hiding the bloodshot eyes underneath.

She leapt at him, and he caught her easily, one handed.

"Hey baby what's up?" He grinned, removed the cigarette from his lips with his free hand.

She nuzzled herself into his chest, locked her arms around his neck and felt the scruff of his beard against the soft skin of her arms. "Please, Dad, please, get me out of here."

"Hey now, come on," he soothed, dropped the cigarette, and rubbed her back. He eyed the mob moving across the barnyard towards them.

"What the fuck's going on, Jan?" He shouted at his ex. "She's terrified!"

Jan shook her head, "She...she doesn't have the faith," she stuttered, shamefully.

"She's afraid of the angel," one of the children said.

"The baby," Aurora moaned. "It's a monster, Daddy." She motioned at the house.

"What baby?"

Aurora turned to the porch. Emily, the infant, the angel—all were gone.

"Emily had her baby," Jan said.

"She did?" Aurora's father whirled and glared at the house. "Is *he* here? Is *he* inside?"

Jan nodded hesitantly.

Aurora felt herself slip free of her father's grip and slide slowly to the ground. She stayed by his side though, ready to watch him defend her against these people, and maybe even call out the bejeweled angel himself.

"Can I see him?" He asked, abruptly. "Is he..." His voice fell into a whisper, "Is he as beautiful as I remember?"

Jan grinned, a slow, joyful thing. "Oh, yes, Woody. I'm surprised by you. I thought –"

"I was wrong," Woody said forcefully, and Aurora frowned up at him. "Once I left, I couldn't help but notice it, you know, the stuff you said to watch for." He gestured at Grandma Patty, who gave a nod and sly smile, as if she'd known all along he'd come around.

"I mean, it's everywhere," Woody balked. "All over the news, social media, the radio. You see people in the streets, and you just know, you can just tell, the evil has penetrated them."

"Amen!" Patty shouted.

"Woody, I've prayed for this day!" Jan said and rushed forward.

Aurora stood back as her mother and father embraced. Her frown intensified.

"Can I see them?" Woody asked, and the family cheered and ushered him towards the house. Aurora found herself helplessly pulled along.

The chanting and babbling began immediately. The bejeweled angel was in the bedroom, and Emily was hunched in the bed, holding the child, but her face had gone blue, her eyes blank, and her chest still.

Aurora glimpsed a small black ring on her aunt's exposed breast, similar to the one on her own mother's neck.

The baby wailed, the sound was more akin to the noise of cats fighting in the middle of the night, but from what orifice the noise emerged Aurora couldn't tell.

Woody fell on his knees; tears streaked his face.

The bejeweled angel looked upon them and smiled his perfect white smile, his red tie strait, like a river of blood bisecting the purity of his crisp white gowns.

The indigo gem swirled, glowed, intensified until the sickening light shone from his eyes as well. He unhinged his jaw and more dark light poured from his maw.

The clan bathed in the indigo illumination.

Rapidly, Aurora felt a loosening, a relaxation that she'd not sought. A fogginess of mind overwhelmed her. She began to sway with the chanting, the words meaningless, but the inflection purposeful, deliberate. She picked up on the rhythm and hummed along with them, then whispered, then sang, danced, cavorted in the passion and presence of the bejeweled angel. She thought, absently, how foolish she'd been to refrain from the rapture for so long. How senseless and stubborn to refute what was clearly a heaven-sent host.

Some people just needed to be shown the light, she supposed.

They all sung his praise, a family, a clan of believers. Even Helga, hunched over from the pain in her abdomen, wore a half grin as she shifted from foot to foot in exaltation.

Aurora's crisp smile appeared which drew the angel's notice. He reached a hand to her which she took at her father's urging. It was damp, slimy, limp like an old banana, opposite of how it appeared, but she didn't mind. Whatever she'd glimpsed while hiding in the cubby was surely a trick of the gloom, for he was beautiful now, so lovely that she wondered how she'd ever been afraid of him.

He favored her with a kiss upon the hand, his breath fowl, like a waft of air from a sewage drain, a peck that marked an oblong, irregular loop in black on her flesh. It hurt, but she also understood it was significant.

Then the bejeweled angel took her mother's hand and led her towards the basement.

Jan blushed, beamed, and her family cheered, whooped, whistled. Woody wiped tears from his face and applauded.

The infant soared suddenly from the arms of its dead mother. It's flower petal wings unfurled to expose the single red eye, glowering, inspecting each member of the gathered congregation. The eye, carried by the fluttering wings, began to emit the same indigo glow as its father, and Aurora understood its birth was a beautiful testament to the glory of their faith.

She silently prayed that she too would someday birth such light into the world.

***

Bryson's stories have appeared in "What One Wouldn't Do", an anthology edited by Scott J. Moses, "Twisted Love", an anthology from Jazz House Publications, and in the upcoming "Mother: Tales of Love and Terror", from Weird Little Worlds, due out Mother's Day 2023.

Heartbeat

Marie H. Mittmann

After the accident, I was like a baby. Not like a one-year-old who can babble and toddle a few steps, but like a newborn: utterly helpless, dependent on others.

I had no control of my arms and legs. I could not make my vocal cords produce any sounds except for a low groan that was the same no matter if I tried to communicate pain or joy or anything else. Even my eyesight was limited like that of an infant during the first weeks of life, and everything that was more than an arm's length away appeared hazy and blurred. What I had left were the senses of touch and hearing, taste, and smell. There wasn't much to taste because the gooey substance I was fed never varied. Smell and touch offered a bit more pleasure, even if only occasionally: when Vanessa bent over my bed, sometimes her hair would brush my skin and I'd catch a whiff of her shampoo. The sense of hearing only brought me joy when I could hear her voice.

Vanessa.

She was my angel. We'd been together for only two months when the accident happened, but she stayed with me. She didn't abandon me for another partner, even though she could have found one easily. Instead, she clung to what the doctor said when she was crying at my bedside in the hospital: that my injuries would have killed me even two years ago, but now thanks to a new treatment method, I stood a chance. It might take weeks or months or years, or it might never happen – but perhaps I would wake up one morning completely restored. My muscles would be weak, my voice hoarse, and the world around me would seem dizzying with a sudden influx of visual input, but I would be my old self again. Vanessa and I both held on to this hope, I supposed.

In the meantime, though, there was little we could do. The treatment at the hospital had been a one-time affair, and all that was left after that was waiting. Vanessa took me in at the run-down mansion she had inherited from some relative. We used to daydream about making it our home and renovating it, even though we had neither skills nor money – back then, before the accident. Now, all Vanessa could do was fix the most urgent things – a dripping roof, a broken heater – with the money she got from my insurance for taking care of me. It wasn't much, but like my treatment it kept things in a kind of limbo. Maybe, one day, if I woke up being cured, we might still make our dream of a shared home come true. In the meantime, Vanessa could at least keep things going on her own.

A nurse came by to wash and feed me and to turn me on the other side in my bed twice a day, and I was glad Vanessa didn't have to do that. Not that she wouldn't have done it; I was sure she would have – but I figured she knew I would have felt humiliated by it. What she did for me, though, was much more important anyway. She let me know she was *there*. A word here and there, the brush of her hair … that was what kept me sane. The few times I was deprived of her presence for too long, a deep despair rose inside me and did what I could not do on purpose: It produced a response from my body. The low groan from deep in my throat grew louder and louder and turned into a wail. A part of me was horrified by this primordial expression of fear and pain, but like a newborn crying, it did the trick: it made Vanessa rush into my room.

Vanessa.

As long as she was there, I could continue this existence.

*

Each morning as I opened my eyes, I tried to roll over in my bed. I gave my body the order to turn, to throw off the blanket and place my feet on the floor, but it never worked. And with each passing day, the despair that only Vanessa kept at bay crept a little closer.

Soon, I dreaded the break of a new day because it would only mean another disappointment. I slept uneasily, waking from nightmares, groaning and still helpless. The sounds I made without wanting to echoed through the rooms of the old mansion. Vanessa came running the first few nights, and as soon as she touched my shoulder, the groaning ceased. I wished I could have suffered in silence in order not to wake my love several times a night, but still I had no control over the sounds that came out of my mouth.

Eventually, Vanessa took to sleeping next to me. After the nurse had positioned my body for the night, she would quietly come into the room. I lay there, facing the wall, incapable of turning around, yet I sensed with every fiber of my body that Vanessa was there. I smelt her shampoo: flowers I could not name; a scent I associated solely with her. I felt her hair brush the back of my neck, and then the mattress shifted under her weight. Her warm body came to rest close to mine, curled up against my back, just the way we had slept when things were different. I listened to the sound of her breath, felt her chest rising against my back, and when I concentrated, I thought I could even make out the steady beating of her heart. For the first time in weeks, I slept peacefully, and from then on, Vanessa would lie down behind me every night.

Finally, nighttime had lost its terror.

Daylight, however, returned it to me.

*

Winter cold was creeping in through the old single-pane windows, together with the early light. Still, I was warm underneath my blanket because Vanessa was there next to me. Most mornings, she would get up before I woke, so this was a rare and special pleasure. My eyes still closed, I scooted down a little on the mattress. So many nights I had thought - maybe dreamed - that I could hear not only her breath but even her heartbeat, and now I wanted to luxuriate in this beautiful, steady sound while awake. I shifted my head just a little to put my ear to her chest and yes – could really hear her heart. I opened my eyes and was about to fully turn around – to kiss her, I think – when I realized what I'd just done: I'd moved of my own free will. For a moment the whole world stood still. Finally, at last, the treatment had shown effect!

The sunlight that fell into the room seemed much brighter than before. The colors of the peeling wallpaper were faded, yet they looked vibrant to me. My vision was normal again. My limbs obeyed me. A laugh bubbled up from deep inside me – a real, joyful, incredulous laugh left my lips that had produced nothing but groans for more than a year.

"Vanessa!"

At last, I was able to say her name again, even though my voice sounded strange and unfamiliar.

"Vanessa, I— "

I had sat up and turned to her. The words died in my throat.

The warm body beside me, the presence I had felt all these nights, the breath and the heartbeat – it wasn't Vanessa. It wasn't even a human being. What lay there next to me wasn't a living thing at all.

A membrane that felt like skin but looked like rubber stretched over a frame in the shape of a woman. The thing had hair that smelt of flowery shampoo, yet the features of a plastic mannequin. My stomach twisted. Still, I first touched the thing's arm and then its chest, which was covered by one of Vanessa's nightgowns. There was no reaction. The fake skin felt warm; the substance underneath resembled flesh and muscle. The inanimate chest rose and fell and some mechanism rhythmically thumped inside. I couldn't believe I'd mistaken this doll for a living person. Suddenly, I felt paralyzed all over again.

Vanessa, what is this?

I pushed the thing away from me. It fell to the floor; sprawled and face down. A white label at the nape of its neck caught my eye. *SootheX,* it said. It was one of those sticker-labels that were meant to be removed, but evidently nobody had bothered. I didn't want to read the rest of it, yet the letters jumped at me with my newly regained vision.

SootheX – the closest thing to human touch, down to the "heartbeat" at its core!

Vanessa hadn't slept next to me to calm me down. Not last night, and perhaps never. My own heart broke while the fake heartbeat within that thing kept pounding on, unchanged.

***

Marie H. Mittmann is an internationally published author living in

Germany. She writes stories ranging from dark and scary to dreamy and romantic, but almost always with a fantasy twist. Her short stories have appeared in anthologies and magazines, both in English and in German, and she has published a dark fantasy novella and a children's book.

Fear Roulette

Paul Grover

"World War Three, again? Come on, this is ridiculous! Give me a staged alien invasion just *one* time!" Agent Ross had reached his last nerve, but the roulette wheel had spoken. The men in dark suits huddled round the casino style wheel which stood at the front of the characterless white room—so deprived of detail it felt like a void in reality. Several sympathetic groans accompanied Ross's complaints, with all the excited anticipation that previously filled the air sucked out of the room. The wheel contained numerous other enticing options after all, along with the alien invasion, such as *cyberattack* and *bio-terror attack*, but alas, they weren't to be. At least not on this occasion anyway.

The hot-headed agent continued his dissent. "For nearly a century we've been coming back to this now. When are we going to display some originality for Christ's sake?"

Agent Knight, the seasoned spinner of the wheel, interjected, "Now, now. You can't say they're hasn't been some interesting diversions these past few years." His cadence was soothing and reassuring, matching his general demeanor. "I know it's disappointing, but we'll just have to make do with the result. Just think. We can mine an energy crisis from this, an economic crash…"

"If the public even buy into it this time," Ross interrupted.

"Please, if it's on the news they'll eat it up and you *know* it!" Knight fired back, less composed than before.

"Fine," conceded Ross. "What's the impetus going to be?" he queried sarcastically. "Let me guess, it'll be the— "

"Guys," a gormless voice in the room piped up. "How long has the new intern been standing in the doorway?"

The agents turned their heads in unison to see the young, wide-eyed, and petrified intern at the door. She had wheeled a cart filled with hot coffee into the room, but the reaction from the agents had frozen her in her tracks.

"What good is retina scanning technology if the last person in the room leaves the door open?" pondered an exasperated Knight.

"Wasn't me," replied an anonymous voice from the herd.

"I swear, I didn't hear anything!" pleaded the intern, in the most innocent tone she could muster. The agents simultaneously looked to the roulette wheel. "I didn't *see* anything, either!" she insisted, facing away from the wheel, as if that was fooling anyone.

"Who wants to take care of this?" sighed Knight.

"Wait, hold up. We can't just kill her!" exclaimed Ross.

"No, please!" cried the intern.

"We'll get blood in the coffee," elaborated Ross in a matter-of-fact manner.

There were mumbles of agreement from the other agents, who in turn gathered round the cart to collect a mug each. The intern looked on in bewilderment and horror alike at the nonchalant attitude the agents seemed to have towards taking her life as they casually sipped away at the refreshments *she* had made for them. Knight returned to his position alongside the wheel. He took a mouthful of the warm, liquidized goodness and reflected upon the current predicament. "Alright, I'll do it myself," he declared. "But you know, it's a shame, this is some damn fine coffee." With that, the veteran agent pulled out a handgun from a holster that was concealed within his blazer.

"You could blow up the polar ice caps!" asserted the intern, out of desperation.

"I beg your pardon?" reacted Knight, confounded.

"You're devising strategies to keep the public locked in a perpetual state of fear, I'm guessing, so they remain subservient to whatever authority figures you put in place...so you can exert even more control over them, little by little?" the intern deduced.

"Hey, what do you know, the kid's got brains!" an amused Ross observed. "What a shame they're going to be blown out now."

"Wait!" the intern continued, "You've got environmental disaster up there on the wheel. I would go about it by destroying the polar ice caps, causing floods of biblical proportions, and switching the narrative from big corporations – who I'm assuming you also control – polluting the planet to them stepping in and offering solutions to the damage, via subsidies from governments. At the taxpayers' expense, of course."

Almost in one collective movement, the agents tilted their heads from the intern to Knight, curious at what his response would be. He squinted at the intern with critical eyes, evaluating her input. Her heart rate increased with every word unspoken.

"Sir," Ross addressed Knight. "It is a bit of a sausage fest in here to be fair, perhaps we could do with a woman on the team?"

The intern carved a cheesy grin from the unbridled fear that was her face, an expression which clearly translated as 'please, God, listen to the guy'.

"Ah, what the hell," Knight broke the suspense filled silence. "You've got yourself a promotion," he informed the intern. The agents broke out into cheers of approval, as the intern, teary eyed, struggled to release the biggest sigh of relief of her life.

"Thank you, thank you," she ecstatically repeated.

The agents gulped down the final contents of their coffees in celebration. Knight wiped away any last remnants of liquid from his upper lip with the back of his sleeve. "Once you graduate, we might even let you have a spin of the— " Knight paused. Something was wrong. Internally. But not just with him. Another agent collapsed face-first onto the ground. "I knew that coffee was too good to be— " Knight failed to finish his sentence. He too hit the canvas like a ton of bricks; or at least a narrow stack of them.

Ross investigated his empty mug and then looked back at the intern, who held a devilish smile. "Ah, crap," were his last words before he followed the other agents in crumbling unconscious to the ground. The rest of the men fell like dominoes, along with their empty cups.

The room was strewn with bodies. The intern admired her handy work with deep satisfaction. She raised her hand and pressed it to a hidden earpiece. "Did you get all that? Good. Ready for my extraction. At last, the world will know the truth." She addressed the downed agents one last time. "Sorry, boys, I've had a better offer."

She glanced at the roulette wheel once more in disgust. "Maybe now you can get a *peace and love* option."

The supposed intern exited the room.

***

Paul Grover is a freelance writer who has scripted videos for YouTube channel Watch Mojo, written articles for What Culture and Screen Rant, and has scripted radio and television commercials. Paul has also written multiple short stories that have been published by The Writers and Readers' Magazine and Tiger Shark Publishing.

Blink and You'll Miss It

bdyer

The table was made of black cherry wood, varnished with the souls of those who left in years past. It was impeccably clean, wiped daily with soap and water and a little elbow grease, then dried with a clean white cloth. There were no knife marks, no scuffs, nothing sinister to mar its presentation. Still, the woman breathed heavily, her head pressed down where she could best appreciate the table. She didn't have much time left.

*

Yolanda was sitting in her car when it first happened, sitting and letting the engine idle at the edge of the field, thinking about black holes and other things that suck. Green and blue flecks in her eyes danced along the glimmer of the sun's slow, aching surrender of the inevitable. She had a decision to make. No, the problem was follow-through, acting on her decision. She needed to leave him, and she needed it to be final. No more returns, no more apologies. She needed a clean break. Her freckled cheeks twitched, the molars within ground together, microscopic granules flew away, an illustration of entropy. She had a feeling she already passed some invisible event horizon in her life.

She had driven here earlier for peace and quiet, for a scenic backdrop to help her think. More, she came for her favorite sight: the sunrise, like a great egg cracked on the horizon, leaking yolk all over the field. She always found comfort in its monotony, its dependability in fulfilling the promise of tomorrow. This little meadow, tucked a few miles off a forgotten exit, was maybe the best place to watch it. She gripped the steering wheel and looked out only to find disappointment. In all her debating, all her deliberating, she had missed it. She wished she had another chance.

Her eyes fluttered and she was outside, ten feet from where she had been sitting. Her sandy leather hiking boots sank in the dewy soil, a cool breeze brushed past her arms and tickled the blonde hairs there. Her legs shook, and she had to hold them to steady them, or maybe to calm them down. Impossibly, the sun rose again. She had gotten her wish.

Ok, she thought, this is a dream. She beamed at the sun, inventing a secret language she could share with it. She smiled so deeply, so purely, her eyes closed without a thought. When she opened them, she was further into the field and the sun peeked over the end of the field again.

Stop moving, don't do anything, she told herself. Stay calm. Think. She had been in her car, then she was outside her car. She had somehow jumped or was thrust forward in space. Something had to trigger it, or she would be flying endlessly forward in space. No, there was a catalyst. The second time, it happened after she opened her eyes. She clicked her tongue.

This time, she made a conscious decision to blink.

There was a flash, and the sun began to rise. Her shoes sunk deeper into an area of the field more mud than grass. Her car sat ten feet behind her, silent and dead. Moments earlier it had been crooning its irregular rumblings of fifteen years. Her memory played back the clipped, digitized voice vomiting out her stereo, a dissertation on chaos and the gravitational effect of black holes. She had been reviewing the paper for consideration, an unhappy task she tolerated for her part of the thesis committee. She dug out the notes she had taken and scanned the words, trying to prove a point to herself.

The distorted movements of the accretion disk as it nears the center of the black hole is in direct proportion to the force being exerted on space-time itself.

She shook her head and stopped reading.

"I'll save you the trouble, it's not a dream."

The rough voice, steeped and serrated, sliced down her back, cutting through the silence like a rusty saw. Only C Martin Peters could make her feel so degraded. What she had once mistaken for character had earned a different feel, and the scars all over her body from the lashings and cuts of his words were proof.

She bit her lip and looked down at the ground, conjuring an image of him: one eye naked, bloodshot from sleepless nights, and the other obscured by a shower of hair; his skin pitted with craters of acne long gone; his fat little nose and strange lips like caterpillars humping whenever he mumbled. Mostly she thought about his eye. It punched through her, judged her, looked down, down, down.

"It's an ingenious little thing I stumbled on a few years ago," he said. "You've heard me mention it, I'm sure. The infinity box. I use it to test out various experiments on physics, quantum mechanics, and unruly girlfriends."

He laughed at this. Yolanda didn't think she would ever laugh again.

When she turned, he was gone. Only his laughter remained echoing around, and right at the end, right on the fringes of his laughter, a strange tone played. It took her a second to realize it was the microwave timer going off.

*

A faint light shone through the curtains, shimmering against the rarely used silverware and the special plates set on the table. Blue fractal patterns on the edge of the plates twinkled in the light which played along them. He had called them 'Welcome Back Plates,' a name to match the nickname he gave her. She hated the name and everything it implied. She wouldn't return this time.

*

She was distracting herself with experiments. People blink around twelve times in a minute, and she couldn't measure the blinks she didn't notice, so her data would be incomplete. She'd manage anyway.

She blinked and the first few rays of the sun pierced the darkness around her. The grass crinkled beneath her boots. The meadow had lost some of its luster. She blinked again and the field had yellowed with age. The car had tipped over in a heap, a decrepit brutalist representation of a 2002 Hyundai Elantra. It had been picked clean to its skeleton and covered in rust; its wheels long gone. Vines twisted uncomfortably around the frame like some bizarro vascular system.

Goddamn infinity box, of course. Somehow, all Martin's schemes hinged on it. The idea of the thing was the ballast of his entire ego. Despite his obsession, he never went into detail about it, so all she could gather was theoretical. It was essentially a pocket universe, a handheld sandbox for whatever physics or quantum experiments his mind could concoct. All that said, it was nothing but a fantasy of his, an invention used to validate impossible theories. Or was it?

She opened her eyes to a field blanketed in a thick coat of white. The sunrise sparkled along the snow-covered field, sending light into her eyes.

Wind howled across the plains, blowing straight through her flannel, blew straight through her flannel, mocking her attempts to bundle against it. She blinked forward in the field and stopped and tilted her head. She blinked again and closed her eyes a moment longer, and there it was again:

Silence.

In the void between blinks there was absolute silence while the world around her was obliterated. The cold, that inescapable ghost flying through her body at every turn, had gone. It returned upon opening her eyes, much like the dazzling spectacle of the sunrise. She made note of this and considered its implications if not applications.

She took a step, then another, appreciating the Styrofoam crunch of her boots through the deep snow. Tracks of various creatures were scattered around here—deer, rabbits, and some prints less familiar to her. She bent down to investigate tracks assumed to be wolven, lupine, when a low guttural growl sounded and prickled along her spine. She shot upright, not daring to turn around. The growl trilled a strange cadence, first twisting and winding itself around unfamiliar sounds until it was able to organize them and then, slowly, piece them together into something she could recognize.

When it appeared satisfied it had mastered those sounds, it repeated them, quicker and closer together: "Yo....lan......da."

She blinked.

Rain flattened her hair against her head, slipped down her neck and soaked through her flannel, making her feel colder than she had earlier. She could hear the quickening of its panting, the rushed movements of its pads vaulting through the snow, snow replaced with mud and muck, maybe months down the line when spring starts creeping in. She imagined its open mouth flailing streams of slobber, a mouth disembodied from a creature she had never seen, never knew, a phantom.

She wanted to check behind her, set her mind at ease. When she tried, she came up short. Her head wouldn't turn, her hips wouldn't cooperate. Nothing she tried would allow her to turn around. She blinked and for a split second the cold left her bones. When she opened them, it returned, rain saturated her clothes again. He too had returned.

"Yoyo," purred a familiar voice. It was bestial, distorted and savage, yet unmistakably him. C Martin Peters. Something pushed up, smushing its fleshy stomach against the small of her back. This sent a chill down her spine.

She blinked.

Strong winds were bending the saplings littering the field, uprooting some and flinging them around. Yolanda watched all this, holding an arm before her face, waiting to be blown away. It never happened.

Clawed hands made their way down her sides, swooping around the curves there, moving past her hips and clasping like a lock in front. His breath came out in quick pants against her neck. The tips of his fangs grazed her skin. His jaws closed and pushed down just enough. Then he relaxed and the skin rebounded into place. A thin line of blood made its way down her neck, wriggling like a thick, slimy worm. He licked it before it got away.

She blinked.

They were in the middle of a dimly lit forest. His arms remained around her.

She blinked.

The trees had vanished. Only stumps were left here and there. His head came down on her shoulder and from the corner of her eye she could see his smile stretch across a wolf muzzle.

"That won't work on me, Yoyo. There's no point running. Here, take my hand. I want to show you something." He grabbed her hand, no longer trying to be gentle, and walked ahead of her, dragging her further into the field. At his height he should have lumbered around, but he walked straight and swiftly. It was all she could do to keep up. The thick coat of fur did little to hide the muscles beneath which rippled and thrusted like pistons in an engine. She smirked, disgusted at all this effort for one woman. After they passed a clearing, he stopped and pointed.

"This is where they remain, Yoyo. Those who left. This is where they will always be, ready at my whim to be pulled up. This is the filing cabinet of my love life. This is who I am."

Stone figures pierced the ground below them, taking the form of teachers, nurses, women in business suits, dresses, women with glasses and frizzy hair, bald women and women with straight hair hanging down to their waist. She estimated at least a couple dozen women in various states of distress, holding their hands to their throats, burning alive, screaming in anguish for an end they would never receive. The theme was death, no one gets out of here alive. Girlfriends check in, they don't check out. Each stood on a pedestal and in the center of the field, in the spot of honor, the sunrise gleamed over an empty pedestal emblazoned with the name Yolanda.

"Dead?" she asked. Despite all she had seen, this seemed like too much. "Are these women dead? Am I next? Did you bring me here to die, Martin?"

He laughed. With his wolven face, the contortions needed made it look horrific, like a rabid animal sneezing.

"You still don't understand this place. No, I haven't killed anyone. That would attract the entirely wrong kind of attention. I'm sure they're all alive, somewhere. The box only takes part of them, perhaps the best part. What's leftover is an empty shell—not exactly long-term material. So, I let them go. Or they leave, whatever." His lips curled back, a low snarl hissing out with each breath with steam.

"For a long time, I was content to let the cycle continue forever. Then you came along, made me think we had something real. It's not too late though."

His voice was getting smaller and smaller the more he talked. He was fading away. She stared out at all those statues and cried.

"You can never escape this place, but that doesn't have to be a bad thing. This could be heaven. You decide. I haven't given up on you yet. Don't give up on me."

The words rotted in her stomach long after he spoke them, long after the tears had dried on her cheeks. Soon after the statues before her crumbled to the earth and were gone in a blink of the eye.

*

Only now, with the hand pushing her towards it, gripped firmly behind her head, did she realize there was something more to the strange white box at the end of the table. She had assumed it was a napkin holder for so long, but then voices started coming out, sensations started to emanate from within. There was a deep hunger leaking from the box, pulling at her. The closer she came to it, the more she knew she couldn't escape. And yet, even here, even in this situation, she was curious. Even with her face against the box, body stretched on forever, a small part of her, the part that wasn't flailing her arms like a pinwheel and screaming at the top of her lungs, still wondered how it all worked.

*

She had been going over the list in her mind, trying to decide if any of it mattered. It was her security blanket. She clung to the structure lists provided.

1. She was inside something called an Infinity Box, possibly sitting on the kitchen table of Martin's house, near the microwave.

2. The trigger for her jumps in time and space was a blink, something she had limited control over.

3. She was safe inside the void between blinks.

4. A recent development, she could no longer turn around, told her the rules of this place change on a whim—his whim—and to be prepared for more changes.

5. She needed to leave Martin. She needed to break up. It was ridiculous, hilarious to reduce it to this, yet it was true. She needed to get away from him.

Yolanda's arms were trembling. She had fallen to her knees at some point, and her weak, wobbly arms were the only things keeping her from falling the rest of the way, planting her face in the soil of this field. The field was a cratered, dead wasteland, devoid of any comfort. Cracks strew the dried-out landscape like the bones of some vast organism.

She wondered if she would ever see the sun the same way again. All the warmth she associated with it was missing from this sunrise. All the comfort it had once provided had fled. It had become a cruel symbol of hope, teasing a future she would never see. No matter how many times she blinked, the sun would rise the same. No matter how many tortures she endured, the sun stole an impish look out from the periphery. Whether she chose it or not, she would blink, she would be thrust forward, and the sun would rise again. Those were the rules. She was a mote of dust floating in the rays of another sunrise, helpless, unknowing of its fate.

Her eyes were getting dry, so she closed them. When she opened them, she saw something new.

A silo of pure black loomed remotely, sun sliding along its sides. Upon the silo sat a figure. She blinked.

The bitter coldness devoured her. She had known this feeling, had felt it seep through her clothes and needle its way through her body, but there was something different about this. Every scab, every grudge, every hidden resentment stuck to the skin of her soul pricked up at this cold. It blew a wind around all her yesterdays and coiled them into a spring that could never release. An ache filled her body, gnawed at her insides. Everything around her within the shadow of the silo had died, shriveled and withdrawn into the cracked and barren earth. Martin stood, stretching his wings atop the silo, flexing his ridiculous demonic muscles in the light of the dawn, then took flight. She blinked.

A tremor overtook her arms, and she held them against herself with wrinkled hands. She looked down at them in surprise. Exactly how long had she been here to degrade her body like this? How much of her life did each blink cost? A day? More? She nodded at this, simply accepting it.

C Martin Peters landed beside her, a massive gargoyle with hair melting over one side of its face. His one visible eye remained to stab a piercing look into her.

"It's time," he said. His one eye was graven, cracked with veins, weighed down with shadow. "You can still save yourself. Choose me, and I can make this all go away. Or you can blink, and, well…" he trailed off, moving his eyes to the distant sun.

"…Your next will be your last. Sacrifices are needed, I'm afraid. But I can save you if…"

Yolanda blinked.

Her momentary smile broke when she saw what Martin meant. The sun rose, and behind it a great eye opened, slowly swilling the sun to sate some vast cosmic hunger. On the horizon she saw great chunks of earth rip from the surface and spaghetti towards the center of the hole. The ground beneath her began to tremble. Cracks ran along the ground like currents of water forming tributaries everywhere.

Above the roaring sounds all around her, another, deeper, tingling sound shook through her entire body. She looked up and saw patterns had grown around the black hole, fractal shards growing out from the center like ice crystals, each ending at a solid border circling everything around which was pure white. White like eggshells. White like the snow she walked through earlier. White like the whites of an eye. Not that eye, though. Not his eye. Martin was gone. This was something else. Sacrifices had to be made, he had said.

The pupil swiveled to look at her and made another noise. This is it, she thought.

Yolanda's body was flung like a ragdoll towards the eye, sweeping along the wobbling pathways of the accretion disc. All she had left was her mind, and that was drifting away, fading with the strength of her youth. Bits of flesh started peeling away from her arms, her legs. Teeth were ripped from her mouth and went swirling into the vortex. The pupil whirled, prickled at her skin and more of her was pulled apart.

Body giving out, she closed her eyes. The wind stopped. She no longer moved. She no longer hurt. She imagined an inverted Schrodinger's Cat. Until she opened her eyes, the entire universe was in a state of flux, waiting to be observed. She was safe here.

There was no Martin. There was no God. She was safe here in the darkness, in the nothing, in the void. She would stay here and wait. Until what? She thought. Until I find myself. And if I never do? Then she would continue to wait. Waiting was better than having to see his face again. Waiting was better than pretending to be happy here.

With that thought, she realized she could stay there in the void forever.

*

Martin's pillow was crumpled in disarray next to her, spiraling into a vortex where his head had lain. She had the dream again. The dream where she ended things. Where she walked up to Martin and told him they needed to talk. It was disturbing, and yet every night she had the dream, and every morning she woke up staring at his empty pillow. He would be downstairs, working on breakfast.

She wanted to smile at the thought of this, at the idea of him working down there to impress her with some silly display, but she couldn't. She had forgotten how. The tedium of getting dressed blew it from her mind. Dressed, she stood looking out the window, arms hanging limp by her side. Sunlight wrapped around her, overtaking her frail form, possessing her, and she let it.

The earthy scent of coffee greeted her, and she followed it downstairs, skipping down the last few in the way he liked. He laughed at this without turning around. The entire kitchen was permeated with smells of bacon, eggs, hash browns. The subtle smell of hollandaise lingered in the background like a murderer.

"Good morning, my dear," she said.

"Good morning, Yoyo," he chimed. He was in a good mood this morning. She wondered what was different. What had pleased him? She wondered if it was her. "Almost ready, have a seat."

She sat down at the table and looked around. Her eyes passed vacantly from the grain of the table to the Welcome Back plates. Her brain said, "Welcome Back plates." She had no idea what it could mean. Welcome back implies she had left, why would she leave? Martin was her entire universe. Nails dug deep within her clenched fists.

She shook her head and then closed her eyes. She always felt calm when she closed her eyes, when she shut out the world. Sometimes she needed help remembering. A voice met her in the darkness, faint and withering.

When she opened her eyes, she was looking straight at the white box at the side of the table. She had seen it many times. Every day she ate breakfast here, every day it was sitting there. She had never been remotely curious about it before.

"Reach out," said the voice from the darkness.

A light rose in her eyes, a spark long eclipsed.

"Find me," it said, stronger.

She lifted a hand and slowly, timidly, reached towards the glowing white box. She reached and stretched and finally made contact.

carfieldsunriseBLINKsunriseBLINKautumnBLINKwinterBLINKwolf BLINKspringMartinmartinMartinBLINKthinkingBLINKexperiments BLINKsiloBLINKmonsterBLINKmartinMartinmartinBLINKblackhol epullingworldcrumblingeyeBLINKeyeBLINKdarknessnothingwaiting nowNownownow

Martin's hair swished to the motion of the eggs whirling about the bowl. He was oblivious to anything else.

Yolanda stood, and the darkness eased into her body like well-fitting gloves.

"What does he deserve?" it asked.

She silently moved to the knife block.

His elbows danced around, working at the hash browns on the griddle.

"How many cuts will it take?" it asked.

She stood behind him, head tilted.

He scooped up the bacon and put it on a plate.

"What will hurt him the most?"

A wink of light shot from the blade she had lifted above her head. He turned around. That one eye stared at her, unbelieving. That one eye that always cut into her, through her, had lost all understanding. He was the mote of dust.

The first cut was easier than she expected. The knife slid into his eye socket, gushing fluid with each plunge. He slumped over the griddle, his hair sizzling. She didn't give up. Again, the blade rose, and again it sank into his face. The glint of the blade became comforting, warm. Like a great egg cracked on the horizon, his head leaked blood all over the kitchen floor. It's going to be a good day, she thought.

Somewhere around the twentieth sunset of C Martin Peters, she remembered how to smile.

***

Bdyer is a cryptid living in the lowlands of the northern midwest where he forages for stories and tales of the fantastic. When not busy watching birds, he devours works of horror and fantasy, regurgitating them onto paper as a way of understanding the world around him.

Isolated

S.J. Walker

I peer through my blinds from my apartment window, overlooking the scenery that looks like my hometown of Charleston, South Carolina. It even sounds like Charleston with cars driving by on bustling streets, the chattering of pedestrians, and the occasional clip-clopping of horse hooves against cobblestone, pulling tourists in carriages. But I can say with absolute certainty that this godforsaken place isn't my home. It's hell.

When I jog down the stairs of my second-floor apartment, and step outside onto King Street, I'm greeted with the familiar, fresh smells of spring: lilac mixed with some horse manure. A display of Palm trees stretch along the road in front of colorful, historic-looking buildings. For a second, I almost believe in the deception that this is real, that I'm alive and home. Then I remember that anyone I touch disintegrates instantaneously.

I huddle amongst pedestrians who are waiting to cross a street at a stop light. I shuffle to get as close as I can without actually touching anybody. After spending an agonizing week here, I already miss companionship and human connection. Occasionally, I accidentally grace someone with the tip of my elbow and the person explodes at the mere contact. There is no blood or anything gory like that. The people I touch simply shatter into pieces against the pavement, like shards of glass. What's even more disturbing is that no one surrounding the scene ever reacts to it. Instead, they continue looking onward, waiting to cross the street so they can head towards their destinations like nothing is wrong. The following day, I'll recognize the people I've destroyed, and they are somehow fully restored, continuing their routines as if nothing out of the ordinary has happened to them. I am convinced this place is designed to make me lose my grip over my sanity.

Like I've done every day since my arrival, I try again to grab someone's attention. I stand in front of a random person on the sidewalk to block him. I wave my arms at him frantically like a lunatic.

"Hello! Can you see me?!" I cry. "My name is Joshua Hudson! Please notice me!"

The person simply ignores me, checks his wristwatch before circling around me and continuing down the path. My nostrils flare. I react by racing after him and poking his back with my forefinger. I feel oddly satisfied when his pieces collide with the sidewalk. It's not murder because he'll be revived by tomorrow.

Everyone here acts like I don't exist. Yesterday, I even tried walking outside completely naked, and no one batted an eye. This must be part of some elaborate dream that I can't wake up from… Or maybe it's an experiment run by aliens to see how long I can manage without going absolutely crazy.

Fueled by my continued frustration, I catch the sight of a couple walking while holding hands on the other side of the street. *Why do they get to hold hands? It isn't fair!* I cross to them, feeling like a mad man with a stride reminiscent of a caveman or a gorilla. Cars pull to a stop to let me pass. Still, the drivers act like they see past me. They don't press on the horn. I extend my hands towards the couple and watch them explode into pieces. *If I don't get a hand to hold, neither should they!* I stare down at their remains and think, *what am I doing?* I'm becoming a monster in this place.

When I return to my apartment and sit on my bed, I wrap my arms around myself. My hands are the only ones I have. I yearn for touch. I crave it like a drug addict going through severe withdrawal. I rock while holding myself, I weep like a baby. In the mirror on the wall across from my bed, I see my reflection. There, in the glass image, is a disheveled, grown-ass man who hasn't shaved in a week, crying while cradling himself.

Pathetic.

I contemplate my last memory before I ended up here. I was in a car accident. That much is for certain. Inside a taxi, my driver turned left on a green light, thinking the road was clear. I lost consciousness right after a collision with a truck. Likely, I'm probably dead. It is difficult to accept that this is my fate. How long am I expected to remain here?

I've tried to escape this place a few times. I shattered someone as he was entering his car, took his keys and climbed into the driver's seat. I drove the stolen car as far as I could, hoping to escape the city. I spent hours trying to leave. No matter how many different roads I take, I am always led back to the main entrance of the city on an endless loop. I realized in dismay that there's no way out of here.

*

Around noon I visit a small coffee shop around a nearby corner. After staring myself down in the mirror, I had decided to clean myself up. I stroke my smooth, shaven jaw-line, feeling fresher. I took a long, hot shower and dressed in a collared shirt and jeans. The bell rings as I step inside the shop but none of the customers react to my arrival. Though they talk amongst themselves, the cashier doesn't acknowledge my presence either. I leap over the counter and serve my own cup of coffee and grab a croissant from the shelf in the process. At least I don't have to pay.

I climb back over and look for a place to sit and eat. I choose a table where a woman is sitting alone. The woman has her nose in a book and a coffee in her hand. She wears a collared pink shirt and jean skirt with flip flops. Her toenails are painted pastel blue to match her fingernails. Her hair is blonde and pulled back into a high ponytail. She doesn't recede when I pull up a chair and take a seat across from her.

"Hi. I know you probably don't notice me, but I'm Joshua. It's nice to meet you." She doesn't look up, but I keep talking anyway. "You're very pretty. I hope you don't mind me sitting here."

I pull a bite from my fluffy croissant, swallow, then take a sip of my coffee to help flush it down.

"I guess I deserve to be here," I tell her. At this point, I start to feel like I'm in a booth in a Catholic church, and she is the priest taking my confession. "I know I'm not a good person. I've never been involved with my daughter. She might be seven now, maybe eight. Honestly, I don't even know…"

The woman's eyes continue to scan the pages of her book. She is completely oblivious of me.

"I never paid child support," I continue. "I made my money through... '*unconventional means*,' mostly selling stolen items.... Okay, fine, I'll admit it. I was a thief, okay? It's not something I'm proud of." I glance at her again, as if I am trying to assess her reaction over my words, but she still looks unfazed. I sigh, pinching the bridge of my nose with my thumb and forefinger. I inhale a deep breath through my nose and then release my hand upon exhalation and place it back on the surface of the wooden table and grip my coffee cup.

"Back in that taxi, I wasn't planning on paying the driver. I was going to skimp out on the bill," I confess and chuckle darkly. The man didn't deserve to be paid for getting us into an accident anyway. My laughter fades quickly when I realize she's still not paying attention.

"What do I have to say to make things better? How can I get out of here? I'm confessing my sins. What else can I do? Should I confess in a church? Is that the answer?"

I grab my croissant and take another bite. I stare directly at her, hoping she'll at least glance in my direction. I lean forward across the table and deliberately start chewing loudly with my mouth open.

Still no reaction.

I swallow and lean back into my chair. Anger boils inside me. After another sip from my coffee, I slam the cup down against the table. I grab my croissant and throw it at the woman's face. She doesn't even flinch. There is ice in my tone now when I speak.

"You know, you look like the type of woman I used to date. I made so many promises to women like you. Told them they were the only ones for me, that I wanted a relationship. They'd then let me slide into their beds and I'd refuse to call them again. Now I probably can't even touch you without you breaking like glass!"

After blowing up on her, I immediately regret it. I huff out a breath but then look down at the table and trace the lines in the wood with my thumb. I'm ashamed of my short fuse. I momentarily close my eyes and shake my head. I make sure to soften my voice when I speak again.

"I took it for granted. Touch, I mean. The experience of being with a woman… or *anybody*." I sigh again before continuing, "Now, I'd give anything for a simple hug or a pat on the back. Isn't that just sad?" I let out another dark chuckle with my newfound, morbid sense of humor. The laughter takes on a sudden life of its own and I force myself to contain it. *Get it together, Joshua*, I tell myself. *Be cool.*

I'm alerted when the woman suddenly closes her book. She stuffs it into her bag beside her and straps it around her shoulder, then stands up with her coffee cup.

"No, please don't leave," I say, but my plea is ignored. I lunge after her and as I grab her arm to pull her back, she suddenly blasts into fractured pieces.

"NO!!!"

Then it happens. I crack. I collapse to my knees in this public place, and cry like a wailing infant. I can't keep the crazy bottled inside. I am a man transforming into a barbarian.

*

Today starts my second week here in this hell hole. I sleep in my bed as long as I can. Unconsciousness is much better than enduring my increasing insanity. At some point though, the morning sun shines so brightly that my blinds can't keep my bedroom dark enough. Soon, the light flickers through my eyelids and I can no longer deny that it is daytime. I sit up with my back against the headboard and wonder how to spend another day in this cruel joke of a world. That's when I hear a strange voice coming from the street below. I mean, I hear people chattering outside all the time, but not like this.

"Hello?! Can anyone see me?" she asks. "Please, tell me where I am!"

I hear a noise like shattering porcelain, and I jolt in shock. I'm only accustomed to hearing that sound when I am the cause of it.

"No!" the same female voice squeals in horror. "Not again! Why does this keep happening?!"

I jump to my window and peer through a crack in the blinds. I see the remaining pieces of another glass person scattered across the sidewalk. Hovering over them, is a woman who is spinning around, scared and confused. I feel a spark of excitement at the possibility that she is a real person like me, maybe I'm not alone here anymore. The others are always looking ahead, walking with intent like they know where they are going. She is not. My heart is in my throat. Hope lifts me by the chest. I immediately grab a robe from my bedroom closet, slip it on, dart out of my apartment, and rush down the stairs.

"Hello!" I shout once I'm on the sidewalk. I wave to her in a fierce gesture. She flashes surprised eyes at me.

"You can see me?!"

"Yes!" my voice picks up with eager excitement. "And you can see me!"

"Yes," she returns, relief evident in her tone.

We walk speedily towards each other, closing the gap until we are about three feet apart. I want to wrap my arms around her, sweep her up in a tight hug, but I stop myself. I'm afraid she'll shatter into pieces like the others. I don't want to break the only person who can see me. Also, what if she thinks I'm a lunatic, hugging a random stranger?

She pauses when I do and we just stand there, assessing each other for a moment. She is a pretty, petite girl, wearing a floral dress and white flats. Her auburn hair is long, flowing in natural curls past her shoulders. She has freckles sprinkled across a dainty, upturned nose, and rounded cheeks. Her green eyes are large, wide, and focused on me. It is the most beautiful sight I've seen in the last two weeks, someone looking directly *at* me, rather than merely looking in my direction through a blank lens.

I wonder what she thinks of me. I feel my chin, remembering that I haven't shaved in a few days. I'm horrified to feel the scruff. I must look like a homeless person since I'm also naked beneath a robe. She doesn't seem bothered by my rough appearance. Her eyes only contain a spark of relief, mirroring how I feel.

"What's your name?" I inquire.

"I'm Piper. Piper Callaway." She has a voice like an angelic, southern belle.

"Hi Piper. I'm Joshua Hudson."

"Joshua, how long have you been here?"

"Two weeks," I answer grimly.

"What – what *is* this place?"

"I still don't know," I answer honestly. My voice croaks embarrassingly when I say, "I'm just glad to finally meet someone who can actually see me."

My eyes swell and I almost feel like crying but I hold it in. A lump has formed in my throat. I work to swallow it. I have to clear my pipes to flush it all the way down and I almost sound like I'm choking while I do it. My social skills are painstakingly rusty at this point.

"Are you okay?" she asks me.

"Yeah. Yeah, I'm fine." My voice is rough while I am speaking. "Just emotional, I guess. It's been a very long two weeks."

"I don't blame you. I just got here, and I already feel like I'm going crazy!"

"I think this place is designed to gaslight us," I tell her.

"Why does everyone break when I touch them?" she points to the pieces of a body on the ground a few paces behind her.

"I don't know. They just do. But they come back to life the next day," I explain.

"Weird. Will *you* break if I touch you?"

"Do you...*want* to try it?" I ask, extending my wide, hairy arm out towards her. She looks at it and considers. She blinks then taps the tip of her forefinger against my bicep. I should feel somewhat disturbed she was quickly willing to do that, to risk breaking me, but I allow her some slack. The reality of this place probably hasn't kicked in for her yet. Meanwhile, my body reacts with a joyful tremble.

Touch. Real, human touch.

"Please do that again," I urge. She takes a step closer, rests a gentle palm around my wrist. Her warm skin feels amazing. A moan of pleasure escapes my breath and then she releases. *Oh, no,* I couldn't contain my crazy.

"I'm... I'm sorry," I say.

"You really have had a rough two weeks..." she appraises me warily.

"Miserable," I agree, speaking the word a bit too harshly.

"Are we in hell?" she suddenly asks, and the question takes me aback.

I freeze for a second. I stare down her hand on my wrist, evading her curious gaze. I can't answer that question, at least not aloud. If I speak the words, I will be acknowledging my fear about this place: there's no end in sight; I'm potentially stuck here for all eternity; I can't do it. The darkness of the reality would be too intense to soak in. I inhale a shaky breath then exhale.

"I make it through each day, only by thinking that being here is somehow impermanent," I manage to choke these words, which I realize doesn't provide her with a satisfactory answer... It's all I'm able to surmise.

"How long?" she wonders. She looks worried. She should be.

An eternity? The question looms in the air between us.

"I wish I had answers for you, Piper. I really do. But honestly, I have no idea."

*

I ran back to my apartment to change into decent clothes, jeans, and a white collared shirt. While up there, I took the time to shave, slap on some deodorant and clean up a little. I feel a lot better, fresher, when I run downstairs to rejoin Piper outside. She flashes a small smile when she sees me, and I rejoice from the expression because it is *for* me, directed *at* me.

"You clean up well," she says.

"Thanks. Sorry, I would have invited you up to my apartment, but I was worried you would be uncomfortable about the mess," I explain.

"It's okay." She seems somewhat absent, looking off to one

side. I follow her gaze and notice a pile of pieces from a shattered person near where she stands on the sidewalk.

"I hope you didn't go too crazy while waiting," I add. "This place can do that to you."

"He passed me, and I accidentally hit him with my elbow," she explains. "I still find it weird that they do that. Are you sure they come back to life?"

"Yeah, they always manage to restore themselves," I reassure her. I tap her shoulder comfortingly, but it doesn't seem to alleviate her tension. Her eyes are wide, bulging as she glares down at the man's remnants.

"This is going to take some getting used to," she says.

"I'm still not completely used to it," I admit.

"Let's go get something to eat," I suggest. I pull her arm to nudge her away from the man she just shattered. She has a lot to work through inside that skull of hers. I can tell. This place is a lot to take in.

The way the sun kisses my skin from a cloudless sky, I'd never guess at first glance I was in a place like hell. It's beautiful outside with that charming southern vibe, people greeting each other politely as they pass each other across the sidewalk – each other, not us. The beat of the city is friendly, uplifting, though we are external to it. I feel a heightened sense of positivity, a fresh pep in my step with Piper keeping in stride beside me. Her presence makes this place almost tolerable—almost. She still looks rigid. Her chest hitches. She walks with one hand to her temple, the other holding her elbow.

We stop in a restaurant and take a seat at a booth. Since the waiter doesn't notice us, I steal two meals from a table of customers. As usual, they don't react. I grab a plate of cheese ravioli for Piper, a steak for me.

"How do they not notice you taking their food?" she asks me.

"They never notice," I answer her simply.

"That's so strange…"

"You're telling me," I scoff. "Bon appetite!"

We unravel our silverware from napkins on our table and dive in. The food is hot and delicious and slides smoothly down my gullet. I pause after a minute when I notice Piper has stopped eating and she is staring down at her plate.

"Are you okay?" I ask her.

"I'm not sure what to make of this place," she explains.

"Yeah. It can drive you crazy. Trust me. I know."

"I don't think I have much of an appetite," she says.

"Do you want to walk around outside for some fresh air?"

She nods and, like a gentleman, I stand from my seat and offer my hand to help her up. She takes my hand, grateful, but something in her expression looks deeply saddened. I understand because I remember that feeling of being scared, hopeless and overwhelmed when I first woke up here.

"Joshua," she says, "I don't want to be here. I want to go home to Charleston. To the *real* Charleston."

"I know," I tell her with a heavy sigh, "me too."

Once outside, we walk in silence as I can see she's still trying to mentally register where she is. We pause at the pineapple fountain in Waterfront Park. The water droplets fall in sparkles, each glimmers under the rays of the sunshine.

"What's that?" she asks, pointing to a random, folded piece of paper on the ledge of the fountain. It is a little moist from its proximity to the falling water, but not too soggy. I grab it and unfold it between my fingers to read a note scrawled across it in messy handwriting. I read it aloud.

"For one of you, this is your chance to get out of here. Take the knife next to this note and use it. One of you will be free and return to your regular life in the real Charleston. The other will stay here indefinitely."

I look back to the ledge, but I don't see a knife. Then I look to Piper and immediately feel uneasy. Her eyes have changed noticeably from melancholy green to ominous black. She is stiff and pale. In her hand, she tightly grips the handle of the 8-inch butcher's knife. I drop the letter and hold my palms out facing her in defense.

"Piper, wait a minute. Let's talk this out. I don't think the note means what it is implying."

"I think I know exactly what it means. If I kill you, I get to go home."

"It didn't explicitly state that," I say and take a step backward from her. "Piper, hold on. Don't do anything rash."

"I get to go home," she squeals right before she lunges toward me, wielding the knife. I dodge her first attack and start to run. She chases after me in pursuit. While enjoying a peaceful day at the park, people don't realize this chaos beneath their noses. While sprinting, I crash into a pedestrian who turns into one of today's casualties. My sneakers crunch over the person's pieces. I briefly glance behind me as Piper sprints towards me with fierce determination in her black dagger eyes. She may be shorter than me, but she is fast. She whips across the field of the park and, no matter how hard I push my legs to keep running, she is only a stride behind me.

I crash into some more random people enjoying the park. They slow me down. I fall onto their remains. The sharp edges of glass slice into my skin. The real pain comes when Piper drives the knife into my back. I wail in agony.

"You're bleeding," she says, sounding surprised. "Real blood. You're not breaking into glass." She almost sounds like she derives some form of sadistic pleasure from her actions. The next words out of her mouth confirm my chilling thought.

"I like this."

She stabs me again, this time in the back of my thigh. I howl like a wounded animal.

"Who are you?!" I demand under my breath. Immense pain courses through my veins.

"I guess I didn't tell you about my life before I came here. I've killed people before. Though, I must admit, this is my first time killing in broad daylight in a public place."

She bends down, her face now by my head, and points the tip of the bloodied knife between my eyes.

"Piper, please stop," I plead with her, but I know it is useless.

"I'm going home," she sings, and my vision suddenly blackens.

*

I wake up in a haze and notice florescent lights along a ceiling. I look around at the teal walls of the room which resembles a hospital. Something is beeping. A heart monitor beside my bed.

"He's awake," someone says. She approaches me, dressed in a nurse's uniform.

"How are you feeling, Mr. Hudson?"

"You can see me?" I murmur.

She looks confused by my question but answers me anyway.

"Of course, I can see you. How are you feeling?"

Everything hurts.

"I'm okay…"

"You suffered a car accident in a taxi. You have wounds along your back, the back of your thigh, and a nasty gash between your eyes," she explains. "You're lucky to be alive."

"Is the driver alright?" I ask.

"Yes, he's recovering just like you."

I sigh with relief. If I'm home, if I'm *really* home, I'm going to make changes in my life. I'm going to call my ex-wife and plead with her to be involved in my daughter's life. I'm going to get a real job. I'm going to pay child support and do whatever it takes. I'm going to make sure I don't end up back in that… *place* where Piper is probably waiting for me, seething.

"Please tell me, where am I?" I ask the nurse.

"Charleston, South Carolina," she answers. The *real* Charleston.

I'm home, I think with relief. I'm really home.

***

S.J. Walker is a mother and a new voice in the literary landscape. She graduated summa cum laude with her B.A. in Psychology and is currently studying to obtain her MFA in creative writing. She has a small scattering of publications and owns a black cat who serves as an adorable muse for tales of dark fantasy.

A Murder

Ai Jiang

The straggler's camel died before he himself, only because the man fought hunger and lost. He whispered prayers before plunging his danger into the beast, slicing its throat. His friends were moving far too quickly for our liking, but this one—

We watched with eyes glinting scattered across the dehydrated, skeletal body of desert driftwood, eager to devour the bleeding beast, dip our beaks in its flesh the same way the straggler's dagger had. And maybe for dessert, the straggler will quench whatever thirst remains within us.

We waited, feathers ruffling, unfurling our wings, cawing in hope the straggler will get on with his hunting rituals quickly so we can get started with ours. It would be best if he could finish his meal before the carcass spoils—it was already beginning to stale. And if he were to also close his eyes for a few brief moments like his companions had after feasting, it would make our process much easier. But the straggler, instead of making a fire like the men who had abandoned him, dropped to his knees on to the desert sand, face disappearing into the body of the beast. There was no elegance, only primal hunger. It was not unlike our own. Though we felt a brief moment of kinship with the man, it soon waned as the gurgling that came from his throat as he swallowed disgusted us more than it pleased us.

We cocked our heads, waiting.

The man's body heaved but his head remained out of sight. Nothing else mattered but the platter in front of him. We eyed a different platter from where we perched above.

A few of us took flight when the man's face appeared once more, covered in the blood of the dead. Patience, patience. Once all of our own settled down, we dipped our beaks and heads towards the man in unison.

"Straggler," we said, our unsynchronized caws followed one another, creating an echoing effect of the word.

The man's head whipped back and forth before landing on our sleek black bodies, eyes fervent, unfocused. Flesh hung from his lips, seeming almost like an extension. Speckles and smears of blood covered his previously unmarked face. A bronze palette with rouge.

"Who's there?"

We smiled and whispered, "They call us a *murder*."

We took flight, circled around the straggler's body as he tried to clamber into the beast he had slaughtered. His hands held the skin of its belly together, but his grip slipped from the blood. Some of us pecked at the leftover organs surrounding the beast, though most worked at the straggler's desperate fingers until they became bones, until the joints became undone, and dropped in pieces.

"Please, please— " the straggler screamed, thrashed, no longer holding the carcass together.

We left his eyes, still rolling uncontrollably until last.

"A murder, a murder, a murder—" we echoed, we laughed, then we blinded.

We reassembled on the driftwood with its curling arms and brittle bark and flaking skin, and fed it liquid. Moisture the colour of rusting iron dripped from our black feathers.

***

Ai Jiang is a Chinese-Canadian writer and an immigrant from Fujian. She is a member of HWA, SFWA, and Codex. Her work can be found in F&SF, The Dark, Uncanny, among others. She is the holder of Odyssey Workshop's 2022 Fresh Voices Scholarship. Her debut novella Linghun (April 2023) is forthcoming with Dark Matter INK. Find her on Twitter (@AiJiang_) and online (http://aijiang.ca).

The Frog Farmers

Lisha Goldberg

> From the Book of the Lord, Chapter 1 Verse 1:
> And in the end, there was Stop-Time. Earth
> had ceased rotating.
>
> Chapter 1 Verse 2: And the Lord created the
> Upheaval, shifting Earth's continents into four
> quadrants: East Edge, West Edge, Dark, and
> Light.
>
> Chapter 3 Verse 1: Then the Lord fashioned
> the Climatologists into Farmers, for the
> Climatologists had failed the Earth.
>
> Chapter 3 Verse 2: Thus spake the Lord to the
> Farmers: For your failures, ye shall know
> Farming. For your sins, ye shall know eternity.
>
> Chapter 3 Verse 7: And the Lord spake to the
> Farmers, saying: Woe onto you. For ye shall
> dwell in a special kind of Hell called Light.

TwoTen sank into his usual spot at the back of the bus. He
hoped the other Frog Farmers would leave him alone with his
thoughts, and for the first two stops, they did. As a dozen lumbering
bipeds hauled the bus across the rocky landscape, TwoTen's genetic-
memory showed him another vehicle also called a bus. But this
vehicle's driver operated the bus without using animals covered in
layers of sweat and stinking of charred air and excrement. *What did
that mean?*

"Bright Day," ThreeFive chirped as she slid into an adjacent
seat.

"Bright," TwoTen nodded.

ThreeFive eyed him. "A pellet for your thoughts," she prodded.

He hesitated. "I'm coming unglued."

"Oh. Can I see?"

He turned, allowing her to study the tear in his nictitating membrane. When she sat back, he focused his gaze out the open slot. *Window*, his genetic-memory prompted him.

"Did you see someone for that?" she asked.

He shrugged. "I could get it re-glued. But that greedy Doctor Farmer demanded too much live food. So, I'll just force myself to keep it closed."

"I could try sewing it," she offered, her voice quavering a bit.

TwoTen shuddered. "It'll get fixed with my next cloning."

"Oh." ThreeFive shrugged, bringing TwoTen's attention to a new, bloody patch on her scaly shoulder. He turned his attention to the view outside the bus.

"Well, today should be interesting," ThreeFive said. Then she paused to follow her friend's gaze out the open slot. "Oh," she frowned, "I hope no one's hurt."

"Small fire," he shrugged. "It's almost sanded over."

Genetic-memory showed him a red vehicle, (*no bipeds?!*), spewing water all over a burning structure. *Freshwater? Wasteful!*

He faced ThreeFive. "Did you say something?"

Her smile exposed the tip of her sticky tongue, a surprising shade of orange-pink. "Yes. I said, today will be interesting. The new eggs should arrive from Dark."

"Yeah," he shrugged.

"They're supposed to be hardier than the last batch."

"Uh huh." TwoTen flicked his crimson tongue, taste-smelling the maddening mix of weary animals, sweaty riders, festering cancers, and overheated metal.

"Did you hear me?" ThreeFive elbowed him. "I said we're getting better Frog eggs. Better eggs mean better Hatchlings. And better Hatchlings fill Human bellies. And well-fed Humans mean you and I— "

But TwoTen had stopped listening. Instead, he chose to relive that hateful task of raking dead Frog Hatchlings out of the gel pools. Sometimes you'd catch a bunch of bloated bodies beneath the rake, and suddenly fingers, toes, ear flaps, or worse, stomach contents, would break free and contaminate the pool. That always pissed off the Supervisor.

"One or more of you will pay for this mess with an early cloning." This was the Supervisor's favorite threat. Usually, she'd forget her harsh words once the Spiritual Court allowed her to release the Snakes. *Usually.*

TwoTen pictured the Snakes, distending their mouths and gorging on dismembered Frog parts. But Snakes also pooped in the gel, and Snake Farmers did nothing about this. That meant Frog Farmers, like TwoTen, had to strain the gel through smaller and smaller sieves. Then, the Supervisor would take a cleansed gel sample before the Spiritual Court and await their pronouncement. The Court rarely declared the gel pure on the first try.

Punishing us just because they can. TwoTen had always believed this of Human Judges. As an earlier clone, when TwoTen had been TwoThree, he had voiced this treasonous notion aloud. "Complain to the Sun," the Supervisor had snorted at him. By week's end, TwoThree had been early-cloned into TwoFour, even though the Doctor Farmer could not find one single speck of cancer on his body.

After cleaning up a Hatchling die off, TwoTen would spend hours on his basking rock, desperate to burn the smell of decay out of his nostrils. He knew he would pass these disgusting memories onto his future clones, but there was nothing he could do about it.

ThreeFive suddenly broke through TwoTen's reverie. "Sometimes, I think I had a different job." She didn't bother to check whether TwoTen had heard her. "In one of my pasts. Before Stop-Time."

TwoTen's wonky membrane snapped shut. "Don't talk of Before," he hissed.

"Others talk too," she whispered.

Dutifully, TwoTen echoed the Spiritual Court's most famous

ruling: "There was no Before. There is, was, and only ever will be Stop-Time."

> **Book of The Lord Chapter 4 verse 2: And the Lord drove the Engineers into the angry seas, and banished all manner of scientist and self-described "ologist" into Dark.**

"Well," she whispered, "a group of us Frog Farmers share our genetic-memories. And we think that Earth once spun. Like the Moon does."

TwoTen folded his arms, absently noting that his claws needed filing. But that thought got swallowed up by another genetic-memory: the day Earth slowed to a stop, with the Americas facing the Sun and the rest of the world staring into blackness.

> **Chapter 5 Verse 4: Behold, I will fashion my followers into Spiritual Beings called Humans.**
>
> **Chapter 5 Verse 5: These Humans shall dwell in the lands of East Edge and West Edge, between Dark and Light. And I shall bless the Edges with moderate temperatures, and freshwater, and greenery.**
>
> **Chapter 5 Verse 6: And the Humans danced, and sang, and made merry.**

ThreeFive leaned into TwoTen's ear cavity. "Some of us think that in Before, everybody looked like Humans."

TwoTen barked. "Are you nibbling rotten pellets?"

"Don't laugh at me." Her face turned rosy.

TwoTen yipped again. "Can you imagine us looking like Humans? Have you ever seen a Human?"

"Well, technically, none of us have." She watched his eyes roll beneath his membranes.

"Okay," he conceded, "you can't see their whole bodies through the protective suits. But you can see their oversized freak heads through their helmets."

"I guess." She brushed her hand against her scaly cheek. "What does it feel like to have smooth skin?"

"Smooth green skin." His lips stretched across his pointed teeth as he said 'green.' "Name one other thing in Light that's green."

He waited until ThreeFive shook her head.

"And how about their eyes?" TwoTen continued.

"You can't see through their goggles," she protested.

"But why do they need their goggles to be so huge and round?" he challenged. What about their feet?"

"You can't see their feet."

He sighed. "The shape of their boots. They look like floppy shovels."

"Floppy shovels?"

"You have a better description?" He arched the scales above his undamaged eye.

"Hoppy shovels," she joked. "Humans do have a funny bounce to their step, don't they?"

He nodded as another genetic-memory hijacked his brain.

Boston Globe, Letter to the Editor: When will our government stop kowtowing to these crazy, so-called experts? When that half-dead polar bear sailed a spruce tree clear into Boston Harbor, well, that should have been the last straw. But no. Now our government's buying that claim about evolution running wild. Just because one lamebrain scientist found a couple of frogs with a couple of humanoid toes, everybody's panicking. Big deal. Why doesn't our government focus on real problems, like education? Call me a Troglodyte, a Luddite, or just ass-backwards, but I want to know: When are we going to bring mathematics back into the classrooms?

The Spiritual Court denied all Farmers the right to an education. But all Farmers could read, thanks to their genetic-memories. *Better still, the Court didn't know this little fact.*

"Come on." ThreeFive put a rough palm on TwoTen's shoulder. "We're here."

Another genetic-memory tugged at the edges of TwoTen's brain as he stepped out of the bus and inhaled the dry air. *What was a scapegoat?*

Together, TwoTen and ThreeFive walked through the Farm's entry gates, stopping only to offer the Supervisor a fingerprint.

"Shedding," ThreeFive blushed when three attempts failed to leave a complete mark.

The Supervisor grabbed her wrist and flipped her palm upward.

TwoTen tensed his brow, noting how the mole on ThreeFive's wrist had begun to ooze through her scales.

"Hmm. Somebody's getting ripe for cloning," the Supervisor said.

"But I don't want…"

The Supervisor frowned, and ThreeFive hurried off, aware of the Supervisor's eyes on her tail.

"I don't want to be eaten," she whispered into TwoTen's ear cavity.

"You've been through it before," he hissed back.

The annoyance in TwoTen's voice made ThreeFive scowl. "I'm tired of being cloned and eaten and cloned and eaten," she said in a louder voice.

TwoTen picked up his pace.

ThreeFive glanced at her unraveling hand. Her genetic-memory distorted her own limb, giving her five, unscaled, slender fingers, and dull, flat nails. *I was a Frog?!*

She quickened her step to catch up with TwoTen. "My friends do more than share genetic-memories," she whispered.

"I don't want to know." TwoTen cut her off.

"We've got a plan," she continued. "We're going to join a colony. On the Moon."

TwoTen bit down on a bark, but the sounds came out anyway, a series of harsh snorts. "Nobody lives on the Moon. How could anyone live on a spinning thing?" Even as he asked the question, his own genetic-memory showed him a populated, rotating Earth.

"Our Farm used to house flying machines," she pressed on. "We're repairing one."

"Repair all you want," he snorted. "What animal can pull you up to the sky? Or maybe you will fill a balloon with hot air, like the Humans do."

ThreeFive sidled up to TwoTen. "Ask your genetic-memory about something called fuel."

TwoTen tried to oblige, but his genetic-memory left him more puzzled than enlightened.

U.S. President Arias has used the executive powers of their office to shut down the use of all solar-powered airplanes and helicopters.

"Two crashes and four emergency landings in one week is unacceptable," the President said. "Until the climatologists tell us that our planet is on the mend, we will all need to use safer, more Earth-friendly modes of transportation."

On several occasions, President Arias has referred to their personal preference for helium-powered balloons. It is believed that the American President will allow NASA to continue keeping solid rocket fuel on hand in case of an emergency in space.

TwoTen rubbed his scaly scalp, praying that his new tumor had stopped growing. In his mind's eye, he recalled one of his previous clonings, when his head lump had erupted right in front of the Supervisor. TwoTen blushed at the memory of the putrid smell, and his embarrassment as his co-workers pummeled each other in their frenzy to lick his tears.

"We just need something to burn for fuel," ThreeFive continued. "Like gel. Or eggs. Or maybe some Hatchlings."

"Treason," he muttered.

"Wait!" She scurried after him, unable to catch up until he stopped beside the other Farmers at the egg pool. The air felt a tad cooler here, thanks to the tarps thrown over the remnants of an ancient structure. Her genetic-memory showed her a Frog, of all things, probably a female, with hair the color of silvery talc. Beneath this image were the words 'President Starr's State of the Union Address.'

> **My fellow Americans, I regret to inform you that all of humanity has been blindsided. We put our trust in climatologists. We believed them when they asserted that human activity caused global warming. But tonight, I'm here to tell you that humans have had little to no impact on our changing climate. Climate change is occurring because of a natural slowing of the Earth's rotation. As the slowing continues, Earth will be drawn closer to the Sun, and will likely end up in a new orbit between Mercury and Venus. Eventually, Earth will stop spinning and one side will forever face the Sun. I'm sorry to say, the results will be catastrophic. On the positive side, we have had a little bit of time to prepare for this disaster. A little piece of humanity will survive. As we speak, rockets are heading to the moon with provisions to keep our growing colonies...**

ThreeFive's genetic-memory snapped shut when a flash of light smacked her face. *Humans.* The reflections off their metallic flying machines always preceded them. That and the smell emanating from their life support systems. She flicked her tongue. *Desalinated air and moldy cloth.* She didn't know what 'moldy' meant, but she knew that the word described the odor coming from the balloon. For an instant, she wondered whether a balloon would provide better lift than burning Frog eggs. *You really are overdue for a cloning,* she grinned inwardly.

TwoTen felt his heart swell as four Mute Farmers emerged from the cabin beneath the balloon. Without hesitating, the Mutes began the difficult task of securing the flying machine to the hitching post. In more than one incarnation, TwoTen had wished that he were one of the Mutes. Mute Farmers probably knew what went on in Dark and in both Edges. Mute Farmers probably knew where Frog eggs originated, and they probably knew how to harvest them.

Maybe they have knowledge that I can't even imagine, TwoTen thought. *Maybe I should rip out my own vocal cords so I can join the Mutes.*

Once they tethered the craft, the Mute Farmers re-entered the cabin. In a few moments, two Humans bounded into view, their silver life suits scattering the Sunlight in all directions.

What's so spiritual about Humans? TwoTen wondered. *Those big heads just squash their little necks into nothing. They can't even stand up straight.*

Humans are amazing, ThreeFive thought. *Look how their long legs dance about. They're just so… so spiritual."*

The Supervisor swished her tail, and the Farmers dropped to one knee.

The Mute Farmers reappeared, two in front and two behind. Between them was the Ark of the Frogspawn, confirming ThreeFive's prediction that Frog eggs would arrive today. Mutes never touched the Ark. Two poles were inserted into slots at the front and back of the Ark. The Mutes each bore a pole on one shoulder.

The gold Ark?! In his current incarnation, TwoTen had only ever seen the Ark made from grey sandstone. He turned his eyes towards the sculpted Human that sat atop the Ark's lid.

Why is a Spiritual Being sitting with his knees folded against his ears? TwoTen clenched his jaws to stifle a laugh.

ThreeFive's heart soared as she sneaked glances at the Ark. *So beautiful! It must be filled with a gazillion eggs!*

"Why don't they put the Ark on wheels?" ThreeFive breathed into TwoTen's ear.

"Stupid," TwoTen hissed back.

ThreeFive had no idea whether TwoTen had just insulted her or the Humans.

At the pool's edge, the Mute Farmers hoisted the Ark, earning a series of whistles and hoots from the Humans. The two leaped at the Ark and helped lower it into the pool, a gesture wildly out of character for Spiritual Beings.

These eggs must be mega-delicious, ThreeFive thought. *I wish Humans would let us taste them.*

These Humans must be mega-pond scum, TwoTen thought, unsure whether this idea came from his current brain or his genetic-memory. *What is pond scum?*

The Supervisor signaled the Farmers to rise. They watched the Humans open the lid and gently coax out the contents.

TwoTen felt his tail prickle. *Not eggs!* He screamed inside his own head. *Not Hatchlings! These are...overripe?* Never had he seen Hatchlings with scalp hair that undulated in the gel.

ThreeFive screeched, earning disproving looks from the other Farmers, including TwoTen. She didn't notice how the Supervisor narrowed her eyes.

TwoTen bit his inner cheek, wishing that the drawn blood had come from another source. *Why do Humans get the tastiest food?* He felt his chin darken, but he didn't care. *Humans do so little. But they enjoy so much. And they never get cloned. How do they survive without cloning?*

The overripe Hatchlings wrapped their limbs around each other, disoriented from their journey from Dark to Light.

TwoTen's stomach dropped. *Their eyes are open. They see!*

The Supervisor extended her arm backward. Instantly, a Frog Farmer filled the outstretched hand with a hooked pole. With great care, the Supervisor pried the pale figures apart.

Six of them, ThreeFive noted. Her rebel Moon group could try burning these Hatchlings, but that wouldn't provide enough fuel to even reach a hilltop. *Too bad they didn't bring us a few thousand eggs. That would get us off the ground!*

Each time the Supervisor freed a Hatching from the group, the animals would reach out to each other with their unnaturally long fingers and their smooth, skinny limbs. A strange word popped into ThreeFive's head: *Children.* She tilted her head. *What was a children?*

The Supervisor handed off the hook, tasking another Frog Farmer with the job of separating Hatchlings. She caught TwoTen's eye and inclined her head.

TwoTen rose and sterilized his hands by rubbing them in a pile of white sand. Then he grabbed some freshly mined pellets and sprinkled them near the Hatchling's faces. One opened its mouth, and TwoTen had to clamp his shut. *Teeth! Tiny, flat, white teeth!* What other surprises did these overripe creatures possess?

"I had a children!" ThreeFive blurted out.

"She's shedding!" TwoTen pointed to his head. "You know how shedding can addle the brain."

The Supervisor frowned and gave a quick glance toward the Humans. They ignored ThreeFive's outburst, their helmets turned towards the Hatchlings.

"They don't act like other Hatchlings," a newly cloned Farmer said. TwoTen thought her name might be EightThree or maybe EightFive. "Why don't they settle down?" the new one asked. "Why do they grimace?"

We didn't raise these Hatchlings from eggs, TwoTen wanted to say, but didn't. The other Farmers also kept their thoughts to themselves.

The Supervisor eyed the young clone. *She's only just emerged,* the Supervisor reminded herself. *EightFour will soon acquire the knowledge of EightThree.*

"Do they come from somewhere different? EightFour asked. "Are these Light Hatchlings?"

TwoTen tilted his head. *Didn't all Frogs live in Dark? They couldn't possibly be from Light. Could they?*

A long ago genetic-memory demanded ThreeFive's attention.

> **From the files of *You Wanted to Know*, the best place on the Web for celebrity gossip: Whenever Nathan Klein grabs the director's chair, you know that another blockbuster movie will be hitting the theaters. Klein is creating a documentary based on the *New York Time's* bestseller, *As the World Croaked: The Amphibian Cult and the Apocalypse.* The Amphibians first made the news when cult member Lucas Carter was arrested in Wellesley, Massachusetts. Carter was using a stolen back hoe to dig a trench straight through Route 16. Also arrested was cult member April Hagee, who disguised herself as a security guard and stole NASA's entire inventory of adult diapers. In preparation for the world's end, Amphibian cultists are digging tunnels all over North America and filling them with provisions, namely freeze-dried insect pellets and water, in the form of diaper gel. Cult leader Diamond Rainbow, a former climatologist, claims that she got the call to prophesize after meeting a bullfrog named Lord. Rainbow is touting a bible that Lord allegedly dictated to her. This bible alleges that Earth will be drawn into the Sun, and the Amphibians will take over the world.**

While ThreeFive stood transfixed by her genetic-memory, the other Farmers remained kneeling, waiting for the Supervisor to react to EightFour's questions about Frogs and Light. But the Supervisor let the young clone's words hang in the air.

Suddenly, the Humans turned their attention to the idle Farmers. The Supervisor jumped into action, assigning some Farmers into the pellet mines, some to squeeze gel from the holy cloths, and some to clean the Cloning Chambers. TwoTen grabbed ThreeFive and steered her towards the white rocks.

"Here," he closed her fingers around a bashing tool. "We'll turn this rock into sterilizing sand."

The tool slipped out of ThreeFive's hands. TwoTen bent to retrieve it, then felt something thick and wet drip onto his back. His tongue caught a hot, rusty smell, and his heart sank. He rose to see ThreeFive, head cocked to one side, staring directly at the Sun. Her nictitating membranes melted down her cheeks while her eyes boiled in her skull. Puss-filled scales dripped from her shoulder and chest.

TwoTen licked a tear from his cheek. He barely registered the Supervisor's light touch on his back, but he grasped the instructions she whispered into his ear cavity.

ThreeFive will just have to forgive me, he thought. *A Farmer can only eat so many pellets.*

After TwoTen harvested the bits of ThreeFive needed for cloning, he ate his fill of his former friend. TwoTen tackled the most precious pieces first, the heart and the brain. *Not your tastiest parts*, he noted with a little regret. *But you'd want me to have first dibs on your genetic-memory and your kindness.*

The organ meats more than filled his stomach, but TwoTen pushed himself to consume her right thigh, too. *Why should those other Farmers enjoy your sweetest part?*

In accordance with tradition, the Supervisor gave TwoTen four days off work: Two for digestion, and two to mourn his best friend. With one exception, the other Farmers gave TwoTen a wide berth.

"Look what I got!" The intruder hailed him.

From atop his basking rock, TwoTen rolled one eye downward at the newcomer. "Bright day," he muttered, more of a reprimand than a greeting.

"Day!" EightFour craned her head up at him. "Come down and look."

"I'm mourning."

"Look!"

TwoTen focused on the object in EightFour's hands. He felt the Sun's heat leave his bones.

"Is that ThreeFive?" he asked.

"Yup," she giggled. "They look really pretty all lined up in my cave."

"They?"

"I've got six skulls so far," she said. "ThreeFive will be number seven. Supervisor says I should start asking permission before I take them. So can I have your skull?"

TwoTen's chin grew black.

"Not now," she cut off his protest with another giggle. "When it's your time. Can I have your skull when you get yourself cloned? I'll put it right next to ThreeFive, I promise."

He tilted his head for a moment. "Why do you need skulls?"

She shrugged. "They keep me company. And they feel like family. Isn't that funny? I don't know what 'family' means. Do you?"

A single word wafted by TwoTen's genetic-memory: *wedding*?

TwoTen shrugged. "Okay," he said. "When it's time for my cloning, you can have my skull. But you have to let me and ThreeFive come visit."

"Yippee!" EightFour trilled.

"Now scoot," TwoTen ordered.

"Yes sir!" EightFour saluted with her tail and dashed off, her claws kicking up tendrils of dust.

TwoTen pressed his chest against the basking rock and allowed his limbs and his tail to dangle freely. Sleep overtook him immediately. As he slumbered, the Moon crawled across Earth's sky, its colonists busily going about their day. The Moon's astronomers took advantage of the Moon's rotation to check out their ancient home. One pointed a telescope directly at TwoTen. But, even with this newest lens, the astronomer could only make out mountains and craters. Another scientist sent a radio signal to Earth. An ancient machine on the Farm received the broadcast, recorded it, and stored it along with hundreds of other words and images that had come from the Moon's citizens.

A loud blast from the Farm bus sent TwoTen tumbling off the basking rock. Rosy cheeked, he scrambled into the vehicle before the driver could blow the horn again. Pleased that no one had taken his favorite seat, TwoTen settled in for the ride. He hoped that the other Farmers would leave him alone with his thoughts, and for the first two stops, they did.

Then a familiar figure slid in beside him.

"Bright Day," ThreeSix chirped.

"Day," TwoTen nodded. "Welcome back."

"Back from where?" ThreeSix asked.

TwoTen felt his cheeks darken. *Did she forget so soon?*

ThreeSix nudged him. "Pellet for your thoughts."

He sat quietly for a moment, envying her unblemished scales. "I don't know what will happen to those overripe Hatchlings."

She tilted her head. "Isn't it obvious? The Humans will eat them."

"Those Hatchlings *knew* things," he whispered. They had facial expressions."

"That's silly," she shook her head. "Frogs have teeny tiny brains and teeny tiny snouts."

He looked at her.

"What happened to your membrane?" she asked.

"I tore it," he said. "That should be in your genetic-memory."

She paused. "What's genetic-memory?"

His tail tightened. He leaned towards her ear cavity. "I've decided to join your group," he whispered. "I want to build a rocket. To the Moon."

She flicked her orange-pink tongue at a passing fly. "This should be a wonderful day at the Farm," she smiled. "I hope the Humans bring us lots of eggs. My favorite day is when the new eggs come. How about you?"

"Yes," he drew out the word. "My favorite day is when the new eggs come."

Together, the two presented themselves to the Supervisor at the gate. The Supervisor turned over TwoTen's palm and clucked at the maturing cancer cells. "A few more weeks," she grinned.

"What will happen to the overripe Hatchlings?" TwoTen cried out, surprising even himself.

The Supervisor frowned. "Keep it together," she hissed. "We already have twelve extra Farmers in the Cloning Chambers. There's no more room. If you can't control yourself, we'll have to waste you. Understand?"

"Yes," TwoTen felt his bowels shrink. "You get eaten. You don't get cloned."

"Precisely," the Supervisor whispered. "I'd hate to do that to an experienced Farmer like yourself."

TwoTen nodded. "Apologies," he said softly. In a louder voice he said, "I want to tell you how much I enjoy working with new eggs."

From the preserved writings of Harrison Singh, climatologist: I'm at Eastman Pond, and I'm observing another clutch of those half-human, half-frog creatures. I won't tell anyone about this latest find. Too many of us are already dead, thanks to all the deniers who claim that we scientists are the crazies. Maybe they're right. Maybe Climate Change is part of Earth's natural aging. Maybe this speeded-up evolutionary process is, too. But I never would have guessed that frogs would be so quick to acquire human speech. In between all their croaking and their ribbiting, I'm catching words like "lord" and "superior being." And maybe I'm mistaken, but I'd swear that one of them keeps grunting the word "bible." And, my God they're staring at me. One of them just said "lizard." He must mean these thick plates of skin that have flattened out my ear lobes and make my arms itch like mad. Everybody's coming down with this skin issue. Reminds me of those old pandemics I heard about in history class, only I think those just affected nasal

passages. I can only pray that this evolutionary process ends before these frogs, before they…. What? What's next?

"Bright Day." ThreeSix greeted the newly-cloned TwoEleven as she joined him on the bus. "Welcome back. The Humans might bring us new eggs today. I hope that's true."

"Bright Day," TwoEleven grinned, then tilted his head. "What are Humans?"

***

Lisha E. Goldberg started her professional career as a technical writer, then switched to teaching science to elementary children. She enjoys writing short stories and poems. Her hobbies include playing piano and creating artwork with mosaic tiles. Her short stories have appeared in TANSTAAFL Press, Mad Scientist Journal, The Blotter, and Chicken Soup for the Soul. She is a past winner of Writer's Digest Magazine's short story contest with a Inspirational/Religious theme.

A Midday Apparition

Julia C. Lewis

Andrej could feel the harsh sun rays blistering his bare shoulders. He had been working in this same field since five o'clock this morning, and was still only halfway done with the harvest. He knew his father was expecting him to finish today, and all hell would break loose if he came home early. Not wanting to anger the old drunkard, Andrej sighed and picked up his tools yet again, even though he could feel the beginnings of a heatstroke make itself noticeable within his body.

A sudden gust of wind baffled the man and made him glance backwards. Out there in the midst of the overgrown field was a beautiful woman dressed in a long white gown. The sun was illuminating her like a beautiful apparition; a mirage in this bleak field. Surely, a creature this magnificent had no place in a grimy place like this, and must have become lost somehow. Enchanted by this sudden visitor, Andrej started walking towards her, now completely unaware of the blistering heat or the throbbing in his head.

"Hello," he approached her shyly, suddenly having lost all the confidence he usually bore around the girls in the village.

The woman gazed upon him, a sly smile on her lips. "Well, hello there."

Andrej studied her closely. The woman had long black hair that glistened in the sunlight, and her dress was plain, yet hugged her every curve. The only odd thing about her were the giant rusty pair of scissors she held in her hands. It simply didn't fit the situation. Yet, being a man in the prime of his life, Andrej didn't worry too much about it and rather studied the outline of her breasts.

"I have a question," the woman said and Andrej blushed with

embarrassment.

"O-ok…" He swallowed hard.

"In the heat of the day, I may appear before you. I'm neither young nor old, beautiful nor ugly. Answering my question wrong may cost you your head. Who am I?"

Shaking his head in confusion, Andrej suddenly felt the hotness of the day overtake him. His vision became blurry as the throbbing in his head became unbearable. It was too much. *I must be experiencing heatstroke,* he thought as he collapsed to the floor, still looking at the woman above him.

"Do you know the answer?" she questioned, her voice taking on a menacing quality as she towered above Andrej.

"No..please…get…hel—"

Suddenly the woman cackled loudly, and Andrej saw her appearance change before his straining eyes. What had once been a beautiful woman was now an old shriveled up hag. Her skin was gray—not unlike rotting meat left out too long in the sun—and her eyes were black like she was devoid of a soul.

"I'm sorry, dear. Wrong answer."

Her shears glinted in the sunlight as she bent down towards the ground, and with one great *snip!* cut off Andrej's head.

"I'm Lady Midday, my dear. You should've known that."

**

Julia C. Lewis is a book reviewer, editor and writer. Her work has appeared in anthologies such as Blackberry Blood, Dead of Night and Slash-Her. She was born and raised in Germany, and also currently lives there after spending some time in the US. Her heart belongs to her husband, two kids, and three dogs. Her favorite book genre is horror with a particular taste in indie horror.

www. http://www.juliaclewis.com/

Twitter: @curiositybooked

High Cowton

Tim Jeffreys

After checking in at the hotel, Benjamin was directed to his
room. Room twenty-four. It was down a set of stairs, and next door
to some kind of kitchen or scullery. Entering, he had the distinct
impression that he'd known that room before, perhaps in a dream or,
more likely, a nightmare. A carpet the colour of red wine had a
disorientating pattern of white flowers and swirling stems. There was
a TV fixed to the wall and a fridge which he was initially grateful
for, but which would hum on and off throughout the night, the noise
of it keeping him on the margins of sleep. And there was a peculiar
odour, ripe and unpleasant, distinct to rooms in cheap hotels. But
opening the window let in the noise of traffic on the busy road out
front and he was left with no choice but to close it again.

A woman of perhaps twenty manned the reception
desk. Though she had tried hard to make herself appealing, her face
was shapeless and forgettable. He couldn't help but think she judged
him. From the train station, he had walked a steep incline to reach
the hotel, and the day was muggy. At check-in, and every time he
saw the receptionist thereafter, he was out of breath, red-faced, and
lines of sweat ran down his brow.

"Yor-right?" she would say, tonelessly, to him; and he realised
it was indifference she exuded, not judgment. "Yor-right?"

No, he wanted to tell her. *No. I am not all right.*

*

The following day, he returned to the station and took a short train
ride to Tanfield. Ignoring the village centre, he instead found a road
that climbed steeply into the moorland hills. Within an hour, he
stood on a ridge where he could look down on the neighbouring

village of High Cowton. Sheep grazed on the football field behind the school building. He ran his eyes along neat rows of clay-coloured houses. He knew the history of the place. The houses had all been built with local stone. It occurred to him that to live in those houses was to exist inside the subterraneous. A house dug up from under the hills. Something subterrestrial.

That's true of all houses.

It was the voice of Doctor Rawlinson, his psychotherapist, that he heard in his head, steering him away from darker imaginings in her matter-of-fact way as she frequently would during their sessions.

Most houses in the UK are made of brick or stone that comes from underground. There's nothing unusual about a house made of stones, Benjamin.

He had to admit, the voice was right. It made sense.

One of those stone houses he'd lived in as a child. But he recognised nothing. The hills he remembered. The hills with their orangey-brown or purple sheen. He'd seen a time-lapse film of those same hills once. It had unnerved him, the way they'd appeared to undulate like a sea. *These hills should all be green*, he recalled being told once. *It's pollution that causes them to look that way. Those colours. Pollution from the Industrial Revolution.*

He remembered too the factory, remembered its dark, looming presence. It was now home to a café and chic little shops, or so he'd read. He remembered the chimney stacks, the canal. But the streets, the houses, he remembered nothing of those. Which one had been his? He had no idea. Could not even recall the street name. Perhaps if he descended the slope of the hill into the village, the memories would come flooding back. This was what Doctor Rawlinson had advised him to do. *Go back to High Cowton. Confront your fears.* But no, he turned away. He would not go there. Not that day. Not yet.

"Tomorrow," he said to himself. "Tomorrow, I'll go."

Arriving back at the hotel that evening, out of breath again and sweating, he realised the next day would be the twenty-forth of August. And his room number was twenty-four.

A coincidence, said Doctor Rawlinson's voice inside his head.

But Benjamin thought it couldn't be a coincidence. "I don't believe in coincidences," he said, as if Doctor Rawlinson was there in the room with him. "It must be significant. Somehow."

*

At some point during the night, he was woken by men talking loudly outside his room.

"Is he in there?" one of the voices said.

Benjamin pulled the duvet closer around his head. Had he latched the door?

"Never belonged here," the other voice said. "Why's he come back?"

"He's not like us. Never was. He's not welcome around here."

"We'll show him. Eh?"

"Yes."

Benjamin squeezed his eyes shut. There was the sound of a door opening and snapping shut again, then silence.

Benjamin lay still and waited for Doctor Rawlinson's calm, reassuring voice to enter his mind.

That's not what they said, she told him. *You were half-asleep. You imagined it. Even if it was, they can't possibly have been talking about you. No one knows you here. Not anymore.*

They know me, Benjamin thought. *They've been waiting.*

*

The next day started off fine, so Benjamin—his mood lightened by the sunshine—deciding he had, after all, misheard those night-time voices; and he took the train straight to High Cowton. He knew if he got off in Tanfield and hiked into the hills he would lose his nerve and not be able to descend into his home village. But the sky had clouded over by the time he reached High Cowton, and stepping down on to the station platform he was overwhelmed with panic. *The twenty-fourth of August,* he kept thinking. *Room twenty-four. It can't be a coincidence. I don't believe in coincidences. It means something! It's a warning!*

He sat down on a bench outside the station and waited for his mind to still and his breathing to return to normal. In front of him was a black drystone wall which marked the edge of a sloping field. Echoing the rolling contours of the landscape beyond, there was a gap in the wall about six feet wide. It looked as if something had bulldozed through it. Some charging beast perhaps. Or a rampaging crowd.

No.

He closed his eyes.

It probably fell down on its own.

By the time Benjamin felt calm again, it had started to rain and he'd convinced himself that the best thing to do was to go back to the hotel.

On the journey back, he thought about what Doctor Rawlinson had said when he told her about that day when he was seven-years old and he'd seen a man beaten to death on the street in broad daylight.

"I was with my father," he'd said. "We'd just left the butcher's and we saw this man come running around the corner of the street. He must have been about fifty. Well-dressed. He looked frightened. Then we saw a big mob of people come around the corner chasing him. They were carrying sticks and metal rods. Anything they could find. I was scared stiff. I wanted to go home, but my father made me stop and watch. They fell on him and they beat him to death, right there in the street, right in front of us. When it was over, I asked my father why they did it, and all he said was, 'Had to be done, son. He didn't belong here. He should never have come back.'"

"Did you ever ask your father about that incident, later in life?" Doctor Rawlinson wanted to know.

"I did, but he just laughed and looked at me like I was crazy."

"Then it can't have happened," Doctor Rawlinson said. "It's a false memory. Somehow, an actual memory of visiting the butcher's shop with your father has become confused with something else. Perhaps you saw something on the TV that you shouldn't have seen at that age, and it shocked you. The content of the memory, and the source have become disassociated in your mind. People weren't beaten to death in the street in the middle of the day by angry mobs, Benjamin. Not in a quiet little village like High Cowton. Not even back in the mid-1980s." She finished with a smile.

"But I saw it. I saw."

*

When he entered the hotel, the receptionist watched him from behind her desk at the far end of the hall. Though her face was blank, he thought there was something studious about the way she looked at him. Quietly conspiratorial. Her mouth opened.

"Yor-right?"

He nodded, wiped a sleeve across his brow, and hurried down the stairs to his room.

*

Sun again the next morning. And the sky, which he scrutinised on leaving the hotel, had only little puffs of cloud. It looked like it was going to be a fine day. He arrived at the train station and bought a direct ticket to High Cowton.

No point beating around the bush. Just go there. Walk around. See that there's nothing to be frightened of, confront your fears like Doctor Rawlinson says.

During the short train ride he thought about his ex-girlfriend, Carly.

"Where are you from?" she'd asked him on their first date.

"Up north," he'd told her.

"Where up north?"

"Oh, some little village. You won't have heard of it." He'd hoped she wouldn't press him any further. And at the time she hadn't, but she returned to the subject a few months later, when their relationship was firmly established.

"What's the name of that village you're from? The one up north?"

They were lying in bed together one Sunday morning when she asked this. At her house. He'd loved waking up at her place, with none of his own possessions around. How light that had made him feel, how free. Carly had been facing him, her head propped on one elbow, her thick orange hair tousled from sleep.

"It's a dull little place, really. Not very interesting."

"What's the name?"

"Does it matter?"

She'd smiled and slapped his arm playfully. "Why won't you tell me? What's the name of the village?"

"High Cowton."

"High Cowton? Sounds very rustic. Don't you ever go back there?"

"I haven't been back there since the day I left for University."

"But aren't your parents still there?"

"Both of my parents are dead. I wouldn't go back to that village if you paid me."

She had laughed at this. "Why ever not?"

"I just don't belong there anymore. I'm not the same person I was then. And I don't want to be. It wouldn't be right to go back."

Again, she'd laughed. "Are you worried the village won't accept you? Is that it? Because you've got a degree? Because you're a teacher? Because you've travelled? Because you visit art galleries and watch films with subtitles, and live in London? Huh? That sounds very snooty, Benjamin. Maybe that's the real issue here. You've turned into an absolute snob."

She had said all this good-naturedly.

"It doesn't matter. I can't go back."

"Well, I'd like to go," she'd said.

"What?"

"I want to know you. I want to see where you grew up. Will you take me there one day? Please."

He must have shown some horror in his expression, because her face changed.

"What's the matter? It can't be that bad, can it? I can't believe you haven't been back, not even once to the place where you were born."

That was when he told her about his recurring dream of being back in High Cowton. Of stumbling through the village streets, knowing there was no way out. Imprisoned by the surrounding hills.

"When I wake up," he told her. "It always takes me a few minutes to remember that I'm not in High Cowton anymore, that I left the village a long time ago. I have to remind myself of all the years that have passed since I left, all the things I've done, everything I've achieved, just to assure myself that it was only a dream, and that I am most definitely not still trapped in High Cowton."

Carly had stared at him for a few moments after he told her this. Then she said, "Trapped? Wow. What did it do to you that place?"

*

He stood for a moment on the deserted station platform and listened to the train departing. When he realised he could no longer hear it, he exited via a wooden gate and took the few steps down to the street. He moved robotically. He had stopped his thoughts. On his right were the church gardens, shrouded by tall conifers. The graveyard looked gloomy and uninviting even bathed in sunlight. The soot-blackened exterior of the church could just be glimpsed beyond the gravestones and crowding trees. Ahead of him, a road wound downwards and he guessed that it would lead into the centre of the village. Instead of following it, he took a left and found himself walking along the canal. A dilapidated barge was moored beside the bank from which a man in a bucket-hat stood still as a statue, watching him pass. Though unnerved by the man's stillness, he kept walking. He knew the canal path led back to Tanfield. It couldn't be more than a few miles. Peering through the trees on his left, he saw what appeared to be a dried-up lake. All that remained was a large area of cracked earth, in the centre of which was a rowboat. Two boys of about ten years old sat in the boat, vigorously working the oars. They looked over the side of the boat from time to time, appearing perplexed as to why they were going nowhere.

You never will go anywhere if you stay here, lads, Benjamin thought.

He stopped in his tracks. What was he doing? Where was he going? All he had to do was walk around High Cowton, just a quick circuit of the village centre and then he could get back on the train. If he wanted to conquer his irrational fear of the place, and it was Doctor Rawlinson who called it *irrational,* and if he wanted the recurring dream to stop, all he had to do was go there and see the village for what it was. A harmless little Yorkshire township.

He began walking back the way he'd come. This time, he ignored the man stood on the barge, who appeared not to have moved at all. He thought about Carly. Maybe she would agree to meet with him if he told her that he'd conquered his fear. When they were together, she'd kept talking about High Cowton, asking over and over again if they could visit the village where he'd grown up. When, eventually, he'd refused to talk about it, she'd accused him of hiding something. Why wouldn't he take her? Was he ashamed of her? She'd laughed when he told her he was terrified of the place. He never told her about the man he'd seen beaten to death in the middle of the street. If he told her that, she'd have thought him mad.

That's what they do if you dare to go back, he'd thought about telling her. *They kill you.*

Ridiculous, said the voice of Doctor Rawlinson. *It's a paranoid fantasy, that's all it is, Benjamin. Going back to High Cowton will be your first step towards conquering that.*

"All right, all right," he said aloud. "I'm here, aren't I? I'm doing it."

When he reached the church again, he saw that a couple of cars were idling at the junction. Getting closer, he saw why. Some geese had wandered into the middle of the road and waddled there aimlessly, in no hurry to get out of the path of the oncoming traffic. Benjamin was going to walk by, but then he changed his mind and stepped into the road, clapping his hands to urge the geese on their way.

"Thank you!" a woman's voice called out of one of the car windows.

There it was. He'd helped someone. And they had thanked him.

Perhaps it isn't so bad here after all.

He felt good suddenly, brave. He began walking the sloping road he assumed would take him into the village centre. He noticed a Tesco, an incongruous sight among all the old stone facades, but a comforting one. As he crossed the street to another row of shops, a man passing the other way said to him, "Good morning."

"Good morning!"

He looked into the baker's window, enticed by the delicious looking buns and pastries on display. The shop girl, leaning over the counter, smiled at him.

I'll be coming back here later. I'm going to sample some of those cakes.

He practically skipped along the row of shops until he arrived at a post office on the corner of the street.

I'm cured, he thought. *That's it, I'm cured.*

"Yor-right?"

Had he heard that? He looked around to see who had spoken, but there was no one around. Perhaps it had come from an open window, or from inside one of the shops. Of course, it couldn't be the receptionist from the hotel he'd heard. The hotel was miles away. Besides, around here everyone spoke in the same way.

Shortly, he decided, he would go looking for the house he grew up in. But first he wanted to sit down a moment and watch the world go by. Watch what went on in this place, if anything! Ha! There was a bench outside the ironmongers. He sat down on the bench and tilted his head back, so that the sun could warm his face. He smiled. *Such a sense of space here*, he thought. *Such openness.* Why had he not noticed before? Since arriving here, he'd been waiting for a sensation of being home, and he'd been mildly angered to have felt nothing for the place. Now it came. *These hills. This is where I belong.* How strange to think he could have lived in London for so many years, and actually feared returning to a pleasant little place like High Cowton. That he could have had nightmares about it. London was where the real horrors happened. Knife crime was on the rise again. Muggings were a daily occurrence. The news reports were always full of rape and gang war and drug dealing. It was amazing anyone dared step out of their front door in London. Nothing like that, he was certain, ever took place in High Cowton.

And it was true what Doctor Rawlinson had said, he couldn't possibly have seen a man run down by a mob and beaten to death in broad daylight. Here? It had to be a false memory. A paranoid fantasy.

He noticed the door of the newsagents on the other side of the street closing, and the blinds being pulled down over the window. Then the same thing happened in the gift shop further along. Then all the shops along the row were closing. He glanced at his watch. One o'clock. *How quaint*, he thought. *The shops close for lunch.* He watched an old woman exit the post office and begin making her slow way along the street, and seeing this he laughed. *Angry mobs? Imagine it! The most exciting thing that happens here is geese in the road holding up traffic.*

Maybe I should move back here. The thought came from nowhere.

Maybe I should move back. I could get a teaching job at the school. Wake up every morning to fresh air and beautiful countryside. Maybe Carly would move here with me. She'd love it here, I'm sure she would.

Before he could pursue the idea further, he heard sounds from a nearby street that made him sit up straight. It sounded like a lot of people running all together, and the bray of combined shouts, like the crowd at a football match.

What's this?

The old woman had stopped ambling along the opposite pavement and had turned to look at him. He raised his eyebrows in query. She merely stared. Leaning forward, he peered towards the far corner of the street, the direction from which the sounds appeared to coming from. And they were getting louder.

Something's happening after all!

He saw it then in his mind's eye. A mob of people would round the corner and halt there, looking at him. And he would see that in their hands they carried trays of pastries, tins of homemade cakes, and bottles of wine and beer. Children would come forward from the crowd, waving little hand-drawn flags and scattering flowers. Then the crowd would move forward as one and, as they bore down upon him they would, in a unified voice, roar, "Welcome home, Benjamin!"

And Carly would emerge from the crowd and embrace him, and tell him it was all her idea. She had planned everything, with the help of Doctor Rawlinson of course, who was also there.

He waited, expectantly, a child-like glee in his eyes, to see them appear around the corner.

***

Tim Jeffreys' short fiction has appeared in Supernatural Tales, Not One of Us, The Alchemy Press Book of Horrors 2 & 3, and Nightscript, among various other publications. His novella, Holburn, a ghost story set in an exclusive girls' school, will be published by Manta Press in August 2022. Follow his progress at www.timjeffreys.blogspot.co.uk.

The Thaw

Amanda Casile

Dara was in a bar when the ice fell. A hand on her waist, her arms pressed against the sticky counter. She took a sip of whatever was in her glass – sickly sweet, he'd ordered for her – and the room swam. The TV above the bar flashed from the intermission buzzer to breaking news.

The plasticky, fake-concerned face of a newscaster appeared. The bar was loud, and the closed captions blurred and doubled in Dara's eyes. But then came the aerial shots of a vast Antarctic ice shelf sliding off into the ocean. For a moment she was back in that frozen desert. Hearing the rough, crunching sound her boots made in that snow, feeling the bite of wind through her parka. The eternal darkness of winter.

The image of that blue-white mass splintering one hundred pieces and drifting off to sea thundered inside her brain. Her vision tunneled, goosebumps dancing across her arms despite the bar's stifling heat. *Shit*, she muttered. She downed her syrupy drink, wriggled out of the man's embrace, and squeezed her way through the sweaty, sardine-packed fans. "Hey, wait!" he called behind her, probably hoping to collect on his investment, but she didn't turn back.

The cool air and silence of the dark street washed over her like a balm. She fumbled with her phone, heels clacking against the pavement. She'd deleted Grace's number years ago, after she stormed out of the project room, slamming the door on both Grace and her career. But she still knew it by heart.

The collapse was on the western edge, so it might be alright. *It might be alright*, she chanted in rhythm with her steps and the long, melancholic ringtones. Grace didn't pick up. *Shit*. She shoved her phone back into her pocket and managed to hail a cab in the sea of college students out on the town without a care. What was another melted ice shelf to them? Nothing. It happened all the time these days.

The cab pulled up in front of Dara's building. She tumbled out onto the sidewalk like she had too many limbs. Beyond the glare of downtown streetlights, tiny sparkles of silver dotted the sky. Nothing like what she'd seen during their fieldwork at Amundsen. Carina, Centaurus, Crux. Long, cold nights of nothing but sky and snow and stars…and Grace's arms around her waist, lips on hers.

Damnit.

Dara's phone jangled in her pocket, cutting off her thoughts. She saw the number, held the phone to her ear, her throat closing over with ice.

"Dara?" Grace's voice was always calm, professorial. Dara loved that about her. *Each piece of Antarctic ice that falls to the sea changes its salinity. Dara, we're talking drastic alteration of oceanic composition. Not to mention rising sea levels – over five feet in some areas – and elevated temperatures. It will change oceanic currents, shift the natural cycles all living things rely on.*

"You there?"

"Yeah. It's me," Dara finally responded. "I guess you saw it. I was…I tried to call you."

"What time is it?"

"Late. I don't know. Does it matter?"

Grace coughed. "It does – how soon can you get on a plane?"

"What?" Dara fumbled with her keys in the old lock.

"Are you drunk?"

Dara bit off a laugh. "Does *that* matter?"

A long sigh on the other end of the line, followed by another cough. "Listen, I could—" Static swallowed Grace's words.

"Grace?" Dara slammed the door shut behind her. Phone switched to speaker, she tossed it onto the bed and peeled out of her ridiculous outfit, a remnant of her college days, now two sizes and ten years too small.

"—happened faster than we expected – don't know what's going – need someone who understands this stuff, like *really* understands it. Like you."

She shifted the phone back to her ear. "Grace you're cutting out. What are you saying?"

"—back on base. The Foundation will pay for you to—Call Dr. Stadler—plane to Punta Arenas. Tonight if you can." She cut off again, this time because of more coughing. "They'll pick you up there. Just get here ASAP. I need you."

Dara turned the words over in her mind, enjoying the way they sounded in the mouth of her former lover. How uncharacteristic. "Grace, are you okay?"

"Just get here, okay? I'll fill you in when you arrive."

*

The props of the Twin Otter sent ice spiraling through the air, tiny fairies in the sunlight. Dara leaned against her safety restraint, eyes peeled for Grace's red hair against the desolate, white backdrop. But the field was empty. Dara chewed her lip.

The base squatted a few meters away, gunmetal gray and brutalist. The heart-tightening nostalgia that rocketed through her at the sight sent her reeling. It had been six years since she'd wandered those claustrophobic halls, isolated for four dark, freezing months, observing the movements of microscopic fungal spores until she went cross-eyed.

She swallowed back a wave of nausea as the plane tipped left before hitting the runway. Her heartbeat pounded in her head, vestiges of a hangover buzzing in her teeth. The flight to Chile had been long and sleepless, rendering her a dry, brittle husk. She pulled up the furred hood of her parka and jumped into the blinding flurry. With a wave at the captain, she shouldered her pack and jogged across the snow to Destination Alpha, the base's main entrance.

Her boots clanged against the metal steps, breath coming out in short bursts. She still couldn't believe she'd agreed to come. Here she was again, following Grace to the literal end of the Earth.

The door pushed open with a groan, and a wave of warm air blew out, followed by the stagnant smell of humans in close quarters. Funny, she hadn't remembered that, but maybe she'd been so busy inhaling Grace's lavender and spice scent, she'd overlooked the stench of their daily lives in the captivity of these barracks.

The hallway stretched out ahead, empty. Her steps echoed in the open space. The building felt like the discarded exoskeleton of a locust.

"Hello?" she called, her voice deafening. "Grace?"

Summer months were always busy. The base buzzed with over one hundred researchers and staff. Now, the silence weighed on her. A massive, catastrophic event like the collapse of Thwaite glacier should have filled the base to the brim.

They could be out in the field, she reasoned. She stepped over the threshold and peered into the empty gym and theater to her left. Surely, even if they were busy, someone would have at least come to greet her. Dara moved deeper into the base, checking more rooms– music room, craft room, conference room – all empty.

Unease prickled at the nape of her neck. The plane was long gone. What if she was alone out here? No, the pilot spoke to *someone* on the radio. She'd heard it. She quickened her steps to the comms room, humming to herself to push away the terror rising in her gut.

As she neared, something clattered behind her. Dara jumped and spun as a man staggered through a door a few paces away. He coughed, raking a forearm over his mouth, and took a few more halting steps. Dara instinctively backed away at his erratic movements, but recognition began to bloom. The glasses perched on his nose sat askew, and the few hairs he normally wore combed over his bald spot stood straight up.

"Bjorn?" she hazarded.

He jerked up, craned his head toward her, blinking. After an unsuccessful fumble at his glasses, he said, "Dara? What are you–" A coughing fit doubled him over, his thin elbows jerking outward with each wave. Dara clutched the straps of her pack, as though they could spirit her away from this empty strangeness.

"Grace called me," she said when his fit silenced.

"You shouldn't have come."

"But the Thwaite…"

Bjorn nodded, the hairs on his head flapping. "The Doomsday Glacier. You don't even know the half, Dara. You don't even– Well. Well, maybe you do." His nodding grew more vigorous, then stopped. His gaze drifted up to the ceiling. "Leptoglossum retirugum, Galerina, Cryomyces Minteri. Which one is it? Which one–" He shook with coughs again, this time releasing a fine droplet-spray of blood. His body twitched, like the start of seizure. "Sorry." He turned and staggered away, muttering to himself as he zig-zagged down the hall.

Dara stood, stricken, her heart thudding against her ribs. The walls pressed in, the quick-rise panic of a trapped animal. Her mind spun, replaying images of the ice shelf – easily the size of Nevada – sliding away, the sea rippling outward. Memories of microscopic mycelia lighting up behind her lids. The fifty page report she'd written six winters ago, which Grace plonked into the lab's recycling bin. *Impossible and irrelevant,* she'd said. *You can't submit this.*

The lab. That's where Grace would be. Forgetting the comms, Dara sprinted down the hall to the left. A din of hushed voices and intermittent coughing bled out into the corridor, and then there was Grace, bent over a microscope. Thinner, but with that unmistakable red hair falling over her face. Small groups gathered around other work stations. At least two people sat on the floor, backs against the walls, eyes closed, faces to the ceiling. Sleeping?

Dara cleared her throat, and Grace jumped to standing. "Dara!" she cried, as though welcoming the sun after months of darkness. "You came!" Tears sparkled in the edges of Grace's eyes, which were an alarming shade of gray, shot through with red. Her thin arms twined around Dara.

"Of course I came." Her skin thrummed with electricity, the way it did every time Grace touched her. One of the sleeping scientists – Davis, Dara recalled – doubled over, hacking blood across the floor. She shot Grace a worried look. "All this," she waved a hand to the room, the spatter of blood, "is from Thwaite?"

Grace nodded, her face crumpling. Dara had never seen her like this – always her mentor, her critic. "You were right," she said, voice trembling. "About the fungi, about everything. I'm so sorry. You could have saved us if I hadn't–" She swallowed. "You still can. Davis took samples, confirmed it's the fungus you…the one you speculated about, the unnamed one. We've been calling it Dara's fungus." She gave a crazy kind of giggle. In the corner, Davis slumped over sideways, unresponsive. Grace's face grew serious. "It's too late, isn't it?"

The air filters thrummed above as Dara's eyes danced over the micro-fine drops of blood spattered across the floor. The sparse groups of researchers all held the same gray twinge to their skin as Grace. Davis lay sprawled, now. Thin, gray filaments rose from his eyes, nose, mouth, and twined over his body, like a time-lapse nature film.

"I can try. Where are the samples? If I can create a fungicide that interacts with this particular strain, then…" Dara paused as Grace caught a bloody cough with her forearm. "If all else fails, we contain it."

"Half the base has already evacuated. And that damn ice shelf is bobbing off to who knows where. Spreading who knows what."

Dara's head swam. She put a hand against the cool metal desk to steady herself, cleared her scratchy throat. "I need some air."

They retraced Dara's steps to the exit, blinking in the blinding sunlight. Grace leaned against Dara, her cough speckling the snow red.

"You didn't call me here to cure this, did you?"

Grace gazed at her and reached down to intertwine their fingers. "You could have, Dar'. You could have."

"But…" Dara prompted.

"It's too late." A thread-thin filament wriggled from Grace's tear duct and probed at the air like a curious snake. "I just couldn't imagine the rest of my life without you." The Antarctic wind grabbed Grace's hair, raising it like a flame.

Dara's heart shattered, brittle ice in a gale. She stifled a cough and pulled Grace's shivering form against hers. "I love you." She breathed it all in – no more stale barracks scent. Only Grace. It was always only Grace.

She squeezed Dara's hands like a lifeline. "I'm sorry, I should've–.

"It doesn't matter." Across the tundra, ice groaned. The probing filament closed the gap between them, tickled Dara's cheek, burrowed into her ear. Their lips met, and the world disappeared.

***

Amanda lives in Vancouver with her partner, two daughters, and a black cat named Lucky Nightmare. She enjoys writing stories with strong female characters and catastrophes both large and small.

I Don't Bother With the Lights Anymore

Zary Fekete

I can't read the names on the door plate. And I've just struck my last match. The last three burned out before I could find the name. I pray that this one doesn't… Yes! There it is. *Ms. Jerusha Wyvern.* She's the one I need. Ninth floor.

I drop the now unneeded match and slowly push open the heavy door; it probably weighs more than me. The hallway inside is very dark, but there is one of those old-fashioned light switches on the wall…perhaps you remember the kind? They light the stairwell for about a minute before switching off. I suppose it's to conserve electricity.

There is enough light-time to get me to the elevator and then, with a click, there is darkness again. By then, however, I have summoned the elevator and it is slowly crawling its way down toward me from the dim place somewhere above.

I don't need the light that much, anyway. I'm going blind, you see. I have become more accustomed to judging things by their sound. I feel like I am becoming sharper at seeing people by their voices and their words. I couldn't tell you what the taxi driver looked like, the one who brought me to this street, but I would remember his voice if I heard him again. When he talked I could feel his smiles. He asked me why I was here in the 8th district.

I probably told him more than he wanted to know. I'm so nervous, after all. My search has paid off, you see. I've found one. And now that I was on my way to see her, I kept closing my eyes and silently reciting the words I'd been rehearsing.

The cab driver let me talk for a while and then we rode the rest of the way in silence. Before he dropped me off he reminded me that *the 8th district isn't safe for young women anymore.* And even though it was still daytime, still afternoon, it was fairly dark and overcast. It looked like it might rain. *A young lady might catch cold,* he said. *You should be careful,* he told me. I told him I didn't plan on being there long. I would only need a few moments with her.

By now the elevator has arrived and I'm inside. It has an old-fashioned accordion door which takes all my weight to close. By squinting hard, I'm able to make out the floor numbers. I press the button for the ninth. There is a metallic groan and an ancient shudder and then the elevator begins to rise. I smell different smells from each floor as I pass them by. Potatoes, something like mushrooms, garlic.

Something about the smells sends me back into the memory from so many months ago when it happened. A group of us, we had decided to follow the path of the last solar eclipse during the last days of 2020 before so many things changed. There was an empty field off of a country road where we waited. We built a campfire. Prepared food.

Those people who write about these things, they didn't lie. The experience was otherworldly. The moment the moon's shadow started to fall across the earth the animals prepared for night. Spiders began to take apart their webs.

At the very instant the darkness was at its greatest, I could not resist. I stared up. Directly at the shrouded disk of solar light, my eyes, unprotected. My friends laughed, but then began to implore me to turn away. I couldn't. Something had overtaken me. Even though I could feel my eyes beginning to burn, still I looked up, resolutely caught and in rapture.

In that moment I felt an ancient mingling of creatures and goddesses. While my eyes burned I felt, perhaps, I could hear them. They spoke their quiet, shadow language to me in the whisper of the insects that had gathered around me in the field. Their dark words were pregnant with personal transformation as well as transformation for the world at large.

When I finally looked down, my eyes were bleeding with my

own tears, and I saw the fiery circle of the sun's atmosphere branded onto my vision for the rest of the day. No matter where I looked, the molten ring of the heavens hung unimpeded before my eyes. And there was a revelation that came with it. For on the ragged edges of the fire, I could see living things that crawled in the dark spaces behind the sun.

Those things out there. Hanging in space. They've always been there. But now I can see them. Now I can hear their mouths, wet with covenantal promise. The tendrils of poisons and sweet pledges.

Shortly after that my eyes began to fail, but by then I had been given an inner view. I believe that I know something now. I see the earth as it truly is: a living island which floats in the blackest darkness of space. And on the day of the eclipse I saw the source of all the planet's energy become darkened; a yawning black hole.

I haven't been able to stop thinking about it and it's been over a year since it happened. I ache to tell others. I feel commissioned. Those things behind the sun…they were the ones who told me about Ms. Jerusha. She is one of them. It's she who has invited me here today…to provide me with an audience.

A moment later, and I'm feeling my way toward her door. It's at the end of the hallway. The hall light stays on long enough for me to find her doorplate. I stand there for a moment with my hands pressed against the wood. It feels warm and wet. I knock twice. There is a pause, a hiss of wind at the threshold, and then Ms. Jerusha is standing in the open door.

Even though she has a face, I can't really see it. I sense the vacant spaces where her eyes must be and the wide slice of a mouth. I can also hear her breathe, sort of thick and filled with tongue. After a pause she says, "Well, then, we'd better have you in."

She brings me down a dark hallway, dark to me at least, and then I'm sitting in a deep chair. She sits across from me, sips something for a moment, and then says, "So, what I wonder then is whether you know how it works?

I can't believe I'm blushing. I give a shy smile. "Yes, I know," I say.

I sense *her* smile and she continues, "There will be plenty who'd say they know, but some of them might fib," she pauses and I sense a small frown, "So what we'll need first is for you to come right out and tell me what you want. To put me at ease, please."

There must be a clock in here somewhere because I hear a ticking in the silence that follows. The atmosphere in this room is close and there's a faint fungal smell of rot. She sips on something while she waits.

I knit my brow and twist my mouth. I take a deep breath and I say, "Ma'am, you know I saw them out there. In spite of the celestial turmoil. Night during mid-day. Fear among men. I heard them. Just like I heard your sweet call," I paused to think carefully. "It's no accident. Eclipses can only happen during the daylight, when people are awake. It's a time for new seeds. I know this now. They showed this to me and made me promises for the future. They promised truth. Now may I have it?"

I'm breathing a little heavy now. In the breathy silence I can hear the ticking and more sipping. The smell of brown rot has grown.

She says, "And what do you suppose you'll do if you have it?"

I am so eager that I close my eyes to steady myself. I say, "If you give me the eyes of the world, I'll share it. I want to invite others."

Another pause. More ticking and the rot smell is stronger. But also an earthy scent of freshly turned fallow ground comes, like during planting time. I sense her look me up and down. Then she leans forward and presses a little jar into my right hand. The planting smell, is it coming from her?

I hear her stand. She says, "We'll have it happen by tomorrow. Tomorrow morning. Will tomorrow morning do?"

"Oh," I say, "Oh, yes! Tomorrow will do."

"Fine then." And now she's ushering me back down her hall and out the door. I cross the threshold and a slight shiver comes between my thighs. A faint tingle. I press my hand between my legs because, for a moment, I think I might not be able to stand it. Then it leaves and I feel wet and weak.

I turn to thank her, but she stops me before I do, and she says instead, "Because you only have until tomorrow morning, you know. Which leaves a long night tonight for all the work."

"Yes," I say, "I know."

By the time I've summoned another cab and made it back home it's just before seven. I take a glass of water from the kitchen. I tip the powder from Ms. Jerusha's jar into it and drink it.

Afterwards, I open the living room window so the moonlight can stream in. I don't bother with any lights. They don't do me much good anymore anyway. Since the eclipse, the moonlight is something now that I can actually feel. I don't have to see it to know it's flooded up the room. I lie down on the carpet and feel gravity gently tug me down against the floor. I feel the powder working. The moonlight slowly begins to coat me like warm honey. I part my legs and stretch out my arms to either side so I can be completely covered.

As I lie there all night, the voices all begin to whisper to me again. Their dewy words and breathy phrases flutter in my ears like moth wings. My legs twist and I turn my feet side to side like a little girl who can't decide. When it finally arrives, the delicious ring of solar fire heats my skin until I gasp and heave and sigh with no shame and a total emptying.

When I finish I lie on the floor for awhile longer and feel myself vibrate. I sense the shadows of clouds move across my face. I breathe deeply.

I don't much bother with the lights anymore. That will all change after tomorrow, I smile. I sit down at my desk and fumble for the laptop switch. I sense the soft glow of the monitor across my fingers.

As my outer sight diminishes further, I'm given an expanded inward view. And Ms. Jerusha promised me the eyes and ears of the world. I have thought through all my words. And her jar has given me the tongues of all the nations. There is only one universal language tonight.

I adjust my screen, blink my eyes, open a portal. I smile. I begin to speak. A kind of rapture begins.

***

Zary Fekete has worked as a teacher in Moldova, Romania, China, and Cambodia. They currently live and work as a writer in Minnesota. They have previously been published in Goats Milk Mag, Shady Grove Literary, Journal of Expressive Writing, Ginosko Literary Journal, SIC Journal, Warp10Fiction, Reflex Fiction, Potato Soup Journal, Cholla Needles, and Rabid Oak. They enjoy reading, podcasts, and long, slow films.

Bone Structure

Keech Ballard

It's all about the timing. If you want to cause the most damage for the least effort. Raise the hammer high above your head. Bring it down with just enough force to break some bones.

For *Homo robustus*, you might want to get a bigger hammer. Just don't overextend yourself. Try not to get too carried away. The purpose is to incite fear and loathing, not to commit murder. That can come later. Much later in your career. It's for their own good. They were asking for it. They needed it. They deserved it.

You are beginning to see the light. See how soft it glows, off there in the distance. You should follow the light. Across the sky. Into the vast reaches of the unknown.

Where it is always bright. Too bright. So bright it hurts. The brightness starts to burn. Slowly at first. Then more and more. Not to worry. It will all go away. You will learn to adjust. You won't feel a thing. You will get used to it. Acclimatization. It's a good thing. For you. And your world.

Welcome to the bright side of things.

***

Recent examples of Keech's grave humors may be unearthed at: Ellipsis Zine, Outlander Zine, Antipodean SF, A World Away, Analogies & Allegories, Gnashing Teeth, The Magnus Effect, The Drabble, Chasing Shadows, and Kalonopia Collective.

What the Storm Brought In

C.M. Forest

"Oh my God, it's beautiful, Hill!" Gemma swung in a circle as she moved from the grassy shoulder onto the sand of the beach.

Hilliard, picnic basket in hand, lifted his sunglasses and took in the stretch of land fronting the ocean. The sun was high in a cloudless sky. Seagulls flew in a lazy circle out over the water. Small, rolling whitecaps appeared atop the waves sliding into shore. The beach, known locally as Clear Beach, stretched for over a quarter mile before rounding a bend and vanishing from sight. A steep, rocky face rose up closer to the bend creating a natural privacy wall.

"I told you! I couldn't even find this place online. It's a local haunt. No tourists!"

Gemma flashed a smile before relieving him of the picnic basket. "Except us! I got to say, you really came through this time, my love."

"Don't I always?"

Gemma see-sawed her hand in the air. Hilliard gripped his chest in an attempt to mend his broken heart.

They moved closer to the water; a bit of sand eclipsed the toe of Hilliard's sandal. A wave of gritty warmth slide across the bottom of his foot. It felt nice.

"Woah, look at those!" Gemma skipped forward and crouched next to, what looked from Hilliard's vantage point to be, a mound of clear slime.

"What are they?" Now that the object had been pointed out, he noticed many other such quivering forms dotting the sand.

His fiancé examined the mysterious thing for a moment, before looking up at him. "They're jellyfish!"

Hilliard had never seen a real jellyfish before. But now it had been made clear to him, there was no denying its species. The graceful creatures were reduced to formless clumps when excised from the water.

Gemma stood back up, gazed out at the pleasant waves, and asked, "I wonder what happened? Why so many washed ashore?"

"Must have been the storms." The entire area had been hit with a chain of terrible tropical storms—the last, gasping remnants of a hurricane—for three days; it had almost derailed Hilliard and Gemma's vacation plans completely. But the weather had calmed since and, other than some roof repair, and fallen tree removal, the jellyfish were the first evidence they had seen of the storms since arriving.

"Must be." Gemma scooped up the basket from the place she'd left it in the sand and continued walking. "Do you think that's why the beach is empty?"

Hilliard had been wondering the same thing. Although Clear Beach was not on any map, it was apparently well known by the locals. He'd heard this from his cousin whom had vacationed in the area the year previous. It was quiet, peaceful, but never empty. A smattering of residents could always be found splashing in the waves, or soaking up the sun. "I guess so. Who knows how bad the damage was for some of these people? Maybe the beach was the last thing on their minds."

"Well, either way, it just means more for us!"

They found a nice area some way from the point of entrance and laid out their towel. Hilliard put a smooth rock on the corner so the wind wouldn't upset their spot. Out on the horizon they could see the faint glimmer of a ship passing along the coast. It looked like a lonely speck of white paint, a blemish, on an otherwise perfect vista of the sea.

The water was chillier than expected, but not so much so to be unbearable. Once they had braved the initial shock, the temperature became tolerable. They splashed and swam and kissed; the latter leaving the taste of salt in their mouths. Afterward, they sat on the towel and ate lunch. Hilliard had snuck a bottle of wine in with the sandwiches and poured them each a measure in the plastic wine glasses he'd brought along.

"I never want to leave here!" Gemma said. Hilliard agreed.

The sun had dried their bodies, leaving their skin feeling tight and slightly itchy. Hilliard had packed the remains of their picnic back in the basket and let the pleasant buzz from the wine spin through his brain unabated. It was a perfect day. But, as he again peered down the expanse of the beach, he wondered why nobody else was there.

"I'm going to take a walk toward those rocks. Maybe something besides jellyfish washed ashore. I'd love to find some nice seashells. Wanna come?" She said and stood up and stretched her arms over her head. Her body eclipsed the sun.

"I think I'll stay. I might even take a nap."

Gemma squatted and kissed him on the forehead. "Thank you for a wonderful time. This was just what we needed."

He watched her pick her way across the sand; sidestepping the occasional jellyfish. A real-life Venus. He shook his head. "How'd you get so lucky, Hill?"

Lying back, staring up at the blue sky—made a shadowy hue thanks to his sunglasses—Hilliard watched the seagulls continue their unending loop above.

*

Coldness at his feet pulled him from sleep. A brief flare of panic ignited inside him when he couldn't recall where he was or why he was there. Sitting up, he saw that he was still at Clear Beach. The sun had begun its nightly descent, allowing a world of gloom to creep in. The tide, which was far from their beach towel earlier, had snuck up the shore and lapped at the edges of the fabric; it had been the surf cascading over his toes which had yanked him from slumber.

"Shit!" Hilliard scrambled to his feet and pulled the towel away from the encroaching tide.

"Gemma? Why'd you let me sleep so long?" He spun in a circle, pulling his shades free, looking for the woman, but saw only empty sand and rolling waves. "Gemma?"

One of the seagulls above landed on the damp sand and let out a mournful squawk. Hilliard noticed that the bird's brethren continued their spiraling dance in the darkening sky. "Taking a break, eh pal?" Another squawk, this one almost indignant, and then the gull was off.

Hilliard piled their belongings farther up by the grassy shoulder, away from the advancing tide, and started toward the rocky outcropping. He thought he could see his fiancé's footsteps in the sand, but it could have been his imagination.

"Gemma!" he called, sure she would appear and be just as dumbfounded at the lapse in time as he had been, but there was no sound; just the ever-present tumbling of ocean waves.

The closer he got to the jutting rockface, the more he was able to decipher something odd on the beach; besides the dead jellyfish. Mounds of sand, each an inch or two high, threw exaggerated shadows thanks to the sinking sun. If not for the angle of the light, Hilliard was sure he would have missed them completely.

He began to have a strange feeling in the pit of his stomach. He tried to brush it off as the weight of the wine, but was unsuccessful. It was dread; a gnawing, rabid sensation that he was about to find something that he couldn't unsee. The nearest mound moved.

"Jesus!" Hilliard shouted and jumped back, waiting for whatever fresh horror was about to emerge. He pictured some monstrous crustacean; all barnacle-encrusted shell and primeval pinchers. But the sandy hill only shivered slightly; just enough to cause a small avalanche of sand to topple from the peak of the mound. What was revealed beneath stole away his breathe as surely as his imagined creature from the depths.

It was a face. A human face.

The first thought that spun through Hilliard's mind was that he was seeing a dead body. A corpse washed up on shore and buried beneath the sand.

"Oh my God!" The words leapt from his lips as surely as if

they had a mind of their own.

Before him, the face shook. One eye flittered open followed by the other.

"Who is it? Who's there?" The face asked.

Hilliard approached; his legs heavy with fear. "Hilliard. Who are you? Are you... Are you okay?"

The face was pale, but a hint of color managed to peak through the pallor of the cheeks. It was a man buried beneath the sand. He appeared to be older than Hilliard, maybe in his fifties, but Hilliard couldn't say that with any authority.

"Of course, I'm okay, my fine man. The name's Clarence. I'm staying just up the road." Hilliard waited for more, but nothing came.

"Why are you buried in the sand?" Before Clarence could give an answer, Hilliard squatted down and began pulling free handfuls of beach.

"Stop! What are you doing?" A bit of spittle followed the words; it sat like frothy freckles around the man's mouth.

Hilliard looked from the buried man to the approaching tide and back again. "You can't *stay* here, the tide's coming in. You'll drown!"

The man erupted into laughter, which sent more of the sand falling away from his face. Hilliard could see bits of gray hair poking through the grains like antenna; a rind of stubble dotted Clarence's chin. "Don't be ridiculous! I won't drown! I've seen the truth. I know what awaits me. I'm ready to join them!"

Even as he spoke, the surging tide snaked up and partially climbed the burial mound before pulling back into the ocean.

"Are you crazy? I can't leave you here!" Again, Hilliard reached out to brush away the grit which encompassed Clarence's face. This time, instead of words coming back at him, the man shifted his head to the side and bit down on Hilliard's thumb.

"Fuck!" Hilliard yanked his hand way and began to shake out the pain. After a moment, he realized Clarence had managed to puncture his skin in three places. "Are you out of your fucking mind!"

The man laughed—Hilliard's blood coating his lips like some sort of macabre lipstick—and said, "We've all seen it. What the storm brought in. I thought I was the last, but now *you're* here."

"The last?" Hilliard stepped back and took in the multitude of assorted lumps deforming the otherwise smooth surface of Clear Beach; malignant tumors of sand. "You don't mean…"

The man laughed again. Unlike earlier though, this mirth was choked short as the tide managed to mount his body and push across his face. Salt water filled Clarence's mouth. Clarence coughed and spluttered. After the water receded, he struggled to breathe.

"I'm ready!" Clarence shouted, even as he wheezed for air.

Hilliard watched horrified as another wave submerged Clarence's grinning visage. When it pulled back it left pools in his eyes. The man's eyeballs rolled in the brine.

Shaken to his core, Hilliard hurried to the next mound and began to brush away the sand. Another face greeted him, but this time, there was no mistaking the fact that the person beneath the sand was dead: a young man; his skin a mottled gray. One eye had remained open; wet grit crusted the lids.

Stumbling forward on limbs numb with horror, he revealed the dark treasure buried beneath the next mound: a middle-aged woman. The one after: a teenage boy. Further still: a child no older than five or six. All drowned to death under their beds of sand. Interspersed with the mounds were the jellyfish. Tiny gelatinous forms complimented the larger mortal remains hidden in the beach-front graves.

"Gemma!" Hilliard was screaming now. He tried not to look at the lumpy protrusions but the human-sized sand hills dotted the beach everywhere. There had to be dozens.

As he reached the rockface, he noticed the beach formed a depression. The advancing tide had already created a pool of the area. Something dark bobbed in the middle, breaking the surface like an iceberg. He set over for the spot, suddenly compelled to do so when his eye caught a different sight: a fresh mound of sand.

The area on either side of the pile was heavily disturbed. The remnants of claw marks revealed that whoever had constructed the site had been almost frantic in their preparation of it.

"Hill! My love! Isn't it wonderful!" Gemma's smiling face beamed from an opening in the beach. Her earthen blanket was so fresh it had yet to smooth out. It looked like she had fallen into a sandcastle and lazily pulled the remains atop herself.

Hilliard dropped to his knees next to her; his breath coming in short bursts. "What's happening! Why are you buried?"

Her fine eyebrows knotted together in confusion. It was an expression that, under different circumstances, he found irresistible. Now it made him want to shriek in repulsion.

"Why wouldn't I? The way is *so* clear. Everything we've ever wanted has been a lie. For the first time, I can see, Hill. And it's wonderful!"

The tide began to climb the part of her makeshift grave where her feet were. Hilliard guessed it would be about ten minutes, at most, before the waves covered the lips he had so recently kissed.

He shook his head. "This is fucking crazy! I'm getting you out." He reached forward, then hesitated a moment when he saw the red, inflamed portion of his thumb which had recently been assaulted.

"Please, Hill, don't. I know you're scared. But the truth is here. Once you see it, we can go together."

Hilliard heard his fiancé, but in the way that a person hears background noise. It was present in his mind, but not clear enough to be fully understood. Instead, he started working at digging her free.

"Hilliard! Please, stop!" The sand mound quaked as Gemma spoke. "You don't understand what you're doing. Go, look, see what the ocean has delivered. See what the storm brought in. Then, if you want, I'll come with you."

What frightened Hilliard the most was the look in Gemma's eyes; it wasn't the mad glint of insanity highlighting her irises as had been present in Clarence's gaze, but rather the cool understanding of complete confidence in her words.

"Fine. Fine, Gemma, but then we're leaving."

Standing up, Hilliard moved closer to the tidal pool. The liquid was exceptionally dark; it looked as much like an oil spill as it did ocean water. Maybe during the full light of day, he would have been able to make out the object resting in the middle, but with the sun waning, it appeared as a twisted piece of driftwood, or a tangled bit of garbage. Wading into the water, which was surprisingly warm, he noticed the bobbing corpses of jellyfish. There were hundreds in the small, natural pool.

"Okay, Gemma, I'm here," he called back over his shoulder. "Can we leave?"

"You still haven't seen it. Not really." Her tone, much lower than his. It carried an almost patronizing note.

Sighing, he returned his attention to the object in the pool. On closer inspection, he noticed it wasn't driftwood or garbage, but rather some kind of dead marine life washed ashore during the storm. Only, even that seemed wrong. He had never in all his years witnessed a fish, or sea mammal, that had clearly defined limbs. They weren't human though. More like a hybrid of arms, legs and fins. And the head was massive; at least a third of the overall body. Its mouth was open so wide that it looked more like a small cave than a proper orifice. A peculiar sensation began to ebb and flow through Hilliard's body. It started like a headache then shifted throughout his being.

"What? I don't understand." He intended this for Gemma's ears, but realized he had spoken far too low for it to carry the distance between them. When he tried again, nothing came out at all.

Sitting atop the great maw in the creature's face were a pair of white, glazed eyes. Darker hints in the middle revealed where the pupils had been, but they had fogged over into a milky haze.

Hilliard tried to turn away, but he found his body had been rendered useless. All he could do was stare into those dead orbs as they stared back. In that white sheen he could see an endless tunnel which cut through the fabric of all reality; a vicious wound in the body of the cosmos. At the end, there was a spiraling vortex where things much older than the universe writhed; twisting forms so big they mocked Hilliard's understanding of size and scope.

When he finally looked away, night had fully fallen. His feet had grown numb from standing in the inky water. Moving up the beach, he passed the spot where Gemma had buried herself only to find it completely submerged. Above, the gulls continued their exhausting aerial ballet; several had already fallen into the surf seemingly dead from the effort. Glancing out into the ocean, he figured the tide would soon reach its zenith for the evening; but it wasn't quite there yet. There was still time. Finding a suitable spot, Hilliard dropped to his knees and began to dig a hole big enough to lie in.

***

C.M. Forest, also known as Christian Laforet, is the author of the novel Infested, the novella We All Fall Before the Harvest, the short story collection The Space Between Houses, as well as the co-author of the short-story collection No Light Tomorrow. His short fiction has been featured in several anthologies across multiple genres. A self-proclaimed horror movie expert, he spent an embarrassing amount of his youth watching scary movies. When not writing, he lives in Ontario, Canada with his wife, kids, three cats and a pandemic dog named Sully who has an ongoing love affair with a blanket.

Cutting Land

Luke Harrower

My sleep was disturbed when the eager rays of the sun plummeted onto my head.

That's when I first saw the jungle.

A thick canopy of palm trees gazed upon my confused face as I stumbled onto my feet and looked around. My toes gripped tight at arid sand, tickled only slightly by tufts of dry grass. I tried to remember how I arrived in this jungle.

But I couldn't.

When I had fallen asleep, I was next to my husband, and now my bare flesh was being attacked by scorching rays. I breathed deeply, trying to work out where I might be by examining the trees for life; birds or insects I might recognize as being native to some other continent.

But there was no life.

While there was plenty of haphazard and unrestrained flora, there were no animals to spy on, and listening carefully provided no further assistance. The thicket, dense as lead. I could see no more than a metre ahead of myself before my vision was cut off by the unkempt hair of the jungle. I looked up to the sky to ease my claustrophobia. The trees were swinging like boat passengers on choppy water, but there was no feeling of wind blowing through. I started to ponder whether I was on an island, or on something moving through the ocean, but regardless of any theory I could make, I knew I wouldn't achieve anything by standing in place. I thought about home, and my family who were probably worried sick and wondering where I was.

I examined my immediate area, and tried to determine which

route would provide the least resistance, but no part of the foliage was going to give way without a fight. I gripped the sturdy reeds which surrounded me, and pushed them, or snapped them, or wrestled with them, until I could move, inch by inch through the spider's web. I worked and worked and worked for what felt like hours, but the sun never shifted position; always overhead and peering through the leaves, every wave of heat feeling like a command to stop. Under the destructive heat, I struggled to stand up; a light head and dizziness were the effects of the curse the sun had cast on me. Without the heat, the task may have been bearable, but as it was, it felt like I was carrying a furnace through the desert.

I soon collapsed to the ground in exhaustion.

That's when I noticed the holes.

Along the path I had hiked, there were holes in the ground I'm certain weren't there before; it wasn't simply a small trench in the ground you could dig with a shovel, but a chasm with no walls or floor, as if the island was made of fabric and had been cut with scissors. I was hypnotized for a moment, a recipe comprising curiosity and fear digesting within my stomach, as I stared down into jet black voids.

The thing that woke me from my daze? Every cavity in the ground was the size and shape of my own feet; it appeared every time I had taken a step, a new chasm had presented itself. I picked up a small pebble to act as my cave canary, threw it into a hole, and watched it fall. I experimented with another stone. I looked directly over the hole to see at what point the pebble no longer became visible, and after ten seconds, the stone became too small to see. I continued my study for a few minutes, walking back down the path I'd trodden, and as I stepped alongside my previous tracks, I realised the older footprints were larger.

They had been growing.

Like fire burning a piece of paper, every chasm I had made was stretching to consume the jungle I was in. I stood still, stiller than I ever had in my life so as to not create any more holes. I thought carefully about my situation. I needed to escape this jungle, that was always true, but now I had a time-bomb strapped to my ankle. If I stopped moving for too long, it would detonate. I didn't want to find out what was at the bottom of those chasms; the thought terrified me.

I ran.

I ran faster than I think I ever have done in my life, despite the heat and the exhaustion. I needed to keep moving before the chasms swallowed me. I tried to stampede through the woodland and gain as much ground on the holes as possible, but they were always one step behind me.

I'd not eaten or drank anything since arriving, and I sweated more and more as the day went on; I wondered how long I would have left before the adrenaline left my body, and I'd pass out. Time went by. I felt more and more that fatigue was establishing dominance over my body, forcing my fingers to miss their marks, and causing my head to sway and bob towards the ground.

I reached my limit.

I crumbled to the ground, unable to hold on to the emotional strength I needed to stop myself from crying. Thinking about my husband and my family forced my throat to cripple as tears rippled to the ground. I looked at the nearest chasm, only a small leap from my current position, and let my head sink into the sand. I cried for God knows how long, only being broken from my spell when the chasm stretched and forced my toe to slip through.

But it was more than a slip.

I could feel my foot being pulled.

As if a scrawny, long-fingered hand had crawled up from the depth of hell, I felt my leg being dragged into the chasm like a vacuum. I grabbed a-hold of the nearest grass stalks, thanking them—they were sturdy beyond belief. I pulled myself from the chasm and backed away, refusing to be taken, or dragged down, or to give up on escaping.

I would see my husband again.

I would see my family again.

I would get out of this jungle.

Mustering what little of my muscles were still prepared to fight this war, I tried to shunt through the brush with my shoulder, leaves and branches taking swings and uppercuts at my body, cutting and bruising my face, but I would not fall. Forcing myself through the wicked shackles of nature, I could finally see blue skies ahead of me; I knew I was mere inches away from escape. I closed my eyes and bulldozed through the last remnant of what kept me from freedom, and when I passed the threshold of grass into open air, I tumbled to the ground. I don't know how long I rested on the sand, but stopping anytime would have felt too soon. I turned onto my back and opened my eyes, swearing at the infernal dictator in the sky that made my fight so difficult, but at least now, I was free.

Or so I thought.

Turning to look towards the horizon, I searched for other landmasses or boats in the ocean, but there were none.

There wasn't even an ocean.

I was on an island surrounded by total blackness where the sea should have been. I wandered over to the edge of the sand, and gazed down over the beach; had I not known any better, I could have convinced myself I was looking at a starless night sky. Looking up, the sky was blue and cloudless, as it had always been since my arrival, and the horizon where the two colours met blended like liquids, dissipating and dissolving into each other.

I started to panic.

Energy surged through my body so suddenly I had to vent it somehow. I ran around the coastline looking for a land bridge, or something I could better recognize, but what I saw was reality.

I was on an island *literally* in the middle of nowhere.

I fell to my knees and cried.

The sudden crushing realization that I wouldn't see another person again smashed into my chest like a sledgehammer.

I cried and cried and cried until I was choking.

The only thing that broke me out of my state was when my leg slipped, and I nearly fell into a hole I created.

Wiping my eyes, I looked at the path I had trodden, and realised I hadn't just run around the island once, but multiple times. My mind was a blur after finding the coast, and I must have convinced myself I was wrong over and over again. The beach was slowly being eaten up by my footprints. I knew it wouldn't be long before whatever demon crept in those chasms pulled me through.

After everything I'd fought against, even crying was a challenge; I was emotionally decayed, and weak as a corpse.

I couldn't move.

I couldn't shout.

I couldn't beg.

The only thing I could do was fall asleep.

**

Luke Harrower is a writer from the UK who indulges in creating twisted characters in horror stories, and making people laugh with light-hearted comedy. Luke has no concept of a middle ground. You can find him on twitter @LukeHarrow.

Chemotropism

Hazel Ragaire

Dusts obscure the sun's light so completely that the sunflowers forget warmth's embrace. Muted yellow petals curl inward, luster diminished. Once green leaves offer grays, photosynthesis forgotten. But the leaves' once fine hairs seemingly giant to tiny aphids lengthen, thicken, and hollow adapting to the changed world.

They wait.

A human emerges, focused on scavenging. The flowers ready, swaying gently without a breeze, preparing.

Eventually, the human walks too close.

Strong leaves capture limbs, holding fast. Smaller leaves vine under clothing, hairs scenting before piercing flesh and anchoring themselves to drain their prey.

Humans above a certain age had enjoyed many years in the sun, and their blood still harbors this warmth's spice. So the sunflowers drink, siphoning what once existed into themselves. When their veins run red under toughened grayed-green stalks, the hairs recoil, and using roots still mastering movement, they shuffle to the side so others can remember the sun's vintage.

Thanking the human for its warmth, the sunflowers each remove a seed and push it deep down into still-soft flesh, nestling their future into the past. Working together, they drag the body to join the farm they guard. Bodies in various states of decomposition host growing sunflowers who turn, welcoming the next generation.

***

Only ideas outnumber the books in Hazel's home. Breathing life into monster monstrosities and the just plain weird with a dash of horror or a sprinkle of sci-fi is kinda what she does. Enjoy published works

in several Ghost Orchid Press anthologies, Halloween Horror 3,
Wimbledon Common, and 42 Stories as well as Fudoki and
Microfiction Monday Magazine. Find her at www.hazelragaire.com
or Twitter @HRagaire.

Gypsy, Go Home

Andrew Roberts

Reece hammered down on the horn. He heard the ugly blat he'd never liked and felt the heel of his hand press even harder, trying to get more out of it.

The car in front stopped hard with a skid that threw it across the middle of the road. Reece hit the brakes and then pulled at the handbrake, barely hearing it grate where he'd missed the button. The brake lights in front came on twice, and then he heard the engine roar in neutral and knew the driver had pushed the accelerator all the way to the floor. The driver reached up and adjusted the mirror. It was too far away for Reece to see the driver reflected in it.

Reece could see the European number plate with its black on white lettering. The left-hand side was cracked and broken off across the circle of stars and he couldn't even see what country it was from. A metallic oval flag sticker decorated the corner of the boot. Reece had no idea where it represented.

The driver reached up and adjusted the mirror. It was too far away for Reece to see him reflected in it.

The passenger door opened. Reece reached across himself and pushed the central locking down—gently, as though not being heard doing it were paramount. His arm moved slowly back to its proper side and he could feel fear freeze his body as the door swung wider.

Someone stepped out and stood by the car, legs planted wide, a twisted smile on his face. His eyes were brooding beneath the band of the woollen commando hat jammed down tight on his head. The door was wide behind him and Reece could hear the engine still idling, choppier and rougher—wilder—than the one he was in charge of. The man's hand came up to chest level and he beckoned

Reece forward with his fingers twice.

Reece knew there was only one way this would go if he got out of the car. He glanced in the mirror and felt his hand move to the gear stick of its own volition.

The man stepped forward a pace and made that beckoning gesture again. There were horses in the field to Reece's left. They didn't care what was happening.

Another pace. Thirty feet between them. Or was it only twenty? No beckoning this time. Instead, the man's hands went behind his back. His right came out and dropped harmlessly by his side. The left came out holding a knife.

His fingers unfurled from the handle and gestured again. He moved the blade down the leg of his jeans and back up again like it was a leather strop.

Reece made a sharp shooing gesture with his hand and heard himself say <u>fuck off</u> weakly through clenched teeth.

The man's smile twisted some more then dropped from his face completely. He began walking towards the car and Reece could see how tightly he was gripping the knife.

There was an engine behind them now. Reece could hear it coming up the lane. The man with the knife glanced towards the corner and then back at Reece. He tilted his chin and drew the knife in front of his throat sharply. Then he turned and walked slowly back to the car.

*

For a moment he is aware of footsteps and a presence too close, then he feels his jacket pulled up and over his head. There is a blow on the side of his face that has his ear ringing, then he is being dragged forward, a hand holding the jacket over his head and another on his belt and waistband. His body resists, leaning back and dropping its weight but it does no good because the hands twist and drag and propel him forward and he leaves the ground as he is bundled into the back of a car. The hands pull him upright and yank the jacket down off his head. The first thing he sees is a pennant hanging from the mirror. It matches the flag on the rear of the car. Reece still cannot name it.

The car is moving now. The man with the knife is sitting beside him. There is space between them and Reece remembers how he always used to fight with his brother and sister on long car journeys as they squabbled for arm- and leg-room. His sister hanged herself before she was twenty-one and Reece sometimes wishes he had had the chance to apologise to her.

The man looks at Reece and smiles. His smile is thin and humourless. So is the knife, and Reece can see its real function is to open letters. He doubts the man has ever used it on an envelope. Then his brain points out what he has already seen: their faces are not covered. They are not afraid of him seeing them close up. That cannot be a good thing.

I just stopped for a lottery ticket, he wants to say. *And a drink. I'm not supposed to be here.* The drink is on the pavement outside the shop. He remembers hearing it hit the floor and roll. The lottery ticket is in his back pocket. The odds are forty-five million to one, apparently.

He wonders why they didn't just beat him up at the shop, leave him bruised and battered on the concrete. Because they want anonymity, no incriminating evidence on CCTV, but also because they want more than that. They want to hurt him properly. Run the knife over his skin, pierce his flesh, maybe even leave him for dead. He wonders if there is a can of petrol in the boot and how full it might be.

The man with the knife is running it over the inside of the door, gouging a line into the plastic. The line is deep and jagged and Reece knows he has no chance here. His situation is without hope. He has been outmanoeuvered and now he is outnumbered and outgunned. He wonders what kind of fool would pick a fight like that. His kind, apparently. He knows he doesn't even begin to compare with these two men. They are six feet tall and look like this is nothing new to them. He is five feet seven and although he is athletic enough he has never really been in a fight—doesn't know the dirty tricks, how to keep his guard up to avoid injury, or where the openings are for a counter-attack.

He opens his mouth to speak and the man at the side of him thrusts the knife into the back of the passenger seat. It goes in deep and the man has to twist it to draw it out. Reece closes his mouth. He doesn't think much conversation will pass between the three of them.

*

The lock-bolt was up on the door, an inch of silver that might be his only saviour. He might not know how to fight but he might be faster than these two. As long as they were both on foot, somewhere the car wouldn't go.

The driver indicated (suddenly so safe, so courteous, so Highway Code) and the car rolled down a short ramp into a small dusty parking area that was little more than compacted earth and a handful of chippings. A tangled knot of hedge shielded them from the road. There was a wood to the right, on Reece's side. The rest of the land was open scrub, perhaps reclaimed mining land or the outskirts of marshland that had been too expensive to develop.

The car turned one hundred and eighty degrees at the bottom of the ramp and pulled up tight against the bank and hedge. Reece saw the driver bite down on his bottom lip as he turned the engine off. The man at the side of Reece waited to meet his companion's eyes in the mirror while the knife traced its pattern in the door panel.

Reece leaned back against the door and kicked him in the face. The man's head smacked against the window. His eyes swivelled towards Reece in dazed shock.

And then Reece was out, flinging the door shut behind him and sprinting for the narrow path that disappeared into the woods.

The driver was out and chasing him but Reece was faster. Fast enough to be able to take a look behind and see the other man join the chase. He was rubbing his jaw where Reece's foot had connected. His stride was lumbering and Reece knew he was quick enough to outpace both of them. He just hoped help was close enough at hand.

Fifty yards in, the path started to peter out and he realised his mistake—sometimes the only way to the other side *is* the other side. He didn't think there was a way out of here without turning back. If that were true, his attackers were probably leaning against trees smoking cigarettes while they awaited his return. Either that or advancing towards him in a straight line like beaters flushing out game.

He surveyed the thick tangle of briars and brambles and ferns and knew if they found him dead in here it wouldn't be until his face had been eaten off by wild animals. If they found him at all, that was. Then he spotted something that was equal parts hope and equal parts ridiculous and surreal. Hope because it spoke of civilisation, of an existence where you didn't lie dead while animals dined on your face and soft tissue. Surreal because it was on its side.

There was a hut in the distance, a hundred yards away. It looked intact and hardly weathered, but the roof was facing him instead of the sky. He made his way towards it, thinking ludicrously that there might be some wide and easy path to escape on the other side of it.

When he reached it he saw there wasn't, but he walked around it and saw it was in good condition from floor to tip. There was even a quartered and glassless window frame in its front. He was thinking of the three little pigs and trying to remember how that had ended when he heard movement. He looked across the woods and saw the man who had been driving. He was holding onto a tree and scanning the undergrowth.

Reece dropped behind the hut, wondering how much of a trail he had left in his wake. Did it even matter? He was hiding behind the most obvious feature in the landscape. He put a hand out against the hut to steady himself. His thighs already hurt. All he could do was wait.

*

His breathing is quiet and easy now, almost as if he is strolling through the shade of the woods, not crouching behind the corner of some mysterious sideways hut with a rock in his hands, but he can hear his heartbeat in his ears and he wonders why his pursuers cannot hear it too, have not called out I can hear your blood stop hiding to him, and he wonders why the drivers whose tyres and engines he can hear the distant swoosh and hum of cannot hear it and why the people waiting for them at the end of their journeys cannot hear it, why they aren't phoning the police, and his hands are slick with sweat as is the rest of him and he can hear twigs and bracken cracking now and the sound is louder even than his heart and he knows this is the moment of his life, it has all come down to this and if this is a test it is a test like no other test, and the next noise he hears is the sound of a footstep in damp mud and he realises somewhere a bird is singing and he considers how tiny the smallest of birds is and how you would feel its heart tripping in its chest if you held it in your fist and how it would know and not know what fate awaited it if the fist decided to close on its bones, and now there is a shadow and suddenly he is rising, exploding upwards with the weight of the moss-covered rock in his hands not a bird not feathers and bones and quieted song and as he rises he is only inches from the man and the man tries to jump in shock but he is too late or Reece is too early because the rock smacks into the underside of his chin and snaps his head back and his mouth spills teeth and next Reece sweeps his hands down like he is wielding a sword and the rock smashes into the man's temple. Reece sees the life leave his body in an instant.

His body falls to the floor with a noise like someone has dropped a heavy hold-all and Reece stares at the man and inclines his head slightly because the man's jaw hangs ruined. His mouth is open as if he has words he needs to set forth. Reece waits but there is nothing.

After he has thrown up, he sees the wallet wedged in the man's back pocket. He pulls it out, not because it interests him but because he is hoping beyond hope that the car keys are hidden beneath it. They aren't and he can see the other pockets will yield no joy either. He opens the wallet for some reason. Fingers shaking, he pulls out a card. J HYNES the card says. There is something wrong with that but Reece doesn't know what. He slides the card back into its compartment and pushes the wallet back into J HYNES's pocket. He straightens up, gets his bearings and moves through the woods back towards where he came from, back towards the car. Not on the path now but pushing through the undergrowth as silently as he can. There is another man in the woods. He is hoping the man has left the keys hanging in the car ignition.

*

The car is locked. Of course it is locked. He should have never left the woods. Kept going until he reached the other side or found the traffic he could hear. Waved it down like a madman. Hidden until dark. Anything but this. There is no defence here.

He doesn't remember what he did with the moss-covered rock but that is what he needs now, so that he can smash the car window. Can he hot-wire it? He knows the theory, but of course he has never done it. Might there even be tools inside? Tools he could use as weapons even if he does run first? There has to be a socket wrench, at least. Then he takes a step back because the car is alarmed. It has to be. He has to go. Run for the road. It doesn't matter that he will be easily spotted, easily found in the open. There is no alternative.

He glances up at the woods and he sees Knife-Man or rather the shape of Knife-Man—he is all in shadow—emerging from the trees. He drops to a crouch. It is like being behind the shed. Knife-Man moves towards the car and Reece edges backwards to hide himself.

*

He is lying on his stomach beneath the car and his amplified heart is back. He can see the man's shoes. They are Nike. Not far from new.

The car shifts and he knows the man has settled his weight on it. He hears fumbling and then smells tobacco. It is sweet and acrid at the same time. He lies still. There is nothing else to do.

The cigarette hits the ground. It is a roll-up and there is plenty of it left. The man's feet turn. One rises from the ground and grinds the cigarette out.

Reece can see the front of the trainer. He can see the tuft of stitching where it has been imperfectly finished. It is so close he could touch it.

The foot moves away and he can see the ruined butt in all its ragged detail.

Then he sees the man's face and the man reaches in and pulls him out.

His face drags along the gravel and he is trying to pull away but then he is all the way out from under the car and the sun is in his face and the man is grinning at him and Reece can see what looks like a letter-opener in the man's hand and it may well be but Reece knows it is not a letter-opener to the man, knows it is a blade, a knife, an instrument of death, a thing to end lives, but the man cannot see Reece's hand, he cannot see what Reece is holding, how it is black and white with a tiny piece of blue at its sharpest edge which is even sharper than it was because of the way it cracked when Reece pulled it from its fixings and Reece knows as soon as the man can see, it will be too late, his advantage will have gone, so he launches himself upwards straight at the man, straight into the man, and he knows the danger of the man's blade is irrelevant now because it will either strike him or not and he is prepared for either of those things and doesn't care which any longer, and then the man sees what he has in his hand and it is too late but not for Reece for the man because Reece's hand is only six inches from the man's neck now and that is close enough so that Reece can push it home and push again as the man's neck offers resistance and again as red spurts from the man's neck in a fount the man's body can surely not sustain and Reece's hands are moving in a gouging or sawing motion now and he has both hands holding firm and the man's eyes are wide as the redness spouts out of him sideways and Reece can see the man's severed blood vessel now and it looks like a piece of gristle in a slice of beef and the wound around it flaps ragged and ruined as Reece works and turns the sharpness of the number plate into it and the man's weight is falling towards him now and he steps aside and the man says you dirty fucker in a voice that sounds as if he has surprised himself, as if the words have bypassed his brain and just spilled out of him with no intent, but beyond the words and tone is the man's accent and the accent is not an accent at all, it is spoken in perfect English and suddenly Reece no longer knows up from down or left from right just as the man with the number plate in his neck will no longer know alive from dead and something is atilt here and Reece doesn't know what it is and then as the man's weight becomes totally and utterly and irrevocably dead and his fall forward becomes a sag, he does. He lets the dead man hit the ground, then he kicks the dead man in the side and he presses his foot against the dead man's back but there is nothing there anymore and he turns to the car. He stares at the space where the number plate used to be. It is pristine, its colour cleaner and brighter than the area around it because the sun has never kissed it. Then he looks at what passes for a handle on a car boot these days and he knows this day is not over yet. It has one more secret.

J HYNES and another dead man with an English voice are travelling in a foreign car and that does not seem at all right.

He takes a step forward and stops because he does not want to touch the car. He wonders if he touched it climbing underneath and thinks about fire. Then he wonders if his fingerprints are in the dirt and dust beneath the car and he stops thinking. Then he sees his hand reach out and test the latch and he does not know why because his brain knows the car is locked. He lets go and takes a deep breath and moves back to the man who is dead and thrusts his hand into the man's pocket and small mercies the key is in that pocket and he straightens up clutching it like a prize which he knows it is not. He looks at the boot and he thinks about what he is going to find in there and the best he can tell himself is that once he has done this thing it is all over and the day can hold no more horrors. Then, as if to chide himself for his optimism, he has a flash of what he will uncover and somehow it is himself lying in the boot space, curled and twisted and bloodied and dead, blank eyes staring up at himself. He dismisses this impossible vision and he clicks the key and hears the thunk of the lock releasing, and then he hears another sound, faint, the shifting of weight or a breath, and he snatches open the boot while he has the courage, before his legs betray him or his hands slam it closed forever.

A man is looking up at him. The man's face is bruised and swollen. The man's legs are bound in duct tape at the ankles. His hands are trussed in the same fashion behind his back. He looks like a question mark because he is too big for the space he occupies. There is a strip of tape over the man's mouth, too. Reece does not know the clinical definition of a giant but this cannot be far off. Over six and a half feet, broad and strong with muscles that are the product of genetics not exercise. The man is staring up at him, his eyes wide. There is fear and confusion and perhaps hope on his face.

Reece reaches down and pulls the tape off the man's lips as gently as he can.

The man waits, expressionless now. Finally, he asks Reece a question. "Good man?"

Reece wonders if he should laugh. Instead, he nods. "Good man," he says and leans forward to stick the key through the tape on the man's wrists.

The tape is tough. He thinks about leaning in further and using his teeth but it brings to mind the sound of the first man's jaw breaking and his teeth scattering into the woods.

As the tape snaps, the man sits up as best he can. He rubs at his wrists. When he is done, Reece hands him the key and watches while he frees his legs. The last of the tape splits and Reece finds himself realising the number plate would have done the job better. The letter opener best of all.

He offers the man his arm and hand so he can climb out of the car. His legs seem steady and firm as he stands with one hand on the lip of the boot. Then, he turns and sees the dead man with the number plate sticking out of his neck. His face remains impassive. "You do?" he asks Reece, and Reece nods. "Other man?" Reece nods again. "Same," he says, and before he even finishes the word the man is saying good. He reaches his hand out to shake. Reece takes it and even though their grip is firm and strong they can feel the tremble of each other's bodies. "Ciprian," the man says. Reece repeats it but does not reciprocate. Even one of them knowing the other's name is too much, he thinks.

The man (Reece is already trying to forget his name even though he knows that will be impossible) seems to understand. He smiles and releases Reece's hand. "My car," he says, brandishing the key. "No police, yes?"

Reece nods. "No police."

"You save my life. No police. All done or you want?"

"No," Reece says, and he reaches out again so they can seal the pact.

"You have car? House? Come—I drive us."

Reece looks down at the dead man but before he can say anything his accomplice—for that is what he is now—strides across, reaches down and twists the number plate from the corpse's neck. "I burn. I smash. I get rid of," he says. "As soon as we are safe." He bends down and drags the plate back and forth across the ground so there will be no blood dripping wherever he will place it in the car.

"Paint stripper," Reece says. "Acid. Whatever you have." He wonders how he knows these things.

"No worry," says Ciprian, the man whose name Reece will never forget. "I do this. All safe. Good men. Bad men. Is no problem."

Reece agrees with the sentiment but is not sure the last sentence is correct. He is thinking about cameras. He is thinking about witnesses. He is thinking about a police forensics team pulling fragments of plastic and paint from a dead man's neck. Fingerprints on trees and rocks and footprints in mud and dust. Sleep too, that might be a problem.

Ciprian crosses to the car. He pushes the boot down. Reece moves to the passenger door. He thinks about not touching the handle but takes hold anyway. He knows if they find the car and find Ciprian, they will find him too. It is inevitable. He cannot picture himself saying no, it wasn't me, prove it. Besides, he is already beginning not to care. Good men. Bad men. There is no argument there.

There is a moment before they leave this place when he thinks they are going to drive over the body, deliberately and at speed, but the giant called Ciprian double-twists the wheel at the last second and the body is behind them, rotting but not crushed.

Reece pushes his seatbelt into its slot and stares through the windscreen. He feels tears spill onto his cheeks and does not wipe them away.

"Is okay," the voice beside him says. A hand pats his knee twice. After that, there is the hum of an engine and the road unrolling before them.

***

Andrew Roberts's stories have appeared in numerous publications on both sides of the Atlantic and also received Honourable Mention in Ellen Datlow's Year's Best lists. He has had scripts produced for British TV and is currently trying to exchange a feature script and children's novel for a large bag of money or magic beans. His novel, World To Come, featuring zombies running (walking?) riot in a 1930s mining town in the North of England is forthcoming. A collection, Unfit for Tombs and Hearse, will be published in 2022. He tweets economically or ludicrously, depending on your point of view, behind the mask of @penofhorror.

First Take

Rae Knowles

Every inhale stung, air burrowing into the cracks of my swollen tongue. The overhead position of my arms wrenched my back into a sharp arch, stretching my lungs even when they were empty. I forced myself to slow my breathing, to keep from gasping. At least two days had passed, though it was impossible to know for sure, the only window high and narrow, the light blocked by velvet burgundy drapes. Fear had long faded into the background, a grating buzz ever-present, persistent, torturous white noise. My own stink wafted up from my battered body, sharp ammonia, fresh sweat atop dried layers, and a metallic tinge. I learned to relax my legs. Flailing meant swinging and swinging meant crashing into the concrete wall behind me. It was a fruitless effort anyway, I thought, as I glanced up at the heavy chains strung over a support beam, tethering me in the air by my wrists. Fruitless and painful, as I was constantly reminded by the ache in my shoulder where it had twisted out of the socket.

When I was still, I could listen. Muted voices above, seeping through the floor, one his and the other feminine. Did she know I was down here? I imagined another chain tucked away somewhere, ready and waiting to string her up. In my delirium, I pictured a collection of us, a twisted mobile of suspended bodies.

"He—" I sputtered into a coughing fit. My lungs were raw tinder. So much for trying to warn her.

Leopard spots obscured my vision, black, navy, and deep purple. The sensation of spinning made me force my eyes open, but whether I was turning on the chain or the basement whirled around me, I couldn't tell. Then, the sound of metal on metal, a door above creaking on its hinges. And footsteps.

Light flooded the room, a blow against my tender pupils, and I squeezed my eyes shut to defend against it. Even through closed lids the light penetrated, sending a pounding headache from my sinuses to the back of my skull. His footsteps were heavy, clunking and clinking in his steel-toed boots, but these were lighter, careful.

Blinking and squinting, the figure before me morphed from an indistinguishable blur to a human shape. She was thin, younger than me by a decade, her hair streamed down either side of her chest in tangled auburn curls. On her face was a quiet determination. She veered to my left, outside my sightline, then doubled back carrying a paint-stained wooden ladder. She held it at an awkward angle, like it was too heavy to lift comfortably.

"Who—" I had to gasp, sending stinging pain through the cracks in my tongue.

"Shhhhh," she said, unfolding the ladder and lowering the safety shelf. Her fist was closed, and I shied away out of instinct, braced myself for another strike against my already bruised abdomen. My chains clinked above in response.

"I've got the key," she said, and climbed one rung after another until she was at eye level. She pressed her finger into my injured shoulder, rotating me, and jimmied a small key into the padlock. Chin tipped up, I tried to watch her progress, but quickly snapped my eyes shut. The glare from the overhead lights sent my head spinning.

She leaned in, soft breath tickling my ear. "We gotta do this in one shot." Her eyes grew wide. I nodded, and she nodded back. "It's gonna be a bit of a dro—"

I plummeted down, my legs breaking my fall but refusing to hold my weight. She scurried from her spot on the ladder, extended her hand. My thighs jellied, resisting my attempt to stand on them, but she pulled hard, lurched me onto my bare feet. Stage lights beamed from all four corners of the room; I blocked the worst of it with my palm.

"What the f—"

"Come on," she urged. "There's not much time." Wood squealed against concrete as she dragged the ladder to the window. I eyed the space between the highest step and the curtain.

"I don't know if I can fit." My mouth and throat wetted themselves, warming up from normal speech but still jagged after the litany of screams I'd sent through them my first day.

"You have to." She stepped down, motioned for me to climb.

I barely trusted my legs to hold me, much less balance my weight on four-inch rungs, but it was this window or that door, and that door led to the house, *his* house. So I stepped up, bracing myself with my hands. One step, then another, then another. My palms flat on the concrete wall, I found purchase on the top rung, which chastised me, *Do Not Climb*. I pushed the curtain aside, startled to find bright daylight beaming in. A matted clump of hair swung into my face, and I pushed it away, the dry black blood crunching under the slightest pressure, speckling my hand with fine dust. The window was painted shut. I had the thought of being trapped down there, of being hoisted back up to hang by my wrists, and adrenaline shot through my veins, pushing me to find the added strength to force it open. It flew up in one shot, and the rapid movement swayed the ladder beneath me. I would've tumbled to the ground had she not held it tight.

"Go on," she said.

I'd have to jump, try to get my good arm under me, gather enough strength to pull myself through. I hesitated, determining the right amount of force to propel myself onto the ledge, when heavy bootsteps above my head urged me forward, and next I knew I was squeezing my hips through the slim window frame, the metal scraping off a layer of skin from my naked waist. Weedy grass made for a welcoming landing pad, and I saw that it stretched out for acres around me on all sides, except for a defunct barn on my left. Rotting farm equipment dotted the field, and I was choosing the best escape route when I heard, "move!"

I scrambled out of the way, watched the red-headed girl pull herself through the window, her thin frame passing easily through.

"If we don't get outta here now, I don't know what he'll do to me." Her bottom lip trembled. Her eyes twitched and she blinked back tears. I thought she might burst into hysterics when her face flattened, her posture straightened, she sighed.

"Goddammit, can we take that again?"

She didn't speak to me, but over her left shoulder. My eyes passed between her and the wall where she stared.

She breathed out slow and steady, shook her head briskly, locked eyes with me.

"If we don't get outta here now, I don't know *what* he'll do to me." Her tone was higher, more desperate. Before I could process the oddity, she grabbed my hand, and we were running.

Burrs spiked into my unprotected soles, and I, deprived of water since my capture, was dragged into keeping pace with her. The farmland warped and blurred around me. I watched the patchy lawn streak by under my feet. Ahead, maybe two hundred yards, the property broke into woods. I didn't care that she yanked my bad arm, that the seething pain arched all the way down into my hips. Every step put more distance between him and me.

"We're almost there," she said.

The tree line still some way off, I was surprised when her pace slowed, surprised, but also grateful as I sucked in breaths and tried to ignore the tingling in my legs.

"This is it," she whispered.

I glanced over my shoulder, saw nothing but the empty field we'd crossed. "It's what?"

"Our mark."

My pulse thumped in my ears. I waited for her to explain.

She clenched her lips together, but a tiny smile fought its way through. She leaned in again, whispered like an excited child.

"What do you want first? The good news or the bad?"

Familiar tendrils encircled my chest. It was the same dread I'd felt that day when he'd clicked the locks on the car doors, when I saw the shimmer of the metal pipe.

She couldn't contain it anymore, joy ripped through her maw exposing her toothy grin.

"We're gonna be in a movie!" Her svelte body vibrated, her

eyes wide and wild.

Flight signals shot from my fingertips to my toenails, but my body lacked the strength to answer their call.

"But," she leaned in close again, spit flying off her tongue onto my neck, "it's a scary movie."

I eyed the tree line. She skipped a circle, harem pants billowing in her wake. My brain compelled me to run, but she would catch me within two strides.

"Baby," she yelled, diverting her attention to the barn, "how's the light?"

She struck a pose, hand on her hip, then another, shifting her weight to the other leg. "You got my good side?" She doubled over with giggles, then turned back to me. "We're gonna be famous!" Her eyes glittered. Not a hint of malice or fear. I thought of June, my niece, at four, meeting Princess Elsa at Disneyland. Pure elation. Unadulterated euphoria.

I spotted an old school camera perched on a tripod beside the barn door.

"You have no idea how long it took me to convince him." She smirked, ushered me a few steps to my left to a pile of bramble. "Come on, you gotta help me get set up."

I was suddenly, painfully aware of my nude body, the crusted wounds in various stages of healing and infection. I folded an arm across my chest to cover my breasts.

She pulled branches from the pile, tossed them thoughtlessly behind her. I studied the back of her head as she crouched. The thickest limbs were an inch, maybe an inch and a half in diameter. I wondered what effect a blow to the back of her head might have. Might give me ten seconds of a head start.

"You gonna help me or what?"

He must be watching. I crouched down, pulled a branch from the pile. Beneath the brush I spotted a board, six feet in length. It was fixed to the ground with some kind of hinge.

"What's this for?"

"The ending," she chirped. "The most important part."

I knew better than to wake a sleepwalker, to challenge a delusion. Maybe if I played along, got her on my side, I could find a way out.

"How does it end?" I tried to keep my tone light, to match hers as best I could.

She stopped unearthing the beam, sucked her lips over her teeth. "Oh," she blushed, "I can't give that away."

"What's your name?" I asked. "Mine's Joanne, but my friends call me Joe." Maybe if she got to know me, see me as a person...

"I'm 'townsperson number one'," she shook her head, *duh*, "and don't be silly. Of course I know you're Sabrina. *You're the star!*" There was sincere admiration in her gaze.

I removed the final thin branch from the pile, revealing the long wooden board.

"I begged Rand for the role, but we both knew the moment we saw you. It couldn't be denied. You were her, plain as day." She stumbled to her feet, grasped the chain bolted to the top half of the board, dug her feet into the dirt for leverage. "I tried to convince him it could be me. Tried and tried and tried. You have no idea." She rolled her eyes, whispered the last part, "He doesn't think I have the acting chops." She scoffed in frustration. Hand over hand she hoisted the board upright. Stabilized by the hinge, it towered about us. "Hold it steady."

I placed a hand on it, keeping it at ninety degrees, and she walked a few feet and fixed the chain to a metal eyehook in poured concrete.

"Is he watching us now?" I searched my surroundings, eyes hopping over the rusted lawnmower, the house we'd escaped from, the open acreage, the looming barn.

"Babe, we're ready for costume," she yelled at the lawnmower. On closer inspection, I spied a pin-sized red light nestled beneath the steering wheel. "He's coming."

My stomach flipped and inverted, bile burned in my throat. I shuddered reflexively, remembering the brilliant sting of the cattle prod, how it bit into my flesh and filled my nose with the scent of my own cooking flesh. I spotted him approaching from the barn, his long strides unencumbered by the gasoline cans he gripped in each hand. Sunlight bounced off his shaved head, nicked from sloppy strokes.

Panic ignited. My body refused to remain still. I snatched up a branch, whipped it into her head like a baseball bat, and sprinted toward the tree line. There were ten feet between us, then fifty. My feet were numb. Pulse pounding in my ears, I couldn't look back. Snapping twigs and footsteps on grasses propelled me forward, I hoped they were only my own. I could make out the texture of the trees, old growth with flaking bark. The heat broke as I entered the shady wood, the relative safety compared to the field's clean sight lines. Then I heard the clink, metal on bone, and fell into black.

For thirty seconds, upon waking, I forgot the nightmare, and was surprised to be greeted by glaring sunlight as my eyelids cracked open. She wore a hooded cape, her auburn ringlets pouring down her shoulders as she adjusted the camera on a tripod, and I heard his clunky movements behind me. Her eyes caught mine, and I thought she'd attack me, retribution for hitting her.

"You're up!" She pushed the hood off her head, revealing smears of fresh blood on her cheek. Her teeth were stained filmy red. "It's almost time."

Gasoline fumes stung my nose and eyes. I heard it splash behind me.

"Get dressed." She tossed a cape, the same muddy color as hers, full length, and I scrambled to my feet, eager to cover my nude figure. The familiar sound of chain grinding against itself alerted me to the cuffs around each ankle, tethering me to an eyehook in the ground.

Behind me, Rand poured gas over the wooden beam, and when he caught sight of me watching him, splashed some onto my robe, like we were play-fighting in a pool. The girl clapped her hands, laughed riotously. Acidic liquid chilled my ribs, reached burn holes in my abdomen where pain flared. He shook the last of the gas over the ground around the beam, stacks of hay that gobbled up the fluid, then slunk back toward the barn.

"I'm sorry I hi—"

She waved off my apology, "Just save it for the camera. We couldn't even get the chase in frame." She shrugged. "Kind of a waste, don't'cha think?"

I nodded. Dull pain radiated through my skull where he'd struck me.

"Camera is here," she pointed, "but remember, don't look right at it. Just keep it in mind during the scene."

I scanned the ground for a key, nothing, then noticed it attached to her waist. Running was no longer an option. "You're really good at this stuff," I blurted.

A coy smile. "You think?"

I nodded.

"I've always loved movies." She twiddled her fingers, picked at her thumbnail.

"You know, when I look at you," I searched her face for any sign of mistrust, "I see Sabrina."

She froze.

I committed. "I see a star."

She glanced left, then right, then lowered her voice. "Do you really think so?"

In her hand I noticed a long plastic object, she flicked it, a grill lighter.

"I do." I pushed down the panic, steadied my voice. "I bet if Rand saw you act this scene, he'd see it too."

She spun the lighter around her finger, tightening and relaxing her cheek muscles, trying and failing to conceal a smile. She clicked the lighter, ignited the flame. Click, then flame.

"We're only set up for one take." She eyed the camera. "If I mess it up—"

"You won't!" I swallowed hard, tried to eat my desperation.

"Someone has to run the camera…make sure we get the right

angles…" She considered. Click, then flame.

I took a careful step toward her. "I don't mind. I've used one of these to film my niece's dance recitals, it's really no problem." My voice hitched in my sandpaper throat.

Click, then flame. She dropped down, the sudden movement paralyzing me as I expected to catch fire, but I felt her fidgeting with my ankle cuff, a sweet release of pressure on one, then the other. She turned, exposing her bloody cheek. "This is my good side," she instructed.

I nodded, took three slow steps behind the camera. She pulled the hood over her head, pushed her hair down her back, hiding her red ringlets.

"You're gonna have to do the special effects." She tossed the lighter which bounced off my fumbling fingers. I scooped it up in clumsy, trembling hands. Kicking off her shoes, she backed herself against the board, then crouched down and secured the chains onto her own ankles, tossed the key out of frame.

Struck by disbelief, I felt a measure of safety. She was confined, and he was an acre or more away, distracted, I assumed, since he hadn't noticed my replacement by an understudy.

"Roll tape!" she commanded, straightening her posture against the board.

I pressed the record button. She tilted her chin to the sky, arms extended. The lighter was heavy in my hand. I knew what must come next. Sweat slicked the grip. The tufts of yellow hay shiny with accelerant would surely explode into a fireball the moment the fire caught. Every human shred inside me screamed for me not to do it, to just run.

"No!" she yelped. The startle jolted me to attention. "You can't do this!" Her eyes caught mine, a tiny, nearly imperceptible moment, when a glint and the hint of a smile urged me to light the hay. I had only a passing moment to decide. If I didn't act now, surely he would know, come barreling out of the barn, chain me to her spot, and I'd burn alive here in the daylight.

Click, then flame. The gas caught. Fire danced blue across the space between her and me, orange crests licked her cloak. Once again, I was running, toes digging into the dry earth, strides punctuated by her howls then shrill screams. I glanced over my shoulder without breaking pace, she was consumed by it, an orange ball of flame, and the field remained empty. I closed in on the tree line. Fifty feet. Then ten. The cool shade engulfed me. Branches snapped under my steps, broken sticks dug into my bare feet, but I felt no pain. Only the whooshing air past my ears, the drumming of my heart. Ahead I saw a break in the trees, glimmers of a white house on a neighboring property, the hum of a plow in the field. I couldn't help but glance back a final time, although the trees obscured my sight line. Her screams formed into words, a pattern echoed again and again, rising over the treetops.

"I'm a star!" There was glee on her voice, pure exaltation. "I'm a star!"

***

Rae Knowles is a queer woman who holds a BA in English Language and Literature with a minor in Creative Writing. Her story, The Last Self Portrait, appears in Annus Horribilis by Bag of Bones Press and Common Oleander will appear in the Moonflowers and Nightshade anthology edited by Samantha Kolesnik in Fall 2022.

Twitter: @_Rae_Knowles

Hook, Line, and Sink Her

Nikki R. Leigh

Staring out at the crystal blue waters, Garrett was reminded of a particular hallway in his older brother's home. A long hallway, filled to the brim with trophies, shining like the glint in his brother's eye when he showed them off.

The sea glistened, just like the patina of the trophies mounted to the walls of that hall. Ten years his junior, Garrett walked those narrow corridors as a teen, running his hands along the smooth exterior of the prizes, all souvenirs of his brother's previous relationships. They took up a lot of space, but his brother was proud of his collection. Garrett often wondered if his brother was as happy in his relationship as he was showing off the trophies that remained once the relationship was over.

His feet dangling over the pier, Garrett set his bait hoping to catch a trophy of his own. He'd paid good money to access the hunting grounds he now peered out at, examining the crests of the waves and wondering what beauties lay trapped underneath. He hoped he had enough time to catch a couple, releasing the undesirables back into the choppy, shining water before the sun went down.

"You got a hunting partner yet?" a deep voice asked from behind him. Garrett craned his neck and shielded his eyes against the sun. His eyes settled on a burly man, his beard wild and his clothes askew. His fishing equipment dangled off his arm, pulling his flannel shirt down across his shoulder.

"No, man. Just me currently. You're welcome to park your stuff here on the pier. I'm hoping there's enough to go around," Garrett replied.

The man boomed a laugh out from his chest, planting his equipment on the wooden boards. "There always is. Enough boon for us mighty men. They've got a guarantee, you know? At least one catch per visit. It's why we pay the big bucks."

Garrett smiled, running his hands through his shaggy brown hair. He wondered if he should have gotten a haircut before coming out for his hunt. He glanced at the man again, noting his shoddy, but formidable appearance. He didn't look dressed up or anything. Garrett figured it didn't really matter what they looked like.

They weren't the ones that needed to be doing the impressing, after all.

Taking a few steps forward to close the distance between him and the newcomer, Garrett reached his hand out towards the man.

"Garrett," he said, as the man's hand clasped around his. "First time here."

The man's eyes sparkled with delight. "Marco. Let's hope you've got some of the beginner's luck, eh? Pull yourself in a real beauty."

"You should see my brother's collection. He's been able to do this once a year for the last decade or so."

"He changes them up that much?"

"He says he loves the thrill. Mounts them to the wall when they're no longer able to live above land. There are some really well-crafted taxidermy artists out there."

"Huh. I wouldn't have even thought to do something like that. Not surprised there's a market for that though." Marco began pulling out his equipment, placing large mechanical rods and a massive reel the size of a bass drum on the deck.

"Quite the set-up you've got there," Garrett said, nodding in the direction of the metal rod and pile of chain-wire, hooks, lines, and sinkers of various shapes bursting from the tackle box. He looked over at his own equipment, a simple fishing rod with a sealable bag attached to it. He was still perfecting his bait, a notepad and paper in his hands.

Garrett liked to believe that he was fishing for all the right reasons, not just to satisfy some primal urge. He was prepared to catch and release, though it did make him feel a little uncomfortable to know that he would be sending perfectly fine trophies back into the water. But now, they'd be scarred, wounded by denial. They'd probably imagine his face at night, as they rested their eyes before another day of chasing the hook.

As the two continued setting up their rigs, their heads whipped to the left across the water to another pier where furious splashing could be heard. Two men were fighting with a large rod, industrial in size and build. Marco and Garrett were rapt in their attention, excited to see whether the others would be successful in their catch.

The two men on the other pier struggled against the thin chain they were pulling, their forearms flexing against the resistance their hooked prey was giving. After three heaves, the line grew taught, and the catch surfaced, a single slender hand breaching the waterline.

Long fingers, pristine nails. A slim arm. A set of shoulders.

A head of blonde hair.

A beautiful face.

A mouth, forcing a smile.

The two men continued to drag their catch to the surface, winding their line to the pier, dragging the woman toward them. From the distance, Garrett couldn't determine if she was struggling. He'd always heard that the women at the bottom of the sea were grateful to be pulled to the land. That they were excited to start a life with the men who took them in.

That was what his brother told him at least.

But as he watched the woman being tugged from the water, taking her first breaths of air on her knees on the pier, the situation felt entirely loveless.

When she caught sight of the two menacing captors, she fought, her hair soaked and drawing her features thin. She beat fists against the men, almost surprised at her own strength, her arms moving faster than she suspected above the density of the water. She was hindered, however, by the thick hook forced through her collarbone. She bled. A lot.

The two men fought back. Their fists gripping her arms so tightly that Garrett could almost feel the phantom grip on his own biceps. He turned away. He knew that even if he met the love of his life today, the savage delight in the eyes of the men would haunt his memory.

His first time seeing the fishing action, and it was not the fairytale that his brother had described, but rather a tense scene of strangers meeting, a woman trapped between a choice for something that resembled freedom *from* the water below, or freedom *within* the water below. It was much more violent than he had suspected, too. He wondered if his brother had shed blood before.

Garrett shuddered and hoped not every encounter was as stilted and dangerous—for all parties—as what he had just seen.

Marco and Garrett turned back to their own stretch of water in front of them, Garrett raising a hand to shield his eyes to take in the majesty of the blue.

"You know what it's like down there?" Marco asked, breaking the silence.

"I never quite gave it much thought. Is it not like what the website advertises? Just like a little town under the water?"

Marco snorted a wad of spit and snot into his throat and hocked it off the pier.

"There's something like a city down there, filled with women of the sea. When underwater explorers discovered their colony in the depths, they wasted no time in sealing it off and monetizing the prey. Everyone is always looking for gold, minerals, and coins in the depths of the ocean, but the big game is where it's at."

"And the ladies can't leave?"

"They're on protected land, of sort. Owned and operated by those that don't care for their well-being, but rather the coin they make. And good for the corporation, anyway. Uncharted waters are free for the taking, these days. To the brave victor goes the spoils." He uttered the last few sentences through pursed lips, almost spitting out the words as though they poisoned his tongue.

Garrett imagined a cabal of women under the sea, faces pressed against nets and walls that drove deep into the ocean floor. He shuddered, wondering if he should carry on in his hunt. He thought again of his brother, the happiness spread across his face when he brought each new trophy wife home. He knew they didn't live long outside of the water, never reaching an anniversary, but he wanted to believe his brother gave them a good life. A life better than the one he was told they lived underwater.

Garrett turned back to Marco. "You don't seem too fond of the fishery," he said. "Why are you here?"

"Better me than men like them," Marco replied, pointing in the direction of the other pier where the two men hovered around their catch, taking pictures of the woman who had fear in her eyes. Bruises had already blossomed on her skin. "Don't hate the players, hate the game, or something like that, eh?"

Garrett liked that philosophy and decided to continue setting his bait. He could be the better man—the real man. The one the women talked about that had kind eyes and a gentle smile. He *would* give them a better life, even as short as it would be for them. He'd learn how to treat a lady right, ready himself for a happy marriage. He scrawled his note across the paper, hoping it would lure a good catch.

"Are they all as beautiful as they advertise? My brother always brought home such pretty women."

"The ones that take the bait, they're usually at the very least slim and able to be carried easily. But sometimes it doesn't matter how beautiful someone thinks they are. If we aren't into it, she goes back in the water."

The guilt in Garrett's stomach bubbled back up again.

Marco continued as he finished setting up his gargantuan fishing rod, then took a seat in a chair next to it. "In the early days, they used real hooks. The sea women didn't know what was happening as the bait fell from the sky and sunk into the water. Stabbed into their reaching hands, just like a fish's mouth. Seeking food, finding wonder, trapped immediately. They were pulled to the surface in pain, and when the men didn't want them, they were thrown back in, the hook marks marring their skin.

"Some still use the hook today, but it's more of a show of purported skill than anything. Reel them in the old way, and all that. But most use the kind of tactics you're trying." Garrett looked at his note again. *23 years old. Entrepreneur and investor. Will take good care of you, like the precious woman you are. Looking for someone who enjoys adventure.*

He wondered if it was too corny. If someone would actually fall for it and fall for him. He had thought about the upcoming moment for years: he throws his bait into the sea; a delicate hand tugs his line, and he carefully leads her to his pier. Her hair is long, and curls over her shoulders to lay *just* right on her chest, which heaves with passion. They fall in love, fast and hard. Marry. Have a kid. In that year, a new experimental drug lets the sea women live on land longer and they get a true life together.

As Garrett drilled his eyes into the blue, trying to see past the shadowy depths, he began to see how wrong he was. He kicked himself for believing the lie.

"Having second thoughts, kid?" Marco asked.

"I don't know, man. Do they even want this?"

"Some do. Some don't. Those are the ones the men seem to want the most. Make the heaviest lines, the sturdiest sinkers. Try to hook the defiant ones who have cordoned themselves off to the deepest parts of the reserve. Some say they've even stuffed themselves full of kelp and fish, trying to make themselves harder to lift."

"Have they been caught before?"

"I've known a few to catch them, pull them to surface after all that effort, and realize they don't want them after all. Toss them back just as scarred by the hook as the rest."

A second commotion interrupted the pair's conversation, this time the pier on the other side of their own. Another woman caught, being brutally yanked to the surface. Her head breached the water, her arm dangling from a hook.

"See?" Marco asked. "Those ones there are going old school." Garrett thought back to the first encounter he'd witnessed ten minutes earlier. Just as brutal. Seems the old ways aren't as passé as they all wanted to think.

Just like before, the men tugged and tugged, heaving the weight of the woman they'd snagged to the pier. As fast as the woman was pulled to the top, struggling against the wrenching of the man at the edge of the pier, another woman emerged, her mouth open in a scream. Her arms circled the trapped woman's legs, and she tugged down hard, attempting to pull her back into the ocean. Garrett could have sworn he saw the woman mouth an "I'm sorry," at the dangling woman before using all her momentum to pull her down. The hook in her arm tore through muscle and skin, releasing her violently back to the water. The two sank back into the ocean, a shroud of red encircling them.

"What the hell was that?" Garrett asked, his disbelief creeping into his voice.

"Promises of surface life don't appeal to all. Especially to those that have already found a life of their own in the sea."

Were there families down there? Garrett wondered. He hadn't even considered that the women below could find love amongst one another. How they reproduced. What life was really like for everyone involved. *Why is life above the water any better?*

Garrett felt more unsure than ever that this was what he wanted. His stomach was gurgling with stress, still teasing the idea that he could be different. Better. More humane. At some point since he arrived, his admiration for his brother had started to shift into a wave of disgust. *Just how many lives had his brother ruined?*

He cleared his throat, tried to still his shaking hands. "Why do you know so much about this all?"

"Just like to stay educated on what's happening beneath the veneer of the waves."

The hairs on Garrett's neck began to prickle, suddenly uncertain about his fishing partner. He couldn't get a beat on what he was all about. Marco seemed to foster disdain for the corporate sensibilities and the violence against the women, yet, here he was.

He took a look at Marco's rig again, noting the fearsome, thick hook attached to the apparatus he'd connected to the pier. The hook looked like it had the strength to hold a shark aloft on a ship. It was almost as wide as Garrett's wrist, with a point that was sharpened and catching the rays of the sun. The substantial barb made Garrett's flesh crawl at the thought of it wedged into his flesh.

Garrett turned away from Marco and his rig, not wanting to show the older man how unsettled he was by his tools. He fidgeted with his note and simple fishing line, pretending to try and situate it differently in the plastic bag.

He got to his knees, looked into the water and saw dark shapes bustling about below. The chop of the water blurred them from above. Garrett's stomach began to lurch as his nerves kicked in. He attempted to talk his way through his nervousness. "The hook seems a little much, don't you think? It sounded like you weren't super keen on using that on the women."

Marco picked the hook up, held it between his meaty palms. "This?" He walked towards Garrett, who felt a drop of sweat make its way down his back. "This isn't for them."

Garrett, from his spot on the dock, his neck awkwardly craned towards the man, didn't even have time to move once he realized what was happening. He tried to dart to his feet, but tripped over a rut in the wood as Marco rushed forward, wrapping the chain around Garrett's neck. "They appreciate a little sacrifice. Who would have thought?"

Garrett was rooted to the spot, his arms trying to fight against the thick metal, his legs, driven hard into the wooden pier.

The massive hook flopped to the side of Garrett's neck as he struggled to breathe, his hands wrapping around the chain in a futile attempt to free himself. Marco took hold of the hook, jerked it upright and into the crook of Garrett's arm. Garrett's eyes bulged as the hook dug into his armpit, through the skin and into the sensitive tissue.

"Let me know what you see down there, would you?" Garrett was hoisted into the air by the stocky man, and unceremoniously tossed off the pier into the water below. His body slapped against the water, and down he went.

The chain around his neck made it impossible to take a final gasp of air before he sank lower and lower into the depths of the sea.

His vision wavered, in and out, but he caught sight of hundreds of women in front of his eyes. His presence barely seemed to faze the dozens of women closest to him, only a few turning their heads in his direction.

Older sea women, scarred from the early days. Younger women prepping themselves for their surface debut. Women with women who wanted nothing to do with the men at the piers.

And all around them, a beautiful city of coral and shells, fish bones and rocks. Houses that bubbled from their chimneys, a park where younger women played with their children. Garrett could almost swear he heard the sounds of giggling, taunting him in his agony.

There was a vastness of life here, all ticking away despite the violence at the surface. A vastness of life, hundreds of women, a city of color.

And just him. Garrett. A sacrifice to show that someone above was willing to go the distance for someone special within. That actions spoke louder than words scrawled on a note. He wondered what Marco's strategy would net. What kind of woman Marco was trying to impress and if it would work. If his life would mean anything to those below the waves.

His vision grew black, fuzzy as his lungs continued to fill with water. His eyes fluttering against the salty water, he couldn't help but wonder one thing as he his feet reached the sand below.

Who would take the bait?

***

Nikki R. Leigh is a queer, forever-90s-kid wallowing in all things horror. When not writing horror fiction and poetry, she can be found creating custom horror-inspired toys, making comics, and hunting vintage paperbacks. She reads her stories to her partner and her cat, one of which gets scared very easily. Her work appears in Dark Matter Magazine, The Book of Queer Saints, and A Woman Built By Man, amongst others anthologies and magazines.

A Nice Day for a Hike

Sarah J. Huntington

Mary had a little lamb, its fleece was white as snow.

Those are the first words that come to her. She has no idea why she is thinking of nursery rhymes, of little lambs and soft fleeces when she currently has no idea what her own name is or even where she is.

All she knows is that her face and body are pressed against a severely hard surface.

I'm...no, I can't remember.

She feels warm, red hot, as if she is inside a powerful oven. Confused, she opens her eyes. They feel gritty, full of dirt, and rife with stinging sensations. The sun is bright and hanging over her. A huge yellow eye seeking to burn her alive, at least, it feels that way.

Where am I? I'm lying on rocks.

Knowledge sparks and not one part of it is pleasant. The awful truth makes her whimper loudly.

Her name is Anna and she fell. She was hiking alone, like always, enjoying the peace and solitude of nature. She was happy, excited, and the day was perfect.

I fell down.

That's why her head hurts so much, her skull bounced off solid rock until she lost consciousness.

She tries to move her legs and finds that only one of them will cooperate. The sensation of brutal pain begins to fire up and engulf her. The nerve endings inside her body burst into vivid life.

Her foot is trapped, wedged firmly in a thin crevice she didn't see in time. The ground has swallowed her all the way up to her lower calf. The pain feels sharp and blinding.

It's broken. My ankle is broken.

She breathes furiously and tries hard not to blackout.

It hurts so much!

She attempts to pull her leg free, but it won't move.

Her vision clears enough to see the truth, there is a piece of jagged bone protruding out through her flesh. A shard of angry white and red. Blood bubbles up and cascades into a crimson river.

Anna swallows her rising panic and sits up slowly and carefully. The thudding in her head increases, her lips feel dry and cracked. Dizziness threatens to overwhelm her.

"Fuck!" She yells.

How long have I been unconscious? This is the worse day, ever.

How could she have been so careless? Now she will have to use her GPS locator and satellite phone, she will have to call for help and then call her partner Adam from the hospital and admit she had an accident.

"I told you never to go hiking alone."

That's what he'll say. He'll complain and whine and she'll have to admit he was right.

She will have to spend six weeks wearing a plaster cast or a huge boot that will make her look as if she is an astronaut going to the moon.

Anna pushes the thoughts away. She needs to think with logic, not chaos. Her ankle is smashed and her foot in its thick boot is wedged so tightly she can't feel her toes.

She is parched, badly dehydrated, and she has no idea of how long she has been lying in the sun.

Too long, her skin feels burned and tender. She checks her watch, its face is smashed but it still works. It's almost eleven.

The beginning of the hottest part of the day.

She reaches for her backpack, she always carries essential equipment, plenty of water, and a first aid kit. Except, she can't see it.

Why isn't it on my back?

Confusion hits, the world feels back to front or upside down. She braces herself and leans around, as far as she can manage, and sees it.

Thank God for that. Did I take it off?

She was hiking through the vast woodland of the national park, she was enjoying herself in the wilderness. It was early in the morning, eight, or maybe a little after. She saw a pretty cluster of trees and went to explore.

Yes, she recalls. A small, slanted rock face that looked easy to climb came into view. It looked tall but not too steep. Not a challenge, but easy. She wanted to race up the front and stand at the top so she could take photographs. She removed her old pack and carried it, afraid she might topple backward with the weight. But no, her foot became stuck and she fell in her eagerness to see the scenes that awaited her.

"So stupid," she whispers. "A rookie mistake."

She stretches for her pack and finds it out of reach by mere inches.

"No!" She wails. Her fear is cold and instant.

This can't be happening!

Her mind fills with static and terror.

Calm down, I can do this. Deep breaths.

Anna focuses hard. It's important not to panic. She needs that pack. She needs her water and her phone urgently.

She shuffles across as far as she can get, the pain in her ankle is brutally raw.

The shock of the quick agony makes her retch and vomit down her shirt. Her body is shaking and sweating. The sun is making her furiously dizzy.

She is in a race against time, against heat.

An odd memory comes to her, the images from a movie she once saw of a man getting stuck down a narrow gap between two huge rock faces. He had to cut his hand off, or something.

Did he survive? Stop it!

She curses her own thoughts, why must her brain torture her when she is already in enough trouble?

She won't have to cut her own foot off, besides, she has no knife. She has no anything.

She blinks quickly, to free her eyes of dirt and tries hard to think with clarity. Perhaps if she could reach down into the thin gap, she could pull her boot off and free her foot? She doubts it will work, the gap feels far too tight and her foot must be swollen.

Water first.

She reaches again, stretching with all her power. Her fingers brush the material of her bag, a barely-there touch before her trapped limb explodes in pain.

She screams wildly.

Black spots erupt in her vision.

The frustration she first felt turns into sharp fear. This is life or death, she understands the cold facts. She is in serious trouble.

She is utterly trapped, unable to help herself.

Other hikers must be around? They'll help me.

She is only two miles or so away from the park's entrance.

The day is sunny, hot, and beautiful. It's an ideal day for taking a long walk in an isolated area. The sky has no clouds in sight. It's perfectly clear and wonderful. It's the reason why she decided upon a hike in the first place: to enjoy the weather, and to get away from Adam for a short time.

She didn't stick to the set trail no, but hardly anyone does.

It's too pretty a day for a disaster. Darkness is the time for terrible things and bad situations, not daylight. The sun should never allow such things under its watch.

But now look. She fell and got herself stuck in an impossible situation.

It's broad daylight, someone has to see me, or hear me.

"HELP!" She cries. "HELP. PLEASE!"

Shouting hurts her entire body.

I'm so thirsty. I need my pack.

For the first time, Anna wonders if she might die. All alone, wedged, and afraid.

What if no one finds her body? She will be just another number, yet another person to go missing inside the boundaries of a national park. Birds might eat her corpse, or greedy bears might fight over her remains.

Will she die of blood loss or dehydration?

She starts to cry. No, she mustn't become defeated. Not yet. It's only eleven in the morning, someone will find her. Someone will spot her and save her.

Still, the heat is becoming more unbearable. She touches her arms, her flesh is red hot and her shoulders are blistered.

I need that water.

She takes off a leather bracelet she wears wrapped around her wrist and puts it between her teeth. She will bite down and reach for her bag, yes the pain will be horrific but she must do it. Her very survival is at stake her choices are none.

One, two, three. No, I can't. Okay, okay, one, two, three. Do it, do it now! No, yes!

She bites down hard and stretches, the agony is white-hot, an inferno inside her bones.

The sounds she makes are inhuman as she reaches as far as she possibly can. Her arm and hand shake with strain. Again, her fingers brush the material but no more.

It isn't possible. She simply cannot reach.

All alone, and with only the hot relentless sun for company, she understands that unless someone finds her, she will soon be dead.

The sun, her former friend, is now her vicious enemy.

*

An hour passes, and yet it feels like an entire day.

Anna is beginning to feel confused. She stares at the sky above her and tries to count the seconds as they pass.

She has forgotten the order of numbers. It feels as if her brain is shrinking.

The blood from her head wound and various cuts has stained the rocks underneath her. She wonders if the mark will remain forever. A small piece of her left behind. Or maybe when animals find her dead body and pull her apart, her foot might remain inside the gap. Someday, it will be found and people will wonder what became of the rest of her. She will be a source of mystery for someone's podcast.

The idea makes her giggle wildly. She is coming undone and she knows it.

Pretty birds with wide wingspans fly above her. How regal they look flying in a circle, how magnificent.

Why can't I be a bird? I could fly away.

Why are they shrieking? Are they waiting for her to die so they can peck at her eyeballs and steal her tongue?

How long will it take?
One day? Two?

Maybe quicker, the sun she loves is killing her. The rays she always liked to sunbathe in, now make her feel revulsion.

I should shout again.

"Help," her voice is little more than a hoarse whisper.

How ironic. The things that can save her life sit right by her side.

Someone will come.

She thinks about the good things in life, the food she will eat when she is as free as the birds, the way Adam, for all his complaining, will look after her. She can rest and watch movies in bed. She will never again go for a hike alone.

In the distance, she hears the sound of whistling.

More birds? Maybe pretty coloured ones that dance across tree branches and sing. The sound of deep laughter erupts.

It's people.

She scrambles up and looks. She is high enough to have a decent view. An ocean of trees face her and a quick flash of red spoils the greens and browns.

Yes! Two people are walking fairly close by.

"Help!" Her voice is torn and ragged. Not at all loud enough to be heard. She slaps the rocks with her hands, gives up, and waves her arms. Each jolt of her body causes fresh waves of hurt.

Desperation swarms her. She is so close to rescue, so very close.

They can't see me!

She tries to scream and still, no one hears. She yanks at her hair in frustration while her blood boils with disbelief.

Please, see me, please!

Anna hears a shuffling sound behind her.

What is that?

"Hello?" She whispers. The single word is little more than a hissing sound.

A deep growl is her only reply.

What the fuck? Please don't be a bear.

She doesn't want to look, doesn't want to see but she must. Slowly, she turns her head.

A cougar. There it stands in all its fierce glory. Its muscular shoulders and legs seem ready to pounce. Its eyes are narrowed and hungry. The rock face and few boulders are no obstacle to it. It sniffs the air greedily.

Blood, my blood attracted it.

The sharks of the wild forest.

Now her fear boils over, her heart pounds rapidly. She raises her weak arms as a shield.

Make noise, I need to scare it away.

Her throat is too torn and dry to make a sound. She searches around her for a small rock or object, something she can throw. There is nothing.

Quickly, she tries to remove the hiking boot on her good foot. Her fingers won't work properly. She can't recall how to undo the tight laces.

The light, the sun, it's all too bright. All she can see are white blobs swarming her vision.

The cougar creeps closer, a stealthy step in her direction. It is not afraid of her. She is weak, done for, and it senses such a thing.

She rips her boot off and throws it. She misses completely.

The creature pauses and lies down under a jutting-out rock, in the shade she longs for. It contemplates her as she contemplates it. Slowly, its tail flickers.

It won't attack. It won't. Or will it wait until tonight?

Anna has no idea what to do. She can only pray other hikers pass near enough to catch sight of her.

Exhaustion, heat, and blood loss are destroying her.

She takes off her sock, balls it up, and launches it at the feline invader. It bounces off thick fur harmlessly. The cougar is entirely unfazed.

If it moves, she'll hear it. She will not dare to take her eyes away from the wretched beast. It is a stalemate.

Her eyes begin to close without her permission.

Just one moment of rest, just one.

Anna imagines being on a boat, surrounded by water, cool and wonderful water. She wants to dive into an ocean or sit inside a freezer.

Is it better to die by cold or by heat?
Above her, the sun continues to scorch her body. She wants to fall deeply asleep but knows she mustn't.

Is this how it ends? No, someone will come.

A large airplane appears and temporarily spoils the clear view. All those people on board and none of them know she is dying beneath them, none of them understands that she needs help desperately.

Mary had a little lamb, its fleece was white as snow.

She realises why her mind played the song to her days ago or was it only hours?

It is the old rhyme her mother used to sing to her as a child, a song of comfort.

But there are no pretty lambs, only a clawed and wicked monster near her.

Where is it?
She turns her head, searching for the cougar. It isn't in sight.

Did I fall asleep? Thank God it's gone.

"Help!" She whispers.

No one can hear me.

Tick tock. Her life is almost an empty sandglass.

Her hand reaches out. For a moment, she believes she can touch the sun with a fingertip. A ball of fire and flames, burning forever in the sky. The concept feels absurd.

I'm dying.

The pain in her body is so bad she almost wants her existence to be over, just so she can feel peace.

Reach my pack, that's all I need to do.

Her body jumps and jerks wildly in protest. She can't feel her trapped foot anymore. It's numb and cold. Yet that could be a good thing.

One last try.

She uses what is nearly the last of her strength to sit up straighter. If she could just reach this time, she will live. She will have an adventure story to tell her friends, she will be brave and admired. She might even get a Netflix special, a documentary all about her survival.

She rubs her face, sweat drips into her eyes and stings. Blood too, she is covered.

The movements cause her head wound to bleed furiously.

Please God, please.

She begs a God she doesn't believe in and stretches out, braces herself for a wave of pain.

Her fingertips touch the material.

A bit more, a little bit more.

She grimaces in agony and forces her arm to cooperate. She nearly has the pack. Hope sparks inside of her.

It still isn't enough but almost.

One, two, three, come on!

She stretches more, her ankle tears slightly. She hears the awful sound of ripping nerves or tendons, the snapping and crunching of bone. It is absolute torture, self-mutilation. Such suffering that her mind threatens to shut down completely.

Almost there.

She grits her teeth and pinches the pack with two fingers.

Yes!

Now come the most vital seconds, she has to pull it towards her, an inch or two and she will have it. She can call for help and drink every drop of water she has. A helicopter will come. She will not lose her foot.

The pack moves across the rock towards her. The noise seems as loud as gunfire.

I'm saved! I did it!

No.

The cougar pounces on her back. It did not walk away or fear her, it simply waited for an opportunity, waited for the temptation of fresh meat to become worth the risk.

Razor-sharp claws pierce her spine, ripping open flesh and tearing through nerves.

Anna screams in shock and bitter pain, in disbelief. The weight of the creature knocks her flat, she sees its eyes, its desire to eat her and tear her to pieces.

She tries to fight, tries to knock the beast away. The shock, the pain, it's all too much.

One massive paw holds her down by her chest. A chorus of hungry growls sounds around her. There are many of them, not just one.

She feels pressure on her throat and knows life is over for her, existence, pain, love, all of it gone.

"No," she croaks. "Plea…"

Strong jaws clamp down, white-hot agony. Her weak fists punch the creature until she falls still. One last gurgle, one last heartbeat, and she is gone. Free, yet not the way she intended.

More blood stains the smooth rocks.

The cougar roars in triumph and enjoys a feast under a beautiful hot sun, for it, it has been a lucky day, one of the best in fact.

***

Sarah Jane Huntington is a horror author and nurse. Her work has been published in several anthologies so far and she is also the author of a few story collections and novellas.

Dance for Auxo

Robin Wallington

I see them there, boy, girl, boy, girl. They are bright in the light, in white dresses, shorts and vests, they dance like an endless zoetrope. I see them, my friends, laughing and beautiful with bright joy on their faces. Around and round they go, hand to hand, like so.

From where I kneel, I squint in the summer sun to watch. That very sun has been delivered from our prayers and in return she blushed our faces dark and bleached our hair light.

There they go once more, the dancers, like a hoop, a circle, the wheel of life. They spin, stepping with bare ankles in a criss-cross form, past my place here in the undulating corn.

Above, a pair of swallows score with energy across the blue sky in bright silhouettes. They celebrate in an aerial ballet but are free to soar away, whilst the dancers flow and eddy toward the barn, where she is readied for them.

Away from this brittle day, at the edge of the trees is a brackened den, where a vixen stalks. She is ragged, a crimson witness with blood on her mouth and no sign of her kill. She watches, stock-still, and above her from amongst the dappled birch leaves a pale oval owl silently sweeps, waving his wing tips in a shooing motion. There's blood on his beak too, and his eyes are black like deepest night. But reflected in them both is the white dancers' circle-shape as it moves across the parched landscape.

Shadows live shortest on the longest day, and today the sun must share her space with the moon, their own universal cycle pairs them together for this precious moment. Beneath that eternal pair the dancers whirl back toward me now, into my vision, in unison. I see and smile inside as some slowing, one by one, exhausted, they drop out. Giddy and exhausted they breathe hard, but do not let disappointment mask their faces for at last just two remain, for the last refrain.

With ceremony, the paint-peeled barn door is opened wide, and there, hulking, she sits, lit from above by shafts of light, the final chosen pair dance before her origami skin. A haze that could be heat or scent lifts from the mass, as she is stretched out, her swollen limbs exposed. Attendants swab at sores and lift great folds as the smiling wide eyed couple, two tiny dolls, twirl before her massive form.

Basking, baking, she opens wide her arms and flesh hangs in draperies of mottled leather. Her damp-mouth widens, tooth-stuck and drooling, it crawls to a half smile. The tiny eyes, like black beetles that hunger for the bright sunlight, are full of life for she must feast now to survive the coming dance of Winter.

From a distance we look like blooms amongst the corn and grasses. Flashes of red, pink and pale blue could be poppies, corn cockle, and cornflower. Closer, we could be statues, a thousand of us or more, all on our knees, hands raised, and facing the direction of the barn. But we are not statues. We are tied, shrunk, dried, wrinkled by the sun so the skin stretches taut, brown as bark. Each face holds a trinity of hollows where the eyes and tongue have been bird pecked. Each of us wears a tight cap of material in red, pink or blue, a field of flowers from afar.

I'm here, crouched, muscles tight, my red cap in place, this is what I will become too, an ode to her, dear Auxo, our perfect Summer.

***

Robin Wallington writes fiction and poetry from his home in the fantastically literary city of Oxford, UK. For the past four years he has run the Creative Writing Group at Oxford University Press. He takes inspiration for his writing from nature, quirky humans and the other strange things found at the edges of the world.

The Rush Baby

Katie Holloway

Our walk was normal, until Poppy stopped. I tutted, craning to watch both her and the dog.

"Look, Mummy, a baby!"

"That's nice," I replied, insincerity dripping, though uncaught. I inhaled: damp grass and near-ripe blackberries. Exhaled: chores, paperwork. I kept going.

She hurried, proffering a thumb-sized doll woven from rushes. It was skillfully made: newborn proportions, dried-out strands woven round and around, knotted and twisted—almost chubby. It had a scratched-on face: gnarled, sleeping...unsettling.

"Can I keep her, Mummy?"

I call Hagrid closer. "If you want to," I sighed.

Poppy dawdled, chatting. She tripped, of course, emitting a sharp, outraged cry. I hauled her up, insisting it wasn't that bad.

"She's ruined!" Poppy wailed, lifting the doll, displaying the smear of blood across its chest.

"Just drop it and keep up."

"I can't!" She was horrified. "She's mine!"

"Fine." I snatched it from her, shoving the thing deep into my pocket. "If you weren't so absorbed in that weed, you wouldn't have fallen over."

Why did I take such a dislike to the baby from the beginning?

I shortened our walk, and we were trudging back when my skin prickled. I stopped, not sure why, exactly, but then I heard it. The faint cry of a young baby. Tiny and shrill, coming from...

No.

Something icy squeezed my heart as I reached into my pocket, feeling something dry, crisp, but undeniably wriggling. Hagrid snapped his head and curled his lip with a growl I'd never heard.

"It's Lavender," Poppy proclaimed. "She's hungry."

With mounting dread, I brought her out of my pocket, and there, laying on the palm of my hand, four woven limbs straining against the air, drawn face scrunched in anguish, was the baby, howling real cries and demanding to be fed.

***

Katie Holloway has always been a writer, but has most recently become obsessed with flash fiction. She is a UEA Creative Writing graduate and is fueled by strong tea and snatches of alone time. Her flash fiction has been published in a number of online journals. Katie tweets @KatieLHWrites.

No Adults Allowed

Bitter Karella

The sun was smiling. Kim didn't like that.

"The sun has a face now," she told Robert. Not that she expected him to care.

Her brother shrugged, his attention captivated by the TV. An animated armadillo was trying to trick an animated cougar into swallowing a bowling ball. Kim didn't recognize this show. It was one of the many new cartoons that had started since the grown-ups disappeared.

The sun had big blank eyes and a wide wide smile; it looked like the awful cartoony pictures Kim had drawn when she was younger, the ones that her mom had nevertheless made such a big deal over and posted on the fridge. Kim felt the sun's staring eyes following her when she went outside, which she tried to avoid. She was certain that it wasn't coincidence; it was looking at her, eyes the size of planets moving with glacial slowness to track her movements across the yard when she had to restock the pantry. The sun's personal attention was making the heat unbearable, enough that the latest batch of cupcakes simply melted on the vine. It was already hot enough now that the sun took up half the sky. Peering through the shuttered blinds at that smiling face, Kim marveled at how much bigger and brighter it was now than before. The sun stared back at her with its rosy cheeks and tight-lipped rictus. Could it see her through the blinds? It looked like it wanted to say something, but it didn't. It stayed silent, big and round and yellow and relentlessly smiling.

They were frightened, at first, when the grown-ups left all those weeks ago. Robert lay curled on the floor crying for days, resisting her feeble attempts to reassure him that Mom would be back any time now. Eventually, they learned that the apocalypse wasn't confined to their household—the Miller twins next door had lost their parents as well and the Steinmarders down the street and the Reynolds and the Foxes and it was with a growing combination of terror and relief that Kim realized it wasn't some fault of her own that had driven their mother away but that it was simply that all adults were now gone.

That's when the world began to change. How often had Kim asked her mother some question only to hear 'Because I say so' as an answer. To think of all the possibilities this world held! And this whole time it was only the adults holding reality in check with their blinkered imaginations.

The TV still worked and, without adults to say so, it showed cartoons twenty-four hours a day. Food was plentiful—hot pizza materialized on their doorstep when they desired it and the pantry was always filled with cookies and potato chips. Kim noticed fat buds swelling on the branches of the old peach tree out back, which improbably blossomed into chocolate cupcakes. A spring of molten taffy spontaneously bubbled up in the green belt and kids from all over the neighborhood came to fill jars and buckets and guzzle goop until they got sick. Somewhere in the distant city, someone imagined the ultimate fort and Kim could see the tower of cardboard and couch cushions growing daily. It was already taller than the old skyscrapers left behind by the adults.

And the sun kept smiling.

Kim sagged onto the couch next to her brother and waited for night to fall. After several more hours of cartoons, a sick knot tightened in her stomach. Daylight still streamed between the blinds, casting striped shadows on the walls.

She checked the clock, even though she already knew the answer. It was ten o'clock.

"It's ten o'clock," she said.

Robert shrugged again.

"It's still light out."

Robert ignored her.

She didn't want to say it, saying it out loud would make it real.

"I don't think it's going to get dark anymore," she said.

"Whatever. That's fine. I didn't like the dark anyway," said Robert. "It's scary."

The next time that she went outside, Kim couldn't help but think the house looked more and more like a mere façade, an empty outline like a child's drawing, a scribbled curlicue of smoke hanging from the chimney even though she was sure there was no fire in the fireplace. Did the house even have a fireplace? Things were changing too fast.

And that was when the sun spoke. It had a voice like a swarm of wasps buzzing inside her skull.

"Hello Kim," it said.

Kim didn't dare look up. The sun was so big and bright now that it just looked like white fire, the dark pits of its eyes and mouth barely visible as dim blurs against the glare. She stared at her feet. She stared at the cracked earth below her shoes and the dead dried weeds that were once the flower bed that her mother had been so proud of before she'd disappeared.

"Hello Kim," said the sun again.

"Hello," said Kim finally. The back of her neck was burning under the sun's glare.

"I'm so glad that the adults are gone," said the sun. "They were keeping us apart, Kim. They said I had to be 92.485 million miles away, Kim. Isn't that silly?"

Kim didn't say anything. She kept looking at her feet. She thought about the dead flowers. She thought about Robert and his cartoons. She thought about her mother, wherever she was. She thought about anything except the warmth on her neck and, despite the heat, despite the sweat forming on her forehead and on her back and under her armpits, she felt a chill deep down. When the sun spoke again, it was right by her ear and she could smell the singe of her own hair burning.

"Why don't you draw me anymore, Kim?"

***

Bitter Karella is a writer, text game designer, and horror aficionado behind the microfiction comedy account @Midnight_pals, which asks what if all your favorite horror writers gathered around the campfire to tell scary stories. Her horror text games, available on itchio, include Night House, All Visitors Welcome, Toadstools, and Santa Carcossa Nights.

Art for Claustrophobics

Logan McConnell

The chandelier swayed, scaring away the birds. They had nested amongst the crystals and candle holders, accustomed to the sudden assault of bright lights, but would not roost through the storm and its gusting winds. As they scattered, their feathers floated down on top of a grandfather clock, a sofa, and Mr. Wallace. Mr. Wallace felt the impending storm as well, but he did not leave *his* nest: a house without walls.

Beside Mr. Wallace was a stack of paintings, each one cocooned in off-white sheets to protect them from nature's harsh elements. He sipped his tea and eyed the minute hand of the clock, his feet tapping in unison with each 'tick' and 'tock'. A field mouse scurried from his front lawn over to the center of the drawing room, then out through the foyer. He smiled.

As the clock struck noon, a white truck appeared in the distance, its tires on the dirt road caused dust clouds to rise into the air. The truck parked in the driveway just as a lightning bolt lit the sky, as if to announce that Mr. Wallace had a guest arriving at his country estate. He set his cup down and walked over to the entrance.

The driver stepped out. An older man, he wore gray overalls and a scruffy mustache above a mouth that gaped open upon approaching the house of Mr. Wallace.

"You must be the contractor," said Mr. Wallace, stepping over the threshold where a door would have gone, were there a wall to hold such a luxury. "I'm Mr. Wallace, we spoke on the phone," he reached his hand out. "It's Pat, right?"

Pat didn't move, his attention entirely focused on the house, staring at the floating roof. "How... the ceiling just..."

Mr. Wallace dropped his hand and looked behind him. "Oh yes, I don't have walls. A bit of a postmodernist flair, I confess. It's nice to have out here in the country. You know I built a house with a floating roof just like this one a few years back in the suburbs, but the HOA was a nightmare to deal with." Mr. Wallace placed his hands on his hips and smiled. "So, I got some land out here, in the country."

Pat remained in awe until thunder broke his fixated gaze at the hovering ceiling. "Yeah… I'm the contractor. Where are the walls? How is your roof staying up like that?"

Mr. Wallace sighed, and dropped his arms to his side. "I like the fresh air."

"But…"

"Honestly, I don't understand why everyone else wants walls. They make me so claustrophobic, and cause a home to get too stuffy. Besides, the climate here is rather temperate, even the winters and summers are very pleasant. Why seal myself away from that?"

Pat turned away from the house, making eye contact with Mr. Wallace for the first time since his arrival. "I'm still confused. You mentioned you wanted some paintings hung up."

"Correct," said Mr. Wallace with a nod.

"Then, how can I do that when there are no walls?"

Mr. Wallace lowered his eyelids and stared at the man for a few seconds before answering. "The ceiling. I need you to attach them to the ceiling. You did bring your ladder like I asked?"

"Yes sir," said Pat, pointing to his truck. "How many paintings you want up there?

"Three. And they're quite priceless," said Mr. Wallace, leaning closer to Pat. "So don't drop them," he whispered. He led Pat over to the drawing room beside the three canvases.

Pat picked one up to gauge the weight. "This is pretty heavy, but I got what I need." He looked up. "Never hung paintings from the ceiling before, though." Pat walked back to his truck and removed a ladder and tool box. Mr. Wallace gave Pat instructions on how to mount the pictures: three in a horizontal row, evenly spaced.

Pat set the ladder in the living room, beside Mr. Wallace's sofa, and ascended with the first painting under his arm. When he reached the top, he gently placed the painting on the ladder's cap, and ran his bare fingers along the ceiling. The material was unlike anything Pat had ever felt. He touched the barrier once again, discovering the solid surface was warm on his skin, yet simultaneously chilled his fingers to their bones.

Unsure if the floating ceiling could be penetrated, he marked with a pencil where the corners of the frame would be positioned, then drilled a screw into the spot, amazed to find it curl inwards without resistance.

Pat proceeded, and asked Mr. Wallace, "So, what line of work you in?"

From the sofa, Mr. Wallace, who had returned to sipping his tea, called up, "Alchemy."

Pat snapped his head down to stare at him. "Alchemy? Is that what you said?"

Mr. Wallace nodded, without taking his eyes from the storm clouds in the distance.

"You mean, like turning lead into gold? Stuff like that?" Pat asked.

Mr. Wallace slowly turned to face him, crossed his arms, and scrunched his lips together before speaking. "It's called transmutation, and no. Turning things to gold is very difficult, actually. Gold is to alchemy what brain surgery is to medicine, if you get what I'm saying."

"I do," said Pat, as he readied to mount the painting.

Mr. Wallace continued. "I can transmute most materials quite easily enough."

"That's very interesting," said Pat as he slowly removed the painting's cover. The image was a bird, a robin with scarlet wings, sitting in a cage. A young woman, with pale skin and wide eyes, stood outside of the cage, sticking a finger through the bars. Pat proceeded to attach the painting, and when complete he descended the ladder to grab the second.

"Going well so far," said Mr. Wallace, who was staring up at the red bird in the cage. He lied down to stare up at the painting, as Pat moved the ladder over and climbed up.

"I was thinking," said Pat, "your alchemy, is that how you got this ceiling to stay mid-air?"

"Yes," said Mr. Wallace.

"I see. How, exactly, if you don't mind me asking."

Pat reached the top and pulled the cover off the second painting. In the center was a massive Bengal tiger prowling a rectangular cage, with a zoo in the background. The tiger's haunches and build were majestic, his expression forlorn. Pat glanced over at the robin, then again to the tiger and stiffened his back.

"I made the ceiling from one of those parade balloons," said Mr. Wallace, breaking Pat's concentration on the art.

"Balloons?"

"Yes, quite. I stole one of those Thanksgiving Day parade balloons, and turned it into a flat surface to serve as a ceiling." Pat looked down at the man, who closed his eyes and shrugged. "Not terribly difficult."

"But," said Pat, "it's not a balloon anymore. So how does it float?"

"Well, there are many steps to transmutation. I don't just snap my fingers and make it happen. No, what you do is you change components of the item one by one. I changed the material from soft to hard, the shape from a cartoon animal to a roof. The part of the balloon regarding its place in space, that is, floating, I did not alter. So, my ceiling is able to stay in the air by itself, instead of depending on pesky walls," he said with a shiver.

Pat nearly finished securing the second painting to the ceiling. "And you don't want walls because of claustrophobia? And fresh air and all that?"

Mr. Wallace nodded.

Pat scratched his head as he descended the ladder. "If I may ask, why do you have these pictures of animals in cages, if you get so claustrophobic? Seems like you would prefer a landscape or wide view of a canyon or something."

There was no immediate response. Pat reached the floor and looked over to Mr. Wallace, who was watching him. Mr. Wallace's nose was flared and his pupils contracted. He licked his lips. The man's stare had an intensity that conjured a visceral tension between the two, as if his gaze could rip Pat's flesh.

Finally, Mr. Wallace answered. "I suppose it's similar to how people often feel cozy locked inside their home during a deluge of rain or an ominous thunderstorm, to observe that threat from a safe distance behind a barrier. Storms aren't frightful to me, small spaces are.

"How calming, how soothing it is, to see others trapped within narrow, cage walls. How I breathe a sigh of relief knowing that somewhere out there, the turbulent entity of small spaces has devoured another. To see that red robin or tiger in a cage, I can relax, knowing it is them and not me that is trapped."

When Mr. Wallace had finished, Pat realized he was gripping the ladder, his knuckles white, palms slipping against the metal with sweat. "Well, I don't want to take up any more of your time. I'll get that last painting up there and be on my way." He placed his hands into his pockets, and gasped.

"Something wrong?" asked Mr. Wallace.

"I'm out of screws. I could have sworn there was an extra pack in my side pocket..."

"Oh, no bother. Allow me to help," said Mr. Wallace. He got up, walked over to the edge of his floor, onto his lawn, and removed four blades of grass. He collected them in his palm, curled his fingers, and whispered words into his hand that Pat could not hear. A moment later Mr. Wallace returned, holding four screws.

"Screws are easy," he said. "That's alchemy 101."

"Th— thanks..." Pat muttered, and took them from Mr. Wallace. Pat picked up the last painting, held it between his arm and torso, and climbed up the ladder.

At the top, he wobbled, lifted both hands to catch himself, and dropped the painting.

The painting was still covered in a white sheet, billowing in the air like a ghost, striking the floor with a loud snap. Without walls, there was no echo, only a crash followed by a sickening silence. Even the wind had ceased. Pat could not bring himself to look at the battered painting inside the sheet, and shut his eyes. He felt Mr. Wallace's stare return on him.

Pat climbed down, skipping every other rung, his shaking legs missed the last step, causing him to tumble. Pat rolled over and saw Mr. Wallace shift the ladder directly above him where he lay on the floor. Pat looked into his eyes and screamed.

Mr. Wallace shook the ladder with both hands. "I told you to be careful," he stated, before whispering words under his breath. The ladder's steel beams wilted like heavy, decaying flower stems, closing in on Pat's writhing body.

Hours later, the storm had departed. The birds return to their nest within the chandelier. Their feathers fell onto the grandfather clock and Mr. Wallace, who reclined to view his two paintings on the ceiling, both beloved and familiar. Occasionally he would roll over to admire his new work of art, on the floor, confined within a cage.

***

Logan McConnell is a health care worker and writer of quiet horror. His work is published or upcoming in Coffin Bell, Diet Milk Magazine, Dark Recesses Press, Vanishing Point Magazine and others. He is influenced by the works of Mary Shelley, Shirley Jackson and Thomas Ligotti. He lives with his boyfriend in Tennessee. Twitter: @LMwriter91

Martyr

Damian Karras

For a house that supposedly belongs to God, it was surprisingly easy to break into. I just walked through the front door. It wasn't broad daylight, but it wasn't witching hour either. The building was unlocked and empty. This town is small, quiet, and completely convinced of its own safety. Around here, everyone goes to sleep with their doors unlocked. Gates unlatched. Windows open to the soft breezes of midwestern America.

Everyone here thinks they're going to live forever.

And everyone thinks they're going to heaven afterward.

I didn't walk directly into the sanctuary. Deciding to bide my time, I took an immediate left and traveled down the well-worn carpeted staircase. The church's basement level was divided into several different rooms by drywall. It smelt like ancient paper and dust. Silent as a crypt at midnight and exactly as ominous.

I carefully sat down everything I was carrying and pulled my phone out of my pocket. The flashlight app cut a blinding slice of light through the darkness. Tacked to the walls were children's drawings of Jesus. Noah and his ark. Sampson and Delilah. All the wonderful stories of torture and murder they teach little kids in Sunday school.

I smiled to myself and began to walk around.

The first room was for toddlers. My light shone over countless plastic containers of crayons, colored pencils, and chalk. Building blocks littered the floor. The second room was for the five and ups. Lots of books, most of them simplified picture bibles for youngsters. The remains of frosted cookies were spread over three different knee-high tables. An old television on a cart was sat in the corner, no doubt already preloaded with a VHS tape of Christian cartoon propaganda. The third room was for the teenagers, and it was bland. Sad. This was the point where creativity was deleted. No more finger painting. No more parables. Just hard scripture and blatant judgment.

My daughter's name was Ruby, and she was beautiful. By far the best thing that ever happened to me. Before her, I was lost. Me and her mom… God, we had no idea what the hell we were doing. Drifting aimlessly through a self-destructive life. She drank anything she could get her hands on, and I smoked anything anyone handed me.

Then Ruby came along.

I remember walking her into every one of those rooms. Year after year, all smiles and hugs. I remember her covered in frosting coming out of the toddler room, smeared in marker coming out of the young adult room, and full of purpose and conviction coming out of the teenager room. In her mind she was prepared, in debt to God, and ready to venture out into the world and spread the almighty gospel to those less fortunate.

Downstairs, this memory felt like a stab in the chest, so I turned and walked away.

My flashlight app led me back to the staircase. I turned it off, picked up everything I had dropped, and began a slow march back up to the ground floor. The containers were heavy. They sloshed and swung almost uncontrollably in my hands. My shoulders and biceps ached just carrying them. Ironically, my first thought was of Jesus, and how it must have felt dragging around that heavy ass cross.

At the top of the stairs I took a rest, dropping my load and taking a second to catch my breath. I knew from experience that beyond the thick wooden doors to my left was the sanctuary. Stained glass. Rows of pews. A stage covered in alter cloths and incense burners with a pulpit standing tall directly in the middle. This mental image also hurt, but enough fury flashed up to offset the sorrow.

Ruby, my daughter, she was a saint. I never saw her swat a fly or heard her mutter a curse. In sixteen years, she never purposely broke a rule or ignored a command. Looking back, I realize I didn't deserve her. If there was a God, he would've gifted me a rebellious, acidic, punk-rock riot girl that spat in my face. After the life I'd lived up the point she was born, that's what I deserved. I wasn't worthy of an angel, and that angel didn't deserve to die.

Atop the stairs, I tried to calm myself. I took deep breaths. I counted to ten, then twenty, then fifty. There really wasn't any rush. The street outside the plate glass doors was calm and serene. All the children in the neighborhood had passed out hours ago while their parents drank wine and watched the news, content in the knowledge that their kids were still drawing breath.

People often take the most important things for granted.

Thinking about all those families infuriated me, but I was well past the point of useless blame. I'd come too far, thought too much, and debated myself into too many dead ends. Mortal man can't even begin to understand the workings of the divine. This tragedy, this atrocity, was between me and God himself. With both of my arms weighed down, I kicked open the doors to the sanctuary and stomped inside.

I hadn't been back in this room since the funeral.

An entire sorrow-soaked year ago.

See, Ruby... Ruby felt like she needed to help. She needed to go out. Spread the gospel. Save souls from the depths of eternal hellfire. For whatever reason, she felt like she didn't deserve heaven. This is that undeniable, half-ton guilt that the clergy loves to drop on people. They filled her ears with tales about the eternally humble Christ, and she bought it hook, line, and crucifix heavy sinker.

So out of nowhere, she brazenly announces she's going off to Haiti. The people there are dying, she says. Poor beyond belief. Starving, dehydrated, and have never heard a single world printed in the King James version. They're perishing, and their souls are doomed. She had to intervene. She had to tend to the lost souls. She had to save them.

Blah, blah, blah, redemption...

Yada, yada, yada, forgiveness...

The number one regret I have, bar none, was letting her go.

Even though the church was closed, the sanctuary was still lit with secondary lights installed in the ceiling. A massive cross hung on the back wall. There was a baptismal tub set up to the left of the pulpit that looked like a ridiculously large bird bath. I walked up to the second row, shimmied in sideways, and sat down heavily in the same place my tiny family had sat for years.

I dropped my containers, took a deep breath, and tried not to cry.

Looking around, so many memories.

My own soul was saved up on that very stage. My daughter was christened and baptized in that stone tub. My wife broke down and took her first communion directly in front of that pulpit, on her knees, choking on tears. All we wanted was to pay for our sins. Absolution. Amnesty. Immunity to the eternal damnation we clearly deserved.

We tried… That's what I want everyone to remember….

*

Ruby, she boarded a plane along with twelve other hardcore disciples and two church leaders. They touched down twelve hours later, taxiing into the Toussaint Louverture International Airport. From the scant evidence the local police could gather, my daughter's body was discovered at around five the next morning.

They found her in a ditch, completely naked.

She had been raped and tortured. Patches of her skin were gone, along with most of her blood and the gold cross she always wore around her neck.

It was hell getting her remains returned to the states, and once she was finally back, law enforcement wouldn't even let us see her until after the autopsy. A full investigation was launched, but no one was ever caught or charged with the murder of my little girl. News reporters flew in and out of our house like hummingbirds. Apparently, I was on television.

I don't remember any of it.

What I do remember is anger. Hatred. Disillusion. This went against everything we were taught to believe, and everything we surrendered our hearts for. If there is a God, why is my baby dead? Why didn't he take me? I deserved to die in agony, not her.

Not my precious little girl.

Me and her used to make paper airplanes, folding pieces of paper over and over, tossing them around and laughing when they crashed. I'm writing this on crumpled notebook paper I brought from home. When I'm done, I'll fold it, open a window, and send it flying out before I dowse the pews and hymn books and alter in gasoline. I brought two books of matches, because I'm used to things going wrong.

I love you, Ruby. If there is a God, I hope he'll be kind enough to let you visit me in the blinding brightness of the all-consuming fires of hell.

***

Damian Karras is a speculative fiction author from Davenport, IA. His debut novel "Avari", along with two short story collections, are all available on Amazon. His first traditionally published story "Deny, deny, deny" is set to be released on horrorzine.com in October. His work is best described as "abnormal" and you can learn more at damiankarras.com.

Ephemera Parasitoid

Alpheus Williams

A good scotch saved for special occasions. Beautiful, tawny liquid silk swirls around icy mystery. Smoky peat, wild North Seas on the nose, visions of long boats and winter bleached Vikings. The depth of simple pleasures when your time's up. A nice drop to go out on. I wonder if my free loading lodgers are as drunk as I am. They've been squirming through my system for weeks, slowly sucking it dry. Almost adults, they will be breaking through their chrysalises. Their time has come to flee the nest.

How does our world end?

If we ever had a choice it doesn't matter because that train has left the station. So many things came with a warming planet: dead seas, fires, extinction, and the coming of parasitoid wasps that preyed on humans. Perhaps they were newly emerged from melting polar ice. The Science is out. Not that it matters. Those we put in power never listened to Science anyway.

Here's the story.

I find the beginning. Cut and paste. Add to the narrative. There's video. All there. A damned fine effort. Edited and polished with all the time and care I had left.

My opus. My best work. Left to wander cyberspace. It's what I leave behind.

Let me tell you about the wasps.

The wasps find a human host, lay their eggs beneath the skin, then die. Two days gestation. Six days larval stage. Six days as pupae. They emerge, fly, breed and die in less than a day.

It was my last assignment.

Dead Parties: Orgies of drink, drugs, sex and mayhem, young people at the point of demise having their last fling.

Speculation: No one really knows what happens behind those walls. It's a farewell kiss to the sensual, to life, private and personal. I was there to record the final act of their leaving.

*

They emerged, shimmering figures, beautiful and young, staggering in the heat like a drunks stunned in sunlight exiting some dark dingy skid row dive. Bubbles rippled beneath their skin. They made their way to the fire pit. Clinging to one another, their passions spent in orgy, touching, tender, tragic. The mammalian need for closeness.

My body cam took the wide shots, the group emerging, their environs, their mass march to the stadium of fire. I used the hand held for close ups, the clinging hands, staggering feet, wild eyes, tear stained faces.

It was love how they clung together. Wept together as they marched to the pit.

After. I reviewed the footage time and again, cut, edited, fused it together. It really was love. Dreadful sorrowful love. So young. So tragic. I'm a hard bastard and I've seen a lot bad shit in my career. Recorded wars, mass shootings, plagues and mayhem, but this one really got to me. It was hard work putting it together and trying to maintain some journalistic objectivity.

Something went wrong. No ignition. No fire. The close ups show the desperation. The knowing. The horror as their skin broke loose, their bodies dropped to earth and wasps escaped, ascended, free from their human prisons. Thousands of thousands. Swarms in a frantic frenzy of aerial fucking. They blotted the sun.

I captured beautiful close ups. Dying bodies, wasps in flight, linked together in sexual grasp, the males, semen spent, falling to their death like black pebbled rain after mating, their hard bodies pattering on pavement. The females, brilliant ebony, slender waisted bodies, red winged, searching for hosts.

I returned home to my office. Shaken. When you're working, you're working. Detached. Mercenary. You concentrate on the images, the pictures, the things that will make the story. I took off my protective overalls, my face netting and gloves. I sat behind my desk, uploaded the images. I cried. I poured whisky in a glass, drank and cried some more. Shook and trembled. My thighs itched. I dropped my trousers. Up through the legs of my overalls they found me. Six tiny wasps, their stingers stuck in my skin. Delicate kisses unfelt. Their eggs expelled. Dead and dying. I pulled them from my thigh. Tiny enough to be framed by a finger nail. Wings slowing in death, ebbing and gasping with each flutter like a last breath. I placed their bodies on my desk. They're there now. Dried and preserved. Gossamer, stained glass wings of red. I drink to them. It's not without some sorrow that I will terminate their line, their desperate effort to leave something of themselves behind.

*

It will be quick. Painless. I will pour the last of the bottle in my glass. Walk into the kitchen where I've left the gas tappets running on the unlit stove on. The windows will be closed, the door sealed. I will sit at the breakfast counter, dip my nose into the glass, breathe in whisky, mask the smell of gas. I will unwrap my last Cubano, saved for a special occasion, earthy tobacco leaf rolled by loving hands as they listened to Shakespeare in lyrical Spanish. Nip the tip. Taste the rich tobacco on my tongue. Finish the whisky. Light the match.

***

Alpheus Williams, curmudgeon, pagan, pantheist, loves his wife, nature, good whisky and dogs, lives and writes in a small coastal village in Australia with his wife and their border collie. His works have appeared in The Molotov Cocktail, Barren Magazine, Storgy, The Write Launch, The Fabulist Magazine, Shotgun Honey, Bristol Noir, Bath Flash Fiction, Ellipses Zine, Danse Macabre, et al. Push Cart nominee 2021.

The Bloat

Bernardo Villela

I am in this multitude afloat among the dead on this river, we call it The Bloat. It's the surest way I could think of to keep myself alive. At least for a little bit.

It's a good thing no waterway in America has ever been considered sacred because they're all desecrated now. Although, even the Ganges is polluted. So much for sanctity. Regardless, our rivers great and small are now free-flowing burial grounds. No one cares to remove the bodies. Sure, sometimes there'll be a murder investigation that'll have the police drag a river, sifting through the flotilla of bodies looking for a victim, like a kid fishing marshmallows out of his cereal, but the rivers are ignored otherwise, like most eyesores and unpleasantries.

If death hadn't become such a casual thing here I never would have found a place to hide, a place to float my cares away. Death is a part of life, death is natural. I've come to accept that. What's unnatural is how we stopped giving a single fuck about how and when in a person's life death occurs. I can't pinpoint when this casualness came about but it was sometime after lockdown drills became a fact of life and COVID became a fixture. Dying became demystified, and into the water the dead went.

Feed the fishes. If we kill 'em, we kill 'em. Fuck 'em. Only billionaires will escape our planet into space anyway.

I don't want to die despite my tenuous peace with it. Most Americans don't, we want to live, which is why this blasé attitude toward death confuses me. I've had a good run for thirty-seven years, though it's felt much longer. To survive I surround myself in the dead and float downriver, sky-gazing and cloud-watching.

The putrescent miasma on every riverbank tells you something macabre lies in the water. The pastoral idyll is destroyed once you see the bodies and flies hovering around them. This is easy enough to ignore flat on your back, but when I need to get vertical to get food, or pee and crap, then I see the maggots and the rotting flesh. The wind is a blessing that allows me only quick huffs of all kinds of bad stenches. The pungent, constant stank of the damp dead only hits me when I'm upright.

Anybody who has seen a mob movie knows you weigh a body down or it won't swim with the fishes long. Gases that build up within a corpse postmortem make it rise to the surface. To blend in with these floating bodies, I smear blueberry juice and leaves on myself and avoid cleaning myself as much as I can stand.

Of course, I'd rather be home, but I'd be dead there. Better to stay adrift.

The reason I'm adrift is dumb. Lost a lousy bet. Twenty bucks. Straight pick 'em, not even against the spread and even odds. But the money was needed 'Tomorrow or you're dead.' I didn't have the money then. I'd die. I knew it. Death's casual now, like I said. Just another body in the river. So the plan was born.

"To float, perchance to live," Billy Shake-a-spear would write if he lived now. And so I did.

Getting vertical every so often also allowed me to reorient myself. I couldn't have a phone; it'd break and track me, so my eyes would need to tell me all I needed to know.

*

One day I fell asleep while floating. My eyes flickered and I felt myself drifting off, literally fell asleep and awoke two hours later, judging by the sun. Traveling by flotation was both a brilliant and an asinine idea: on one hand keeping time was made easier, on the other, I contended with mayflies, dragonflies, mosquitoes, waterfowl, and that puckering sensation of biting fish thinking I'm among the dead and decomposing.

A week into my river-bound journey I had to sneak back into civilization. Doing so to get sun-block once was easy. Doing it over and over to dry clothes and get new ones was exhausting. This, all because I realized I was tanning and the dead don't tan.

Thinking my journey over on the first overcast day of my journey got my mind going in circles. Maybe it was the cumulative effect of the heat, but I drifted off again, this time I'd no idea how long I slept.

To float is to dream, to float and sleep is to awaken to a nightmare. Standing, I looked around and knew I'd gone off-course.

It was swampland, probably The Bayou.

In the clearing between bald cypress and tupelo trees I saw two corpses which had separated from The Bloat. One was being fought over by two gators. Bullfrogs croaked in the distance. They sounded more like disturbed spirits than living creatures.

The pickings weren't slim in these waters for the 'gators and whatever else hungered. Those who died in the Bayou nowadays knocked around the waterways like pin-balls. What I couldn't figure out, as I waded in the algae-infested waters, was how I could get back on course or amend my plan.

I'll go down the Mississippi, I'd thought to myself. Cairo, Illinois wasn't too far from where I'd once called home.

I'll be Huckleberry Dead, I joked as I plotted my macabre journey.

I'm Huckleberry Fucked, I thought as I gathered visual information and strategized.

Still overcast, but late in the day.

When will I eat? When will I sleep? Where can I find refuge?

Before I always had dry land. Now at most there are wetlands, which may offer safety, but not shelter.

"Well, ay-uh'll be," I heard.

Somehow somebody'd seen me and I'd not seen them. The drawl was unmistakably Bayou. Turning to face where the voice came from, I felt the sun was strong through the cloud cover. It was hot, the air was thick with humidity and dense with mosquitoes.

"Well, praise be to Gawd!" exclaimed a voice I knew much too well. It felt like I'd sunk into the Bayou, but that was just my heart.

How in the hell had that scumbag found his way down here? This seemed more amazing than my making it here.

My sodden clothes threatened to pull me under. I glared at Carl, the jerk who'd sent me on the run.

"It floats!" Carl rejoiced. "I was right. I was telling my cousin, I said 'This Lenny is a welch.' If I were him I'd pretend to be a goddamned body and whaddyaknow?"

"Why don'tcha c'min, have your last supper?"

This supposed cousin made this offer so Carl could feel like the goddamned Godfather allowing me a nice meal before being rubbed out. But I stood firm, live or die, I was doing it in the water; it'd gotten me this far.

My kingdom for a reed that could double as a snorkel, I thought. However, I wasn't unprepared for such a situation. With daily reminders of the real ever-present dangers of the world afloat in every river, I anticipated needing survival skills both in the water and beneath the surface.

Hyperventilation was easy to achieve as I was halfway there. I just hoped I was retaining enough oxygen.

To Carl, I must've looked nervous. We were about a hundred yards apart. His cohorts often joked he needed glasses, so he'd not be able to tell what I was really doing.

Submerged, I was in a new world. There had been so many times this summer where I had to plunge into Big Muddy. When I did she sure lived up to her name. The horrors I encountered were usually things I felt: errant severed limbs, driftwood, fish fins, aluminum cans slicing at my kicking legs, and weeds.

Diving in the Bayou brought a different kind of fright. The swamp water was tinged green and more stagnant than what I was used to diving in. Its brackishness made it hard to keep my eyes open. The bodies in my immediate vicinity did not glide around me on a current like vehicles driving on a highway but rather bobbed and swayed like boats in dead tide. The flotsam and jetsam here seemed more abundant and obtrusive than I'd come across before.

Then I saw a short, scaly arm with sharp nails pawing at the water. Jokes about a zombie apocalypse had long since ceased to be jokes, but an anticipated future based on the present. This seemed like the real thing until the reptilian maw opened wide about twenty yards in front of me—facing but not looking at me due to its sideways-facing eyes, was an alligator. It was a behemoth, fattened on the endless smorgasbord these waters offered it.

Reaching into my pocket I confirmed I still had my Bowie knife. Forward I went whipping my legs in unison like a fish while cutting my arms through the undertow freestyle. Funnels of bubbles flew into my line of vision. The 'gator's legs writhed and it rolled—it looked like it was trying to eat a cormorant. The 'gator rose out of the water. It plopped back in. I felt the current push into my back.

The bird must've gotten away. An angry, hungry 'gator was out there now. It propelled me onward.

Looking over my shoulder, the 'gator was fifteen yards back and closing. It knew I was fresh meat. Facing forward again, through the green, I saw arms reaching for me. They grabbed my shoulders. If it was Carl or his cousin, I didn't know. I reached for my knife. Hands around my neck tried to choke me out.

Knife in hand, I swung at his leg. Blood in the water, his grip loosened. I swam around him, another approached. The knife went into a leg once more. It stayed there and I swam until the world started graying at the edges.

When I came to the surface I caught my ragged breath and swam over to a sandbar. In the water I saw blooming red blood-clouds. Out of it came a rosy spume. It was the cousin. Sliding back, I thought I may need to stand. The ground was loamy beneath me. Fear etched on all the cousin's features, a momentary pang of guilt seared through me that this man was caught up in Carl's nonsense, maybe through no fault of his own. My hands found purchase. Could I raise myself up if I needed to and keep an eye on the danger in the water?

Ripped violently into the water, the cousin vanished into a new larger red bloom. The 'gator saved me from a decision. My body relaxed, I needed to catch my breath all over again.

As I sat amid cattails a-sway in the breeze, the clouds were painted in technicolor shades as the sun set behind them, and I marveled at the fact that the water saved me. Most of all there was an emptiness, now that I had survived, accomplished my mission, I felt I was adrift.

* * *

Bernardo Villela has short fiction included in periodicals such as Coffin Bell Journal, The Dark Corner Zine, Sparked Literary Magazine and forthcoming from Eerie River Press. He's had stories included in anthologies such as From the Yonder II, Queer as Hell, and Disturbed. He has had poetry published by The Ekphrastic Review, Zoetic Press, and Bluepepper among others.
Website: www.miller-villela.com

The Legacy of Ol' Peg

Ilyn Welch

Throughout years prior to 2022, Shelly lived in the riparian hills, her body and knapsack absorbing earth and woodland odors. Because of the recent bad fire there, she migrated to the shadows of nearby towns, unfurling her sleeping bag in nooks of buildings, snuggling up to structure walls, lump of her nylon-encased body like a giant egg sac.

The night she snuggled up to Ol' Peg's fence, a man with a revolver and a long beard tickling his beer belly had just sicced his dogs after her. She scrambled over a likely unpermitted brick wall, height medium, too high for canines, low enough to clear with her bindle. On the other side was a two-foot-wide dirt path, county-mapped as an alley, overgrown with grass. She traversed forward, dog snarls fading behind her. The curving trail paralleled various fences of various properties. Compared to the vinyl and cinderblock fortresses, Ol' Peg's fence was homey and rustic.

Shelly slowed her pace, entranced by light glimmering through the fence slats. Eye to a wood knot hole, she discovered little flickering tonsils of fire inside wide-mouthed winter squash lanterns, all with small slits for nostrils and almond-shaped eyes. *Late or super early for Halloween*, Shelly thought. The squashes were arranged throughout the yard as if cocktail party attendees. White-haired Ol' Peg relaxed in a rocking chair, the sway causing her smiling, wrinkled face to alternately shadow then illuminate in the pumpkin flame light. A sizeable pendant shone on the old woman's sternum.

Tired, Shelly encamped for the night alongside that fence.

The next morning, Shelly peeked through the cracks and watched a voegelin emerge from Ol' Peg's cellar. Its tail pointed straight up toward the bright morning sky. *Like a baby possum's tail,* she thought. The rest of its parts were reminiscent of a prehistoric terror bird, including short sinewy arms, with a touch of Puck, horns on head. It camouflaged into a sapling copse, scaring away a flock of bushtits. Through the wood-fence slats, Shelly saw the voegelin's tongue lick bugs off the leaves and tree bark before it disappeared in the shade.

It was the second voegelin sighting in Shelly's lifetime. Sometime after the fire, she had seen one from a distance on a misty Sunday, scurrying inside a morgue carport. One of her two guidebooks, *Illustrated Spirits Almanac*, helped to identify the creature:

> *Voegelin—a malevolent spirit permanently tethered to the exterior property around a building. It is permitted in uninhabited spaces such as basements and chimneys. Magical guardians of the property control a voegelin. A voegelin serves as a minor counterbalance, in that it is used to manage life cycles. Its duties include pest control.*

Shelly's other book was *Birds of the Southland.*

The remainder of Ol' Peg's yard was plentiful with flowers, fruit-bearing trees and vegetable patches, one dedicated to squashes. Near the center stood a wood post more than a yard tall, topped by a compartment. Like a birdhouse. Or the little free library where Shelly acquired her two books. Unlike the little library, the door was a face carving, just like the jack-o'-lanterns, instead of a window.

A screen door squeaked open. Ol' Peg stepped out, stretching arms, one dangling a basket. Sunlight glinted on her pendant. Her white T-shirt image was the three little kittens, of the ancient nursery rhyme, who lost their mittens.

And they began to cry, thought Shelly.

The old woman approached the wood post, touching the amulet to the compartment's lock. The small door with the face clicked open. Reaching inside, Ol' Peg retrieved a pair of garden shears, so tarnished the blades were rusted blood red.

Ol' Peg tended plants and harvested. When the basket filled with food and blooms, she returned the shears, locking the box.

Shelly stayed put, claiming the secluded weedy alley as her habitat, losing track of time in a steady cycle of chilly nights to hot days. *A lucky spot*, Shelly thought. If her presence was known to Ol' Peg, the elderly woman never let on.

Every few days when the home occupant ventured out to run errands, Shelly risked her convenient circumstances by removing two loose fence boards to pick fruit in the yard and access the never-locked back door to use the bathroom.

While Shelly raided the icebox and pantry, she admired Ol' Peg's bric-a-brac. Up-close photos of Ol' Peg showed her ever-present pendant to be a naïve face within a skull shape, bordered by etched lines reminding Shelly of sunrays.

Sometimes Shelly snuck to the front of the home to check out the scene. Ol' Peg's property was set deep within a cul-de-sac, slightly isolated from other homes, some flying militaristic flags. The street-facing exterior of the house was boringly neat, barely accented by a couple unremarkable hedges devoid of blossoms—no hint of the slice of beauty on the premises' flipside. The driveway was dotted with oil stains from Ol' Peg's faded-gold Camry. Once Shelly witnessed the lonely old woman wave to a neighbor who ignored the gesture.

The warmth of the sun woke her one morning. Through dewy weeds, she saw the two planks removed. Sitting up, she felt the weight of a necklace: Ol' Peg's pendant between her breasts. Shelly quieted her breath and crept to the fence opening.

Holding a watering can and wearing the cutesy kitten shirt, Ol' Peg stared directly at her, waving. "Goodbye," she said.

The old woman approached a row of pumpkins, pouring H_2O, picking off a yellowing leaf, quietly examining the ripening bounty.

Crackle.

Shelly thought it was the bushtits hopping. But the stir wasn't routine, it was disruptive. Bursting from a corner of shrubs, the voegelin bipedaled to the garden shears cabinet, its door ajar. It snatched the shears, bounded to Ol' Peg, who turned, accepting the first stab under her left clavicle. The old woman fell among the vines, the voegelin repeatedly thrusting the sharp object into the center of an expanding crimson stain, the color saturating the shirt fabric, obscuring the heads of two kittens.

Ol' Peg stilled. The voegelin licked the dripping blood off the garden tool.

Stomping back to the wood box, the creature placed the shears inside. Tail quivering toward the sky, it defecated at the foot of the pole, burgundy scat rough and bumpy with seeds. Then the voegelin crept into the cellar opening, pulling the single door shut, handle ring clanking against the weathered wood.

Shelly heard only her own shallow breath, until a gentle stir from the tops of some foliage-dense trees.

It wasn't bushtits, but a few golden-furred creatures climbing down. Walking on teddy-bear legs, they approached the squash patch, placing prehensile hands on Ol' Peg's corpse. The tallest one broke away toward the wood post, giving Shelly a full view of its monkey face: earnest features amid blue-white, all framed by dazzling orange fur.

The amulet face, thought Shelly.

The monkey face locked the shears box with a click. Grabbing an ordinary trowel, it scooped up the voegelin's feces and moved to the cellar. Hoisting the door open, the being hurled the poop into the nether and let the panel slam shut as it trudged back to Ol' Peg.

With paws and shovels, the creatures dug a hole alongside the body. After gingerly rolling her into it, they covered Ol' Peg with the earth, patting it with nimble hands, feet and tails into a slight mound, arranging squash vines around the shape in an act of reverence rather than camouflage.

When the big monkey face approached Shelly, she hid under her sleeping bag. The bag rustled with caresses and light reappeared as the creature pulled the material away. The others joined the task, gathering her things. The leader, a couple feet shorter than Shelly, assisted her in standing. The group coaxed her through Ol' Peg's garden, into the house.

Inside they gathered at a round table, where the leader dug

Illustrated Spirits Almanac out of her bindle. Opening the gilt pages to section S, it pointed a leathery digit at an entry:

Snub—magical, benevolent guardian of property. Considered a deity.

She squinted at the illustration of a face, identical to the faces around her, like the amulet, the carved symbol on the garden shears box, the jack-o'-lanterns.

From a nearby desk drawer, the Snub leader extracted an envelope, handing it to her.

Addressed to *Shelly*, she read the neatly printed letter inside.

Dear Shelly,

It is your turn to be sheltered here. You will replace me. To the outside world, you will be me, as nobody pays attention to Ol' Peg anyway. Just as well, right? With the amulet, you will be protected from any hassle from outside. Most importantly it will protect you from harm within, from the voegelin, who lives here in eternal limbo.

All legal documents for the property show Ol' Peg Shelly as the outright owner. Those documents and others are in the same drawer where the Snub retrieved this letter. All bank accounts and the Camry are in the name of Ol' Peg Shelly. The same for our shared driver's license; its photo as well as photos around the house will change to resemble you and will age as you grow older. Once you assume the position, the Snubs will ascend the trees out of sight. Even the voegelin can't find them. They are guardians of this paradise.

Devote time to maintain the garden, tending with the sacred shears—but always lock them up when not in use! It's Ol' Peg's one vulnerability to the voegelin, to be embraced when you are ready to transition. Eat the food the garden bestows, rejoice in the flowers, save the seeds to replant, keep the cycle flowing. At harvest and throughout winter, carve the pumpkins in the likeness of the Snubs, to honor and celebrate them.

You will know when it is time to reabsorb into the earth: when someone like you appears to take up your role as Ol' Peg. You know what to do. Your death will be a rare sacrifice for this small bit of enchanted land and space. Believe me, the anguish will be short and sweet. The Snubs will ensure your burial rites. We will meet in another incarnation.

We are the same,

Ol' Peg

P.S. Put this letter back in the drawer, where it will recycle and adjust for the next Ol' Peg.

Shelly looked up from her reading, finding the Snubs gone. She moved toward the yard, seeing their backs ripple and tails undulate as they walked to the trees. Their coats flickered, translucent in the sunlight, becoming invisible as they ascended into the leaves and branches.

***

Ilyn Welch (she/her) writes horror and mystery from the Inland Empire in Southern California. She has contributed articles to Flagrant Media and flash horror to PANK. Connect with @IlynWelch on ye olde Twitter.

No Land for Man

Emma K. Leadley

Special Agent Harvey Drake watched the feed in silence as the drone flew above the treeline, HD camera capturing every precise, sunlit detail of the terrain below. Steam spiralled from his third coffee of the morning, the previous two next to it, cold.

His first drone had gone down last week. Three experts had scrutinised the recovered footage and all reached the same conclusion: a freak accident. The drone hit a tree branch that had swung into its path, probably blown by the wind. However, when they recovered the machine, they discovered it on the periphery of the woods, rather than at its last known GPS co-ordinates, close to the centre.

No scientific records accounted for the isolated few acres north of Houston. It was a mandated 'no fly zone' but no documentation existed and after satellite surveys showed no apparent cause, Harvey and his covert team were told to investigate. Reports showed no radiation damage, chemical leakage, or unnatural growth patterns. Heat scans reported no sign of life. The entire team knew the existing data couldn't be right, but there was no time between drone launches to requisition a fresh batch of readings.

Now, the second drone was flying in. Static crackles popped sporadically from the microphone. Harvey crossed and uncrossed his arms, his attention entirely on the trees coming into sharp focus. They were tall conifers, forming a dark and dense mass that filled the monitor.

More static pops and crackles broke across the near silence, becoming a constant background hiss. The drone was now above the edge of the firs. Harvey and his technician leaned forward. The screens pixelated and flickered, filling with static snow and the background hiss increased in volume. Both men clamped their hands over their ears. Then, nothing. The screen cut out and once again, heavy silence filled the room. The hairs on the back of Harvey's neck prickled as he frowned at the void in front of him.

"Okay," he said, rubbing his face as the buzzing in his ears faded. "Bring it back and we'll try again tomorrow."

"Chief?" the tech's voice wavered in panic. "Chief!"

They stared at the screens. The static flickered and danced in technicolor, pixelated whirls and loops. Harvey squinted at different angles, as though it were a lenticular photo. The image resolved.

"Is... is that a face?"

Eyes flicked open to show black pits devoid of pupils. A mouth widened into a gaping maw. Sounds warped and twisted from the monstrous construct until words formed, thick and oily as they were uttered.

"This... is... no... land... for... man...."

The screen blanked. Silence grew.

The tech coughed and broke the tension. "We lost another drone, Chief." He slumped forward, whole body shaking.

"Did we get a copy of... of... whatever that was?" Harvey took several deep breaths, wiping his clammy palms on his trousers.

"It's blank. We have no data. There's... nothing?" The tech's face drained of colour, his eyes wide and unfocussed. "Where did it go?"

"We'll send a team in on foot tomorrow, find out exactly what's going on."

*

Early next morning, an unmarked truck crawled down the road running parallel to the woods. Dawn was breaking over the treeline and long shadows formed in the first light.

One of the detectors beeped more insistently and Harvey looked out. "There! What's that?" he pointed. "Stop the truck!"

Logan and Jay, both in hazmat suits, jumped out and carefully approached the object. Their cameras showed the warped and twisted wreckage of a drone spilling out on to the road.

"Bag it. Looks like ours. We'll check it over later," said Harvey, massaging his jaw to unclench the tightening muscles.

The truck crawled further and the detector sounded its warning again. The vehicle camera and thermal scanner showed a pile of hiking equipment with no heat signature.

"What can you see?" asked Harvey, as Logan and Jay approached.

"Backpacks, clothing, tents. There's a wallet here, too."

Harvey winced. "I'll deal with it. You need to go in. We need to find out what the hell's happening here."

The two in hazmat suits exchanged nods before heading into the dense firs. Logan, the taller of the two men went first, Jay scanning the rear. Their microphones caught light breathing and small twigs snapping underfoot but were otherwise silent. A few metres in, most of the light was blocked by tall trunks and thick branches.

"Do you hear that?" Logan asked. His camera showed him lurch to a stumbling halt.

"What?" Jay replied, catching up.

"Nothing audible roadside," said Harvey. He frowned as Logan's gaze darted in random directions.

"It's everywhere," Logan whispered, camera reporting him sinking to the ground and leaning back. A groan filled the microphone. "Everywhere."

"There's nothing here," Jay replied "Literally nothing but trees. It's creepy as fu—"

A crashing din, like an elephant stampeding through the woods, resonated through the microphones. As quickly as it sounded, it went.

"Where the fuck did Logan go?" screamed Harvey. "He just vanished off all comms."

Jay's camera transmitted clear images of the forest looking undisturbed. "I didn't see, Chief. He's just... just... not there."

"Back to the truck, Jay. Now!" Harvey's voice cracked and he balled his fists, thrusting them deep into his pockets.

The tracker showed Jay turn and move back towards the road. Harvey observed him covering the distance at a good pace, shouting for Logan as he ran.

A beeping grabbed his attention. "Logan's back on cam, Jay. Get out. We'll grab Logan then come for you. Wait roadside."

Moments later, the van drew to a halt. An orange hazmat suit lay crumpled on the forest floor, one leg caught on a low branch, waving like a flag. Harvey picked it up in trembling, gloved hands and turned it over. All electronics were intact, and there were no rips or signs of a struggle.

The sound of vomiting coming through his headset broke through his panic. He sprinted to the van and stared at Jay's visual, clamping his hand over his mouth as he himself tried not to retch. Logan was suspended high in the trees. Multiple branches pierced his torso, blood dripping from his wounds to the forest floor. Sunlight flooded in between the treetops to create a haloed outline emphasising Logan's twisted and broken limbs. His face was contorted in wide-eyed terror and his head lolled to one side, neck snapped.

"Oh god, oh god, oh god, oh why the fuck?" Jay drew in quick, sharp breaths, rocking back and forth on his heels. "Oh god."

As Jay and Harvey stared at the vision, vine-like fronds slithered to wrap around Logan's face and upper torso. They worked his jaw and chest until his voice rang out in angry jerks.

"I... warned... you... and... still... you... came... This. Is. No. Land. For. Man."

The vines and piercing branches receded until Logan's lifeless body thudded to the ground.

Jay's monitor flickered and Harvey started shaking, as a network of slithering vines filled the screen. Jay screamed, a piercing, agonising cry.

Harvey found his hazmat suit in the same place as Logan's, several hours later.

***

Emma K. Leadley (she/they) is a UK-based writer with multiple published pieces of speculative flash fiction and short stories to her name. She was a Grindstone Literary 2019 Microfiction Winner and Publishers Weekly once described one of her stories as 'standout'. She lives in Nottingham, with her husband and a rescue greyhound.

The Scent of the Sea

Jonathan Willmer

For a while now, Julian had been smelling the sea in the strangest of places.

"What was that?"

It was only for a second, but it was strong enough to smother the smell of the bins around the back of the Travel Inn, and the cigarette smoke.

"What was what?" The other guy looked at him without much interest. Julian hadn't learned the other guy's name. He didn't like him much; he didn't take the job seriously.

"It's gone now. You're not telling me you didn't catch that?"

In that instant the air had born every unmistakable quality of the sea: the salt, of course, the wafts of seaweed and brine and wet sand, but a great deal more besides; a particular kind of bracing freshness that can't be found inland, mixed up with the sickly candy floss and the doughnuts; a singular cocktail of varied odours which all combined in some finely balanced alchemy to become: the sea.

"Nevermind." Julian stabbed out his cigarette on the side of the bin and flicked it in.

It was only later, during an early evening lull, forcing himself not to look at the clock, shifting his weight from one foot to the other behind the reception desk, moving the sign-in book uselessly a few inches to the left and back again, watching the sky fade beyond his reflection in the glass doors opposite, that he realised this was not the first time he had smelled the sea without good reason.

The last time, a day or two ago, he'd been alone. It was late in the night, crossing the hotel car park under the orange street lights, pulling off his tie even before he reached the car. It had made him stop. Step back a couple of paces, sniff the air like a dog on a trail. But already it was gone, and there'd been someone coming towards him across the car park. He didn't linger.

And, now he thought of it, that hadn't been the first time, either. It had happened before, just the same, a few days earlier. Then it had barely registered, but now he was sure. And what about—

"Erm, hello?" The woman peered across the desk at him, not angry, but nonplussed. A small wheeled suitcase stood at her feet. "Hello? I said have you got a single room, please?"

"Sorry, madam. Of course." The formal manner clicked in instantly. Automatically he drew himself up, arched his shoulders back; his facial muscles, without prompting, arranged themselves into a smile expressing the perfect balance between amiability and solemnity. It was only a Travel Inn, but he prided himself on offering as high a standard of service as could be found anywhere.

The shift dragged on, one of those deathly quiet nights that presented no distractions. Even a hen party, floundering loudly across the foyer around two in the morning, gave him nothing to do. He scarcely felt the heart-shaped balloon, which somehow they'd managed to keep hold of for the whole night, bouncing off his forehead.

"All right, love? Anyone in there?"

The booze-sodden guffaws drifted away into the elevator, the raucous hollering barely piercing his consciousness.

Julian had left his car at home that day, as he sometimes did if he wanted to force himself to exercise. Usually he walked briskly, exhilarated by the cold and the rare solitude, the strange stillness of streets built for noise and bustle. But tonight the walk home was slow. He found himself stopping at every turn, retracing his steps, inhaling deeply, moving on. Was that the sea, then? No, not that time. What about that? "Sorry," he said, as some shadowy figure knocked into him from behind. He stood by to let them pass, and they grumbled something indistinct as they disappeared into the dark. He dimly remembered hearing something about smelling things that weren't there as a precursor to a stroke, or a heart attack, or at any rate something he'd rather not succumb to on a deserted side street at four in the morning. But he thought some more, and he was fairly sure that that was burnt toast, and not the sea. Was that it, that time?

But when it happened, there was no confusing it. He knew that for sure by noon the next day, after it hit him twice before breakfast: once on a gust of wind as he opened the bathroom window, and then again in the kitchen, a sharp saline blast that seemed to come from a jar of instant coffee granules as he tore off the foil. Each time, it hit him with all the dizzying force of a seaside waltzer.

The smell peeled up corners of memories that had lain dormant for years, exposed frayed threads that he spent the rest of the afternoon unpicking. The family dog they walked along the beach every Sunday without fail, the dog that he could only remember as a very old dog, its name lost to him; the hole he'd spent the day digging with his brother in the sand, so deep that neither of them could get out of it, but had to wait in there for hours, or maybe just minutes, shouting for help as the tide trickled in; the wind farm on the other side of the estuary that you could only see on a very clear day. His brother had told him that the windmills were aliens, like the ones from War of the Worlds, and that they were only waiting until the tide was out far enough to walk across on their spindly white legs. For a while he'd believed him.

"You're looking very lost in thought," said Jenny. He hadn't heard her come in. He sat at the kitchen table while she bustled around him, emptied her lunch box into the bin, washed it up at the sink.

He looked up at her. "Do you fancy going to Cleethorpes this weekend? Day trip?"

"Can't this weekend, can we? Got Hannah coming to stay." She looked round. "Don't tell me you forgot?"

"Oh yeah, no. No, of course I didn't. Never mind."

Jenny emptied the bowl out into the sink. "What's brought this on, anyway? You've never talked about the seaside before," she said, wiping her hands on the tea towel. "I thought you hated travelling."

Julian shrugged. "Hardly an intrepid adventure, is it? Thought it might make a nice change, that's all."

He wasn't sure why he didn't mention the smell. Because it was stupid, that's why. How would the conversation go? 'I smelt the sea today.' And what could anyone say to that? 'Oh'.

He didn't mention visiting the seaside again. Nor did Jenny bring it up. One of the cornerstones of their life together was a shared contentment in staying just where they were. He wasn't sure what had made him suggest the trip. Some ill-formed idea that the sea might be summoning him; that maybe he could exorcise the phantom aroma by answering its call, by going there. But the more he thought about it, the more irritated he became that the idea had occurred to him at all. He couldn't believe the world worked like that. No, the only thing to do was ignore it, wait for it to go away. It worked perfectly well for the sprained ankle he'd copped for at five-a-side last year, and the bout of flu he'd picked up before that. It was foolproof.

And it was easy to ignore, at first. It was easy not because it went away, but because, before long, the smell was everywhere; another part of the backdrop to life, like the dislocated shoulder that never healed properly, or the niggling worry that there might not be quite enough money in the bank for the month's standing orders. It was only at dinnertimes it was a problem.

"Mmm, what kind of fish is this?"

"Fish? Julian, it's chicken. You saw me cooking it. Are you all right?"

It was annoying, the smell of the sea covering up everything else, spoiling his food, but he could live with annoying.

It got harder to ignore when the ground underfoot turned to sand.

The first time it happened was when Hannah was over to stay. She'd just turned up, late because of train delays. She'd dumped her bags in the hallway, and then they had to dash out to catch their reservation. The restaurant was at the end of the road, so they walked. Jenny was telling her about the fish faux-pas. They were laughing about it.

"And there was me thinking I was quite a good cook," Jenny

was saying.

"Urgh, oh god."

It was only a fraction of a second, the length of a single footstep. He didn't know what had happened. He thought he'd trodden in something, maybe some discarded food, or worse. Jenny and Hannah stopped, looked back at him.

"What?"

But there was nothing on the floor; nothing on his shoes. "Sorry," he said, meekly.

"Come on then. We're already late."

It happened again on the way home—half way across the road. That same sense of the ground giving way. He stopped, looked down, saw nothing, stepped back over the same patch of tarmac. Perhaps it had gone soft in the heat; but it wasn't hot, and it wasn't soft, not any more. The blaring horn of an approaching car cut his investigation short. He dashed across the road to join the others, waving his hand behind him in a vaguely apologetic way.

"Jesus, Julian! How much did you have to drink?"

The third time it happened, it could only be sand. He was on his own, indoors, about to step in the bath. The sensation of grains of sand sliding between his toes and over his feet, of silk and grit simultaneously, was impossible to mistake. He looked down, and saw only the faded linoleum of the bathroom floor, peeling up at the edges, that he'd been trying to get the landlord to replace since they moved in.

Jenny was beginning to notice something wrong. He hated watching her trying to piece it all together; his sensory confusion, the lack of focus, the inattention.

"Have you heard of anosmia?" she said, looking up from her phone at him over the kitchen table, as he was eating breakfast, and she was eating lunch.

"What? Yeah, I think so. Loss of smell?"

He played out the conversation again in his mind; imagined her response, if he told her that it wasn't anosmia, it was the sea, and now the sand as well. It wouldn't be a mildly puzzled 'oh' any more. It would be panic, phone calls to hospitals, tests, the furrowed brows of a dozen doctors, and he couldn't deal with any of it. He couldn't tell her about the sea, but perhaps it wouldn't hurt to talk. He'd never told her, for instance, that he'd had a brother, once. But now was not the time.

"No, I don't think it's that," he said, gathering the last few wilted cornflakes on his spoon.

"You could take an interest, you know. I'm thinking about you."

"I know. Yeah. Thanks. I just—I don't think it's anosmia, that's all. I don't think it's anything. I'm fine, honestly. Sorry, I have to get to work."

At work it was easier to hide. He had the act down to perfection. Since he'd started at the job, the moment he drove into the hotel car park each day, he left himself behind, and became instead the archetypal Hotel Receptionist. He allowed nothing through the façade of etiquette and manners. He was proud of how completely he inhabited the role, and his pride wasn't diminished in the slightest by the occasional indiscreet sniggers from his less diligent co-workers.

But as he pulled his car into his usual space at the far end of the car park, turned off the ignition, opened the car door and swung his feet out over the tarmac, even this meticulously maintained wall was not enough. He stepped out from the car, and his feet sank into the sand. He didn't bother looking down. He locked the car and started toward the hotel building, bullishly ignoring the ground underfoot. It wasn't far, but the short walk was dogged by the sand, each step a struggle in polished black work shoes which were not designed for this kind of ever-shifting terrain. Ahead of him, he was painfully aware of three or four of his colleagues loitering beside the door. He was careful not to meet their eyes, but he knew they were watching him, and he could picture exactly the way they'd be looking; the glances they'd be exchanging.

"You all right?" said one of them, with scarcely contained mirth, when at last Julian had waded within speaking range.

"Yes, thank you. How are you?"

The sand didn't leave him all evening; the smooth, bone dry kind that fell away with every step, that his feet sank into when he stood still, but each time he looked down he saw only the marble floor. It meant he didn't get across the lobby in time to open the door for the elderly couple struggling with three suitcases. They made nothing of it, but the young man, later on, was less forgiving. He should have just let the man take the suitcases himself, but his professional instincts had kicked in.

"Please, allow me," said Julian, but when he then commenced to walk around the desk in such a slow and laboured manner, the man scoffed.

"Forget it," he said.

The relief of his cigarette break, round the back by the bins, was soured by the presence of the same co-worker who had failed to smell the sea. That was only a week ago; it felt much longer. Julian tried to hide his irritation at seeing him there. Did this man never work?

"You all right mate?"

"Yes, yes I'm fine. I'm fine." Julian lit his cigarette. It took a few tries to get the lighter going. He inhaled deeply and lent back against the wall as he blew the smoke out. He wished he could smell the smoke over the smell of the sea; some of the pleasure of smoking, he found, was lost. The two of them stood for a while.

"Weird," said Julian.

"What?"

"Traffic. At this time. Never thought you could hear the motorway from here."

"What you on about?"

"Traffic. Cars. Listen."

They stood for a moment.

The other guy shrugged. "Nope."

It took Julian until the next day to realise. He woke with the roaring loud in his ears. Even then, it took him a while to figure it out. His mind was cloudy with the remnants of a dream already forgotten, and his eyes were glued together with sleep. He flicked them open long enough to check the clock on the bedside table. Eight thirty in the morning; Jenny wouldn't have left for work yet. It was only three hours since he went to bed, but he wouldn't sleep again with the noise. He climbed out of bed and stumbled toward the window. He was expecting a storm, a gale, leaves blowing furiously in the wind, debris strewn across the lawn, but the day was calm. Nothing stirred. Next door's cat stood gazing into the pond at the end of the garden, and the water was still. But the howling continued, and it wasn't the wind, he knew that now, and it wasn't the traffic either, but waves crashing atop waves, and those cries; weren't they seagulls?

Jenny was in the kitchen. She said something, but he couldn't hear what it was. He threw his coat on over his pyjamas. He told her he was feeling sick; that he needed some fresh air. He told her it was nothing to worry about. He could only just hear himself over the waves. He hoped he wasn't shouting.

Outside, the wind whipped the sand up like needles. He zipped his coat up to his chin. He bent his head downwards and pressed on. He still had his slippers on; they were useless in the sand. He kicked them off and left them at the side of the pavement. Progress was easier, but walking into the wind was exhausting. He looked up, only for a second, wincing so the sand wouldn't scratch his eyes. He saw a woman approaching with a dog; a reddish-brown Afghan. He recognised it from a few doors down. The woman's hair was unruffled by the wind; the dog's long coat barely stirred.

Spray from the sea mingled with the sand. It was freezing on his face. He pulled his coat up further, so that it covered his mouth and nose. He felt pressure on his shoulder. The woman with the dog was grabbing him, trying to get his attention. His hands in his coat pockets, he shrugged her off. She wanted to help him, or fetch help. Perhaps she knew where he lived. He didn't look round. He couldn't hear her if she was speaking. She couldn't help him. He pressed on, each step a struggle, into the wind, and the salt spray.

The mist came down suddenly. When he next glanced up, he could see nothing. He didn't know where he was any more; had no sense of how far he'd walked. He'd forgotten how quickly the mist could descend by the sea. The weather worked in a different way by the sea; it followed its own laws. He'd forgotten how quickly the tides could change. He remembered the signs that stood at regular intervals along the beach like totems, warning about the changing tides. He remembered how silly they looked on a calm sunny day, ineffectually stern amongst the day-trippers and the dog-walkers.

He was at the water now. He felt it between his toes. It lapped around his ankles. The odd larger wave reached his knees, and the cold made him gasp. His pyjama bottoms were sodden. He stopped trying to move forward, as the tide advanced. He was fixed to the spot by the cold, and by the force of the waves, and the wind. He threw his coat off, and soon lost track of it as the sea carried it away. When the waves reached his chest, he lifted his feet off the sand and kicked forward through the water. He tried to keep his head above the waves, but it was impossible. He tried to swallow as much air as he could before he went under. For a long time, for almost too long, the waves kept him under. They spun him around like a plaything until he didn't know which way the sky was, and then they spat him out, and for a while he bobbed atop the waves like flotsam, filling his lungs ready for the next time, and as the waves pulled him down again, he heard a call, his own name, distinct over the noise of the waves and his own manic breathing, a call in a voice he thought he'd forgotten, and as the waves tossed him up again, again came the cry, fainter this time, maybe close, but surely too far, but he had to try, this time he had to.

***

Jonathan Willmer lives in Sheffield, UK, where he works as a postman. His stories have been published in Makarelle, the Templeman Review, Bandit Fiction, and Personal Bests Journal. As well as writing and posting, he plays guitar and keys in a number of bands.

Placements

Stephen Lang

All I have to do is spend a day on the surface. It's an achievement to proceed further than the written examination to qualify for placement. And I'm here early, which will make a good impression. This place—this city—is my first taste of their natural habitat. And no matter how much I've prepared, all the reading, note-taking and revision, it's still a shock when I see my first humans in the flesh.

I'm not supposed to draw attention to myself, but I can't resist the compulsion to do something before meeting the instructor; to make an impression, a connection. It's like I have to pinch myself to prove that I'm still really me, deep beneath all these layers, this guise, the one I might have to wear forever.

A mother and child cross the park towards a playground, the boy dashing ahead of her. I have to narrow my eyes to keep sight of them. There was no warning about the fierceness of the sun up here.

The boy sits on a swing and kicks his legs, wanting his mother to push him, but she recognises another parent. They're soon deep in discussion, shaking their heads. I need to listen and learn, but I only catch fragments.

It happens.

They are conspiratorial, united, as they continue to shake their heads over some calamity known only to them. *It happens.*

I stand in front of the boy and pull out the sixth and seventh fingers on my left hand. His eyes widen as I wiggle them, but it's more in surprise than fear. He doesn't look away as he tugs at his mother's skirt. *Mum, Mum.* She is too busy talking. *Mum, that man.* I am gone before he can get her attention.

Following them was difficult. It was easy to learn to walk

upright for prolonged periods, but shoes are hard to master. I've practised so much, but it only becomes real on the surface when you are interacting; being part of life up here and fitting in as a placement.

The instructor arrives and sits beside me on the park bench. This is only the second time I've seen her in human form. Like me, she is dressed smartly, although the fit of her suit isn't perfect. Most noticeably, the collar of her shirt sticks out in a triangle, making her neck comically thin. It's the same problem as my shoes. We can get the details of the anatomy right, but not the dressing.

I turn to face her, and we press our foreheads together in the standard greeting. Our thoughts intertwine. Mine are anxious, unsettled. Hers are soothing, the headrush a tonic to kick-start the day.

The instructor pulls away. She frowns.

"You're squinting," she says.

She hands me a small oblong box. Inside it, I find a pair of dark glasses. Sun theory is the first part of the curriculum. We learn the paths of the planets, so we are best prepared, although it's more about feeling the sun's warmth and understanding its role as a life-giver. I get that now.

We leave the park and walk downhill to a more populated area. The surrounding roads are full of traffic, eager to arrive and conduct business. The instructor gestures at a sign above a glass-fronted cafe. Costa Coffee.

"I'll wait here," she says. "If you can get me a skinny latte. And whatever you're having, of course."

I've rehearsed the first test so many times, the art of the transaction. Words tick over in my head. Tall. Take out. Contactless.

There are three baristas—one to take the order, one to prepare the drink and one to serve it. I pay and give a name—Rich. The first barista writes on a plastic cup with a squeaky pen. *Rich.* The instructor stands outside as I wait, hands in her pockets and watching me through the glass.

The third barista calls for Rich and confirms the skinny latte as he places it in front of me. His eyes widen when he catches mine, and he tips the cup over with his elbow. A wave of dirt-coloured liquid rushes across the counter, reaching as far as my sleeve, staining the white cuff. The first barista helps to wipe up the mess, and the second prepares a replacement drink for me.

"I'm sorry," he says. "I'm *so* sorry."

"It was an accident," I say. I pick up the new cup and nod by way of thanks. "It happens."

*

The second test is the art of blending in. We walk on, merging with the crowds, and I take the opportunity to improve my shoe technique. I ask more questions. The instructor must have heard them dozens of times before, but she's happy to answer. I'm feeling more at ease now, confident.

And then it does happen.

I see a man with auburn-coloured hair, brushed back untidily from a low forehead. He's wearing a dark suit, similar to mine. We're not supposed to recognise other placements, but he sticks out.

The suit doesn't fit. The sleeves are too long and cover both his hands. His presence might spoil the second test, and instinctively I do the one forbidden thing. I call out to the instructor as she crosses the road ahead of me. Passers-by stop and look at her open-mouthed. It's not a word in their tongue, nor a sound they could easily repeat. I call her name again.

The instructor turns to me. I can see it in her face. *What have you done?* She drops the coffee cup. Is it really that bad? Judging from her expression, I know it is, but I don't have time to react as the van slams into her. The force of the collision throws her into the air. She lands with a crack on the surface of the road.

Humans run to her. Others hold back, deciding who should make the emergency call. It's like the incident in Costa Coffee. Humans are always ready for disaster to strike, collectively poised to take immediate action.

I watch from the edge of the pavement as the driver jumps out of the van. He steps into the puddle of coffee.

"She just walked in front of me," he says. "She wasn't looking."

His voice is pleading. He's scared of what might happen to him. Nobody appears to be listening. What he said, though, is accurate. A pedestrian walked into the traffic without checking if it was safe.

In this form, we are brittle. We run the risk of being so easily killed.

*

I retrace my steps to the park. I don't know what else to do. The death of an instructor on duty must be unprecedented. I wait on the bench, watching the humans exercise the animals they keep as pets. I envy the dogs their freedom and long to be back walking on four legs again.

I see a woman in a dark suit, similar to mine. She approaches me on the path.

"Is there anyone sitting here?" she says.

I shake my head, and she sits beside me.

"Forecast stays nice until Saturday," she says.

I turn to her and take hold of her shoulders. She opens her mouth in surprise, perhaps expecting more of a preamble to our greeting, and I press my forehead against hers. She tries to push away as I probe. I hold tighter, but it's flat inside her mind, two-dimensional. There's no connection.

She shudders. Gently at first, like she's cold, but she can't be on this warm summer's morning. She starts to shake as her life drains away.

I catch her as she slumps, and her head falls on my lap. I push the body up and rest her head on my shoulder. Passers-by are looking at us, and I pretend to whisper something as I brush the hair from her face.

She was not a placement. It was unfortunate, like today's other accidents. It happens.

I position the body upright on the bench with the head leaning back and facing the sun. I put my dark glasses on her. She looks relaxed, like she's enjoying the day. Somebody will come along soon and ask if there is anybody sitting here. This is how they will find her.

*

I climb the steps of a tower standing at the top of the park. From here, I watch the day end and begin again in the morning, left to right, because the tower is south-facing, as sun theory has taught me.

Blue and white tape marks out the surrounding area of the bench far down below. It reflects tiny glints of sunlight as it quivers in the breeze. A police officer turns away a curious jogger from the crime scene.

I can see the road from here where the instructor died. The human authorities will find out that she isn't traceable. She had no identity on the surface, no pretend placement details or made-up name to give to baristas. I must find her body and take it home.

It might help if I ask a familiar face where the hospital is, so I make my way to Costa Coffee.

I order a skinny latte, and the first barista asks for my name.

"Don't you remember me?"

"Sorry?" he says.

"I was here yesterday."

He shrugs. I point to the third barista.

"And you. You tipped over my cup."

I hold out my stained shirt cuff so they can all see it.

"Surely we can remember this as a collective?"

"A what?" says the second barista.

They stand staring at me; the production line of coffee-making stalled. We all wait in silence.

"Can you hurry up, mate?" says a voice behind me. "I'm due at the hospital in half an hour."

I turn to see a man in a tracksuit, and from how it hangs on him, I can tell he's wearing it more for convenience than to exercise. He has zipped it to the top to keep his thin body warm.

"The hospital?"

"Yeah," he says, "and I hope they give me some drugs as good as the ones you're on."

I take hold of the tracksuit, the teeth of the zip biting into my hands.

"Where is it?"

He doesn't answer. I've lifted him an inch from the ground. I feel the fabric of the tracksuit begin to tear.

"Where is the hospital?"

*

Patients look at mobile phones and glossy magazines. If I've learned one thing about human life, it's the sitting and the waiting. They know what to do and how to deal with the tedium.

The receptionist doesn't look up from his screen, but he knows I'm here.

"I'll be with you in a minute," he says.

I count sixty seconds as he pushes a mouse around the corner of the desk, clicking.

"I want to know about someone who died yesterday," I say.

He looks up.

"Sorry," he says. "Can you say that again?"

"Run over," I say. "She wasn't looking."

"Just a moment, please."

He rises from his chair. He goes over to another human sitting in an office area behind him and whispers in their ear.

Humans are so easily prone to excitement. The receptionist is summoning others to help deal with the problem, that collective thing they do.

I trip and fall as I run from the hospital reception. Both of my shoelaces have come undone. The spilt coffee, the van collision, the woman on the bench and now I'm surrounded as I lie on the floor. It happens.

*

I stare into artificial light. The room is roughly ten feet square, with walls, floor and ceiling tiled in white. My hands are secured behind my back.

There is a door, also tiled, but no window. I want to be outside. The forecast stays nice until Saturday.

I push the door with my foot. It clicks open.

"Knock knock," says a voice.

A man stands by a desk and two chairs in another tiled room. He has a bushy moustache, and his sandy hair is receding. He's wearing a leather jacket, a shirt and tie and jeans. Smart casual, somewhere between the man in the tracksuit and me.

"What's your name?" he says.

"Rich," I say.

"Okay, Rich. I'm Detective Inspector Howard. I think it's time we had a chat. Don't you?"

He's holding a plastic folder, fat with papers, which he places on the desk as he gestures for me to sit. I have missed many mornings on the surface. I do not want to be here.

"Can we talk outside?"

He shakes his head.

"Here is fine," he says. We sit, and he opens the folder. "So, I have you down as assaulting a pensioner in Costa Coffee on August the ninth. Sound familiar?"

He places a sheet of paper in front of me on the desk. I don't look at it. I'm more interested in him and how he avoids eye contact. He lights a cigarette, unusual as I thought humans had as good as outlawed smoking. He examines the burning end. Perhaps it's a prop to avoid looking at me.

"Oh, and it says here you're a witness to a road accident that happened the day before. August the eighth."

He positions a second sheet of paper beside the first. I don't look at it. He inhales and exhales from his cigarette.

"One of our men in suits trailing you says you saw the incident and walked away."

"A man in a suit?"

Howard balances the cigarette on the edge of the desk as he studies the paper.

"Oh, and I nearly forgot, you're a murder suspect."

It's the word murder that forces me to look. Murder is a thing that humans can inflict upon each other. It doesn't feel real that I am now their murder suspect. The third sheet of paper is a monochrome copy of a photograph. It's the woman I killed on the bench in the park, smiling into the camera. The sun is behind her, lighting the back of her head. I imagine how the photograph might look in colour; her fair hair made more golden by the sun.

Detective Inspector Howard clears his throat.

"We have testimonies from two dog walkers that you were with the deceased in Brandon Hill Park on August the eighth. The post-mortem found the inside of the victim's head crushed like the remains of a cracked walnut at Christmas. We're still trying to work that one out. Fair to conclude it was an eventful couple of days for you that week?"

"Yes," I say. "Is this the test?"

Howard laughs, although his eyes are cold and humourless as he catches mine for the first time.

"A test?"

Howard presses a finger down on the face in the photograph.

"This is the deceased. Diane Bosniak. HR manager for the local council. Aged forty-four. Married with two children. She loved walking in Brandon Hill Park in her lunch hour. What happened, Rich? Why her?"

*

Howard comes to see me every day, although I'm losing track of time. He asks the same questions as he fills the room with smoke. Why her? How did you do it? I have only one question for him.

"How long?"

He never tells me. Howard wants to make a deal if I answer his questions, although I don't know if this means he will leave me alone or let me go. He removes my handcuffs, but he doesn't say what he wants from me in return.

"Is this a test?"

"I'm a very patient man," he says. "Here's something to think about."

He leaves the folder with me, the wad of papers detailing Diane Bosniak's life.

*

The new man combs his auburn-coloured hair from his forehead with his fingers. Something about him feels familiar to me.

"Where's Howard?"

"Detective Inspector Cruickshanks," he says.

"How long?"

"Tell me. Did we evolve from you? Or you from us?"

"What about Diane Bosniak?"

I've studied the contents of the folder. During the training, we learned about geniuses on the surface. Einstein. Lennon and McCartney. Da Vinci. Shakespeare. It was interesting to find out what the human race had achieved, but I learned much more from the biography of an ordinary woman who loved walking in the park at lunchtime. Diane Bosniak's lifeline also told me about the importance of family. Children and a seemingly endless succession of cats. Her husband must have loaned all this priceless information to aid whatever investigation he thinks this is; photographs, postcards, even old shop receipts.

I must not allow Cruickshanks to take the folder away, but he's more interested in the pictures he shows me on a computer. There are photographs of me, the instructor, and many others I don't know.

"Do you recognise them?" he says. "Are they placements? Or humans?"

He flicks through faces, all nondescripts in ill-fitting suits. I think these others are humans styled to look like placements, watching us.

"Now answer the question," says Cruickshanks. "Did we evolve from you? Or you from us?"

"Is this a test? I thought you were detaining me as a murderer."

Cruickshanks shows me a film. Humans surround a mortuary table where the dead instructor lies, stripped of her smart suit and dignity. There's no sound, only images, and I watch an electric saw silently slice off her arm. The humans take the severed limb to the corner of the room and flock around it like hungry birds, each eager to snatch a piece.

"You know," he says, "you haven't been doing a great job up here. You're so easy to spot."

Cruickshanks loosens his tie. Perhaps the film has made him nauseous, or he's preparing for his next move. I don't know why I find him so familiar.

"Your faces are blank," he says. "They're expressionless. And you don't move in the right way. You're easy to impersonate."

He launches himself across the room in a stiff march. He reminds me of the man who caused the instructor's accident on my first day on the surface. He pulls the sleeves of his jacket down over his hands. I realise it's the same man.

"How do we get down below?" he asks.

"You'll drown," I say.

His eyes widen.

"So, there is a way?"

*

The desk and chairs have gone. The new man stands in the corner of the interview room. His tie is undone, the ends falling halfway down the front of a blue shirt. There are circles of sweat under his arms.

"Where's Cruickshanks?"

"Detective Inspector Aristotelous," he says.

"How long?"

"As long as it takes."

Aristotelous leads me deep into the Earth. The humans have dug so far. We descend in a lift and then further by foot, where the burrowing is tight. The narrow corkscrew steps are the same as the tower on Brandon Hill.

The ground is rough stone, hacked away at a gradient. A human in a glass helmet, pale grey overalls and metal boots stands near a puddle of black oil. He reminds me of photographs I have seen of astronauts. He waves a mittened hand at Aristotelous.

"Good morning, Sergeant," says Aristotelous as he waves in return.

"You'll drown down there," I say.

The oily black raises thin fingers to feel. Aristotelous takes a step towards it, curiosity willing him forward as he realises that the black is a living creature. The fingers wrap around the Sergeant's leg, and he slips. I understand now why Aristotelous and the Sergeant waved to each other in greeting. The Sergeant's voice is inaudible from inside the helmet, so we are deaf to his screams as black overcomes the pale grey. He bumps across the stone, an inch at a time, as the fingers drag him down. He tries to pull them off, but his mittened hands are useless.

I want to remove my human layers and slip into the earth. Not to attempt to rescue the Sergeant but to go home. To breathe, to walk without discomfort and flex my limbs. Fingers and toes free. Me. But reverting to my natural form means I will have failed as a placement. I am not even inclined to reveal my sixth and seventh fingers to Aristotelous.

I follow him up the corkscrew steps. He is muttering and shaking his head, but I can tell from his hastened pace that he is satisfied. The Sergeant was sacrificed for this test to determine if I would attempt to escape. And I did not.

"You can never go down below," I say.

*

Aristotelous threatens me with the electric saw. It screams like it will scythe me in two any second. The unbearable sound serves to block out any attempt I might make to reason with him. He abandons the saw and prods at me with instruments as blunt as spoons as he tries to peel away my layers. I resist like a crab retreating to hide inside its shell, curled up as small and as tight as it can manage, waiting for its tormentor to give up and go away.

The papers cover my tiled floor, a timeline running left to right and top to bottom. Aristotelous fails to understand that if he threatens to remove the life of Diane Bosniak, it will make me do anything, say anything. It would make the most effective test.

Aristotelous invades my space, treading on a collection of memories - Hastings 2011—like he does not even notice it there.

"We've widened the sinkhole," he says.

I shake my head. There's still a lot to do. I need to sort through Padstow 2015. Whitby 2018.

"I confess to the involuntary manslaughter of Diane Bosniak," I say, knowing he doesn't care about her.

Aristotelous turns his back on me, his blue shirt soaked in sweat.

"I'm prepared to play a waiting game," he says. He closes the door behind him as he leaves.

*

Weeks pass, months. The sun is forever hidden from me, moving from left to right. I have missed so many days.

"Knock knock," says a voice.

The man on the other side of the door is familiar to me. The thin hair at the sides of his head has now turned white. His jeans are baggy on him.

"Detective Inspector Howard? Is that you?"

"Just plain old Mr Howard these days," he says. "Call me Neil, please."

He uses a walking stick to cross the interview room. He studies the interior, but there are few changes. The only difference is the missing desk and chairs.

"How long?"

"How about I take you up for a stroll?"

It's mid-morning when we reach the surface. I widen my eyes, letting the sunlight feed them.

It takes me a moment to recognise the hospital car park. I have travelled no distance in all this time, only underground, but far enough to hide me from the sun. Howard has fallen a few paces behind me, and I wait for him to catch up.

"I need a better pair of shoes," he says.

"I studied every moment you made available to me," I say. "Of Diane Bosniak's life. Did I pass the test?"

He takes my arm.

"I had a fabulous idea. That's why they brought me out of retirement to come and see you again. It takes an older mind to crack a difficult nut, doesn't it?"

"What happened to the others?"

He hesitates before answering.

"Cruickshanks is still around in a different, er, capacity. Aristotelous has gone. Reckless man." He bites his lower lip. "The stupid fool wouldn't listen. Or did you mean your own kind? The placements? Nowhere to be seen, I confess. We failed to catch any. Recalled or abandoned to die after they lost you, we've concluded. That was our long game, you see."

"How long?"

He shakes his head as he gently squeezes my arm.

"Have they looked after you, Rich?"

"Mostly."

"Ten years."

"Thank you, Neil."

"I think it's time to run my little idea by you," he says.

*

My students are keen to assemble and start the curriculum. They'll work together as a team. That collective thing humans do.

I've promised little, only that the human volunteers can begin to experience life below the surface. What it was like for their ancestors, or what might be their destiny. I don't know who evolved from who.

It's a beautiful bright day up here. Ten years is not even a heartbeat in the sun's lifetime. I'm due at the simulator, but I have a job to do.

I didn't know what type of flowers to buy. I decided on a variety of bright colours for Diane Bosniak. There is a gold-lettered plaque on the bench, but not dedicated to her. It names a stranger who loved walking in Brandon Hill Park and admired the view from this spot. I sit down, placing the flowers beside me.

I see a child in an oversized hoodie. His mother pushes him on the playground swing.

"He'll grow into it," she says when I join them.

I show him how to tighten the Velcro straps on his trainers. She adjusts her t-shirt that has slipped to reveal a bare shoulder. The differences are now more subtle than cheap off-the-peg suits. Neil Howard and his associates have missed their recent visitors. The placements have learned, adapted and evolved.

The boy wiggles the sixth and seventh fingers on his left hand. He's one of us.

I press my forehead against theirs in turn and urge them to go. All placements must leave before they acquire a taste for the sun, or they will mourn it forever if separated. I warn that the humans are preparing to descend, but they will likely drown. I tell them that no test results are conclusive.

*

So much has changed. The crowds are denser, and there is more traffic. Costa Coffee has gone, but the layout of the roads is the same, and I have no difficulty locating the spot where I saw the instructor for the last time. The sky is azure blue, spotless of clouds.

All I have to do is close my eyes and step forward into the road.

***

Stephen Lang has harboured a lifetime love of all things terrifying. His short stories have appeared in the six, seventh and eighth volumes of the BHF Book of Horror series. He is working on his first novel, scheduled for completion in 2023. Stephen lives in Bristol with his family and an elderly black cat.

Find him on social media @LangWriting

I'm a House but I Must Scream

Basile Lebret

The house lay adorned and alone, a long-forgotten cathedral. Cecilia didn't see it at first, for her eyes were tied to dark figures hovering over a purple background while "We're All Going to Die" by Zheani played along. The art side of TikTok.

They were only two in the car, her and her dad. Timothy had oddly succeeded in not coming—God only knew how. Her mom had simply refused. "I don't see why she should be allowed to fuck with us after she's dead," had been her exact words, but underneath them in the deep streams that sprout life that slithers laid a perfect and still lack of motivation. Some basic needs to not help with golden parted eyes.

Cecilia knew they had arrived, even before her dad absent-mindedly said "We're there," for the vehicle began to shake as it crossed onto some tough gravel.

The house laid there and it seemed … spiky. Gothic would be a better term, almost baroque, so adorned with tiny sprouts Cecilia could not yet discern, that it seemed the abode was alive, spreading. A cancerous cell.

On closer inspection, the concrete fistulas weren't buds or design flaws. Seemed like the vast majority were santons. Gazing upon their porous nature, Cecilia couldn't help but touch the moldy ornaments. As the mineral void caressed her digits, she wondered if every face of the structure were covered with the tiny Catholic figures.

"Your mom used to take you buy some around the holidays. D'you remember?" Asked her father as he tried to unlock the door.

Cecila searched her memory 'til she found a blurry fragment of a child version of her begging to bring back home a cement figure of a tiny farmer. The air smelled of love apples, and a warm flavor she would, in time, discover to be warm wine. Before entering the village, she hadn't known that such characters could be put in a nativity scene. There were modern-day representations of blue-collar workers, bakers, enough plaster sculptures to muster a whole town.

The teenager didn't answer, instead going:

"Is the whole house covered like this? That's very Facteur Cheval."

"Fac…" wondered her dad as the door finally unlocked. "Ouh, yeah. Dude who built strange structures all over his house, right? Throughout all his life? Is that it?"

"Yup, sorta like the Abode of Chaos, over there near Lyon. It's funny what this man went for is now called art when THEY have to fight for the freedom of…"

But when she turned around, her dad wasn't there.

Cecilia stopped her explanation and followed through. The darkness of the house felt cold and smelled of dust.

*

The living room was as big and empty as the stomach of a roaming cat. Glimpse of sunlight creeping through the shutters caught flakes of dead skin whirling in the stale air which smelled of cold rock tiles. Everything stood still. The bulky cupboard on the other side, the giant table which seemed useless, the empty plate with its fork and knife beside it. A bottle of red wine laid open that her dad instantly took and brought to the corner that formed the kitchen and emptied in the sink.

If it wasn't for the dust, the place seemed almost clean. For an old folks' home.

Cecilia guessed that the only doorway she could see must lead to the bed and bathrooms. Above her dad's head, firmly stuck in the ceiling, a group of santons formed what seemed like a spiral from where she stood. Cecilia stepped in to try and light the whole place. As if the lamp overhead could diffract the hopelessness of the whole affair. Switch clicked uselessly.

"Forgot to turn on the fuse box. My bad," said her father. "Your grandma was special, you know?" As if his question could break the sigil.

"Guess that's why we never saw her, then."

The first answer of her dad was the empty bottle hitting a basket with a hollow sound, before he turned around.

"We never saw her because she went insane once Papy died."

"You shouldn't use such words."

"My mom was mentally unstable. When I was a kid, she used to tie my left hand to a chair so that I become right-handed."

"You…"

"That's what folks used to do. And still, this was before your grandfather died."

"Papy seemed like a nice guy."

"Let's just say Grandma was bulkier'n him."

"He liked to garden. A lot."

"He was fleeing from his wife."

"I thought she was an artist of some kind," said Cecilia as she stepped into the light, trying to regain some warmth. "I mean, when I saw the house."

"When he died and she got stuck in there, with her sins and her memories and her lack of children coming to visit, senility hit her. Hard and fast. Started protecting the house, she said. It's what the figures are for, she said."

"How do you know?"

"Not because I never took you that I never visited."

"Oh."

Sunlight cast the shadow of the teenager on a lozenge at her feet. Ceclia shyly stepped from one leg to the other.

"I'm sorry you went through this. As a kid, I mean."

"I know you are," said her dad absent-mindedly. It was clear he was scanning the environment to try and decide what to do next.

"Hrm, the fuse box?"

"Ouh, yeah, the fuse," said the father while snapping his finger.

As he disappeared in the doorway to the right of the tv, Cecilia barked.

"Dad, am glad you're my dad, you know that?"

"I'll take it," was his sole answer, but he was gone and only the darkness spoke.

*

Despite the gray clouds hanging overhead, a sharp light peeked through, as though diffracted by a gray veil. It clung and hit the façade and the statues which composed it with a rare violence. Painting sharp shadows that linked the whole plaster mess, burying the faces of many of the figures in delicious Tenebrae. Cecilia had no doubt, if she were to stay there and stare at the wall, the shadow would draw unscathed motifs of terrible knowledge.

The very phallic nature of the santon figures gave the house a resemblance to a scared puffer fish. Really was it any surprise that Catholicism had chosen to set up plaster figures looking like erections in their nativity scene? Remnants of the Briton dolmen, probably... What her grandmother had done with this tradition, the way she turned these symbols of the patriarchy into a forest of standing penis seemed both an unveiling of the hypocrisy behind it as well as a shield, a metaphor to an army of uncaring young men waiting for the glorious seppuku that'll cleanse their country. Maybe Cecilia was reading too much into it.

She sighed. A part of the teenager wanted to clean the darned structure. A green mold had started to spread over everything, erasing the bleak contrast that the whole composition must have had in its heyday. Closing her eyes, Cecilia could picture her grandmother, slightly bent, pressing on the tiny figures against the outer walls of her abode until they stuck. In her mind's eyes, the old lady had started with the upper right corner. The granddaughter imagined her, standing on one of those rusty, slick chairs that adorned every old folks' home, standing there, as the shadows of the few santons she had already put up turned clockwise all around.

"It must have taken some time," whispered the teenager for no one really but herself.

Mentally ill or not, this was some long-ass work. The immensity of it crashed across her skin like the smallness one might feel while staring at the ocean. She didn't deem herself an artist although she wrote from time to time, yet she could not fathom someone spending so many minutes, hours, whole-ass days, assembling such a weird composition.

Sure, the insanity might have helped. 'But where does the mental condition stop and where does the art start?' she wondered. Cecilia was of the school that there exists no clear answer to such a question, only vague concepts which float on the shitty river that's life.

She stood up, some gravel stuck onto the skin of her thighs, and began to circle the house. At this time, she didn't think of her father. She thought of the old lady, who dreamed plaster figures could protect her home. She thought of le Facteur Cheval Henry Darger. She thought of the Mighty Throne of James Hampton. How the grandeur of some endeavors makes you feel humble.

As they spread towards the back of the house, the figures started to grow in scale. They became grotesque. Underneath her feet the sweet sound of crushed gravel, all around cicadas chanting to find mates. The figures that started catholic and neat and nativity friendly turned more naïve. As if her grandma had given up on buying the damned things and began to mold them herself.

At first, it seemed as if the old women had tried to emulate the style of the saint figures she bought. Her first attempts looked like rocket made of clay, with eyes that were mere slits, remnants of prehistoric representation of vaginas. As her confidence grew, so did the plaster mouths. She had also certainly tried different formula of plaster. Here and there figures were either a sickly white or an odd gray. Sometimes, a hole, filled only by a circle made of glue could be found. Two third down the wall, the SpaceX shapes disappeared turning tsunamis, tornado. What could have passed for a Christian army turned into rolling wave dying by the sea.

Mouth became bigger, wider. Sometimes devouring the whole silhouette. The damn world. Staring at it for too long, one could feel the shimmers low growl bring to one's gut. Silent jaws twisting bodies, calling for help.

Cecilia put her hands on the clay she believed her grandmother had shaped, trying to find the digit of this ancestor she would never know. It made her feel dizzy for a bit. This, all of this proved the vacuity of life. As a snare choking on her trachea, she realized nothing really mattered. You may do something your kid will remember, but their children will certainly forget by the time the children of their children are born. You do not exist anymore.

With her Converse stuck to the ground, crushed by the sun, Cecilia for the first time experienced the spiral that is life that dissolves us all and when she came back to herself, her hand laid tightly gripped around what she thought was some proto-Christian Mary-Magdalene but could have been a demon.

For all it mattered.

*

The back of the house, the back of the house was mesmerizing. The structures grew in shape exponentially. One could witness the betterment of her grandmothers' craftsmanship as she continued her final days' work. If the right and left walls started unskilled, they ended in what seemed like art nouveau gargoyles. The waves had been tamed by the expert fingers of the elderly woman. While the overlapping of the beginning of the wall made Cecilia first think of Munch, she had to abide, it looked like Masha. Like Polish posters from the 70s. The search for details disappeared as though her ancestor had tried to mass produce the sculptures. Very art deco, très industrialism. It was both a rush and a quest in efficiency. The proof of the confidence her gran had grown in her bowels.

As if she'd hit this moment when she knew, given the time she had, she would cut on eyes and gills and digits, for what mattered were the mouths.

They were everywhere, like the eye cavities of long-lost species, trying to decipher the child's body language through holes in time.

*

When Cecilia came back inside, her dad was crying.

The overhead lamp, covered in stained glass, spread an infectious light upon the scene, both red and green and this gold only tungsten and the sun can really create. With her back to the open door, a small wind blew which brought the scent of dried wheats crashing into the damp interior. All around her father, the pieces of furniture now seemed like hungry animals lying in wait.

As he heard her footsteps, the father tried to regain composure, gulping on a sob or two. He felt more than he saw the shadow his child cast, covering him as a warm blanket against the cold, cold atmosphere.

"I don't know where to start," was all he said, smiling despite the recent traces of tears upon his face.

Cecilia scanned her surroundings, the desolate kitchen which smelt of old soap, the vast quantity of trinkets whose dusty smell didn't spread yet but would as soon as someone would touch them. With an inspiration, she took in the vague imprints of this life already gone, firmly forgotten.

"We could do the kitchen," she finally said. "Like, finding which ED has passed and all that."

"Yeah, that's a good idea," asserted her dad, standing up.

"Then we'd move on to the living room."

"But first, we need some plastic bags."

Tidying the kitchen was surprisingly easy. Maybe because old folks devoid of unexpected guests tend to eat less. One of the underestimated benefits of having estranged your progeny.

Overhead, the santons, the last her grandmother had set up, hung from the ceiling as sharpened teeth. Their ephemeral nature raining plaster on the father and his daughter. Despite this, Cecilia would often look at them. This was how she discovered the composition of the ceiling spiral wasn't random. The figures emerged from the back wall of the house as if they were following a procession which entered from the warm outside through the walls. Many of them had been cut in half to create this effect, growing out of the stones like ghosts from the past.

Cecilia was now sure the spiraling effect, à la Van Gogh, started outside before crashing in.

Sort of like religious movements invading your private spaces, like the spiritual education of your elders slowly strangling the adult you were supposed to be?

Or was it an allegory for dementia? An allegory that despite how many defenses one might put up, the disease finally rolls on like the tsunami it always was. Always will be.

Cecilia could picture herself, knee-deep in the sea, facing the rumble that's coming. Except blue veins crept across her hands like vines. As if she was some frozen abode, having held so still, the vegetation finally thought it safe to invade her immobility.

Those were roots that enthrall and keep dreams in check.

The rumble she heard from afar, as it got closer sounded like a cacophony of voices. Voices she'd never heard but already knew.

*

Her father had noticed there wasn't much food left, still he claimed they'd crossed a bakery going in. Lunchtime was upon them.

"What d'you wanna eat?"

"Tuna… Hm, I mean a veggie sandwich, and if there's nothing vegan, something that's cheese only, okay?"

"That's cheese, only, 'kay," answered her dad as Cecilia stared at her slick reflection in the aperture of the VHS player. She had never used one. Her face distorted slightly on the dark mirror, lamps burning bright as ghostly stars all around. Air smelled of this acrylic scent only film really holds, but she didn't know that.

When the roaring of the engine of her dad's car could be heard from outside, she inserted her finger into the gap. There, in the innards of the VHS player, lay a tape. The sticker facing her, stained by a blue marker, appeared homemade.

The teenager gasped. For she thought she could make out her name written in a blurry, hastened manner.

She scanned every button on the device before pushing the one with the eject symbol. With the sound of a mechanic roll, the tape exited its lair. "For Cecilia" was written upon it. She took the artifact and turned it around, enjoying the cold texture of calcified petroleum beneath her fingers.

"How could've she known me?" she wanted to think but said aloud instead, "This is stupid."

Pretending to scan for options, she searched for the remote. It lay naked and shiny on the plastic cloth that seemed to strangle the living room table. The sticky feel of the tarp, the cool breeze of the remote underneath her digits.

Her nan was there, on the tv. Cecilia couldn't remember having pressed any button. It was the manic stare of her elder that made her uneasy. Part of her knew the woman was here, painstakingly looking at her, not on the same plane, but in the same timeframe.

The smell and the aura and the presence of the deceased polluted the whole residence. It stunk and it clung onto the walls, onto her son's body. Onto her every child.

"We all disappear," was the first thing the past said. "We pretend to forget and we busy and we make children and they leave and we realize we don't love anymore but we stay. We build this shell we think is robust, fill it to the brim. Just like ships sinking. But instead of taking the water out, we pour it in. Until this mechanic motion we've accomplished so many times becomes us."

It was at this moment, Cecilia noticed that the camera which was pointed at her gran seemed to breathe. As if someone was holding it. But the elderly's words drowned the teenager's doubts.

"We accomplish it so much 'til our back hurts. 'Til when the task disappears, we don't know what we are anymore. Smart people, they'll go ahead and find a new routine. As if what we're doing isn't just preventing boredom, worries, death.

"We erect useless statues and put words on pages no one will ever read. 'Til everything ends up in a cardboard box even our kids don't know the innards of. We. Never. Was.

"Did you know people used to adorn churches with gargoyles so as to ward off evil? It is said that, should the grotesque statues be faced with pure evil, they would scream indiscriminately. So when their twisted bodies began to appear on the ceiling of my bedroom, I knew what I had to do.

"I erected mausoleums and statuaries to keep them and their red eyes at bay, but every time they'd find a way. And the work went on.

"Of course your grandad didn't care and got mad and rebelled. But that's solely because he couldn't see them!

In a whisper she added: "They crawl upon your sins like aphids." But Cecilia thought she meant skin.

"Luckily, he died and I didn't even cry, for I knew I didn't love him. Hadn't in so long. What I needed was to protect us, was to protect me against the tide that's coming.

"D'you see my fingers?" asked the gran holding up her hands. And in a tangent world her granddaughter answered: "Yes, I can see 'em." Therefore realizing the digits were covered in some gray goo. Plaster.

"You'll drown in the work 'til you can't recognize your hands no more," asserted the elder.

Grandma, the old woman in the tv, she put her fingers onto the tv screen and Cecilia knew, knew she hadn't done it on the camera lens. The goo, it spread on the glass, so thin Cecilia could picture her elder's digital imprint. Pressure so tight it shattered realms.

The tip of the finger split, a gland piercing through foreskin, a malformed baby cranium coming out of some insane womb. The flesh that shone through glistened and smelt of flowers drying under the sun.

As the naked digits pierced through the screen, Cecilia took in the flesh, getting stuck and piling up on the other side of reality.

"We. Never. Was."

*

"Even if it was dementia, it's still art. You can't just go and demolish the house!"

"I won't," answered her dad, who had come back from his grocery trip minutes prior. "I'll sell the land and someone else will destroy it."

Part of her was glad he had found her a veggie sandwich. With a little bit of imagination, she could picture the lonesome dad asking a middle-aged baker for something that would only contain tomato, salad and zucchini. Her heart melted a bit.

"But this is special, can't you see?" yelled Cecilia, letting her lunch drop on the way-too-large table.

"I can't," her dad said, and it resonated like a whip lashing in an empty cavern. "But am glad you see some worth in it."

"Some worth? For fuck's sake, dad! This some Henry Darger type of s-"

"Language."

"This just like the Abode of Chaos!"

"Isn't the owner still fighting his mayor in front of the European Supreme Court nowadays?"

"Oh, so now you know about it?"

"His updates are the only thing you post on Facebook. 'Course I know the Abode!"

Cecilia grabbed her sandwich with a fierceness that even surprised her.

"I'm no art-dealer, Cec'. I don't have the money to turn that into something. Neither do you. We'll talk about that once you graduate."

"You stalling because you think I'll forget about it once I go to uni."

It was her father's turn to stop eating.

"Whadda you want me to do? I should come here and sell tickets to stranger so that they'll witness what old age'll do to them? Fuck! Even if I were the least interested, d'you know how time and energy consuming that would be? But NOOOO, all you have in this teenage brain o' yours is a fucking project and I'm the one who should think of how it needs to be done. RIGHT?!"

The yells, they echoed hard enough that Cecilia worried the statues above the kitchen could fall. But they were sigil, protection. They didn't flinch as the scream reverberated among their bulky structures.

"I'm not saying that," said Cecilia, returning calm when faced with her father's anger. "But maybe you could buy me some time until I come up with something? This is important. She did it for us. She transcended."

"If it wasn't for the harm she inflicted to everyone around her, your grandmother would never be remembered. I don't think she deserves recognition."

*

The shadow of the grandmother loomed large, like that of a circus. It swallowed everything, every dream. Outside, the sun had started to fall, the blackness the house spread on the ground grew and grew 'til it crept upon the nearby trees. In the uncertain dusk, or was it a rising storm, the plaster statues seemed to wriggle like maggots inhabiting a cetacean carcass.

In the car, a few boxes had been piled up as Greek columns and Cecilia knew that once back home, they would disappear in the garage to gather dust and cobwebs 'til they never were.

"No tourists for you," she whispered for her only, as the sharp shadow of the house dosed her feet in a distant cold while the declining sun bathed her naked knees in heat. The dying day bought a cold wind which howled like a famished dog.

"I think we'll have to be back tomorrow," said her dad. "You sure you didn't forget anything inside?"

Tomorrow seemed far away because tomorrow didn't exist. Would never be.

As darkness took a hold of the world, the cave-like interior of the abode seemed to start glistening. An orange aura that could only come from flickering candlelight which did not exist. Cecilia felt drawn to its warmth, lying to herself that she had come back only to make sure she didn't forget anything.

The teenager spared a glance at the statues stuck high above the kitchen. Stalactites frozen in time or the teeth of some dangerous mammals. She thought of getting the VHS, the tape her gran had made just for her, and knelt by the tv set.

It was then she heard the chitinous stumping of a myriad of legs above her head. Thin flakes of plaster snowed down from the ceiling. Their scent making her nose irritated. She looked up.

Above her head laid what she could only assume to be a statue of Balthazar. The figure which had always been looking east now stared intently at her. Its mouth and eyes wide open as those of rabid sharks.

The terror, the pleading in its lifeless eyes.

Cecilia gasped.

The Magi began to howl.

Shrieks, wails, they came through the walls as if the whole world had begun to scream in pain. Cecilia knew that if she were to walk out, get far enough from the house, the countryside would resonate from those same cries coming from the closest church. She pictured the tourists in front of Notre-Dame stopping dead in their tracks as the chorus of millions suffering souls rose to the Heaven. The dread of stones.

"Cecilia!" Cried her dad while entering the house, panting. "Something's wrong with the sky." Behind him, heavens seemed to have gained in luminosity, yet the lights seemed grainier. Not the pale pink a summer evening lays upon the world but the hard grey of a miner's morning.

Air that came from outside spiked the nose as often do acidic agents.

Squatting by the tv set, the cold feel of the VHS player beneath her fingers, bathing in the plastic scent of the tape, Cecilia looked at the scared man, saw the child underneath, the old man he would never be.

"Gargoyles," she stated. "They're bound to scream only when faced with pure evil."

Cecilia sang along as the world disappeared.

***

Basile Lebret is a French blogger who lives south of Paris where the cities meet the trees. His work has been published in SlicedUpPress' Monstroddities, Donnie Goodman's Strange Weeds, AEL Press' Monster and Off Topic Publishing's Home. Find him on Twitter: @evoripclaw or Medium: https://basile-lebret.medium.com/

You and Yours

Matt Elphick

You don't remember your father. Not really. Not as well as you'd like or perhaps should.

There are snatches of images - a dimpled chin dusted with blonde stubble like a freshly harvested field. The smell of tobacco. Fingers worn thick and hard through work lifting the delicate cup of a Bluebell to show you the bee feeding within. A dock leaf rubbed against an angry sting. Nothing more, just fragments.

And stories.

So many stories. Always about the woods and the boating lake, long reclaimed by nature, at its heart. You've known these woods since childhood, took your first tottering steps underneath a canopy of hogweed, dragged a gasping carp onto the bank on a fishing line as thin as spider's silk. Poked at the worm-like guts of a squirrel that hung lazily from the still-smoking hole where the shotgun pellets struck it. Even after the passing decades, walking these paths makes you feel as you did then. These are your woods. This is your home.

You remind yourself that home isn't always a sanctuary.

They scared you then, the stories from Dad. Stories of the pale woman that crawls from the lake at night to stand dripping and hungry in the moonlight. The monstrous owl. The trees that move when you aren't looking. The ghosts of the young lovers that died in a boating accident. You remember one summer that left the grass dead and ground iron, when dehydrated birds died mid-flight, seeing the rotted skeleton of a punt emerge from the black mud as the water receded. You could've sworn you saw the bony curve of an empty eye socket among the wreckage and that, underneath the smell of stagnant water and rotting vegetation, you caught the metallic tang of death.

Of course, you're grown now and don't let your imagination run away with you anymore.

And yet.

And yet you still shiver despite the late-spring sunshine warming your cheeks. You still feel unseen eyes crawl across your back, still flinch at the call of a wood pigeon.

My toe bleeds, Betty.

Your dad whittled a hazel stick as he told you of the green man. This was one of his favourite stories, and he told it often, but something about this telling has stayed with you. It might have been how the blade of his penknife, worn thin as sunlight through years at the whetstone, flashed out a beat to the tale. Or the way the hazel stick turned into a spear under his careful hands, linking you to your earliest ancestors that would have hunted this land when it was first coughed up by an ancient sea. Ancestors that knew the green man all too well.

They knew to thank him when the bushes dripped with berries, and when the fish were fat and many. They thanked him at the thaw when the first new green buds unfurled. But they also cursed him, quietly of course, when a breaking stick alerted the deer that had been stalked for over an hour. A stick that had not been there when the foot was lifted. The green man loves his people but he grows restless. Sometimes, much like between siblings, love is shown through pranks. Or a balled fist to the guts.

Dad spoke fondly of the green man, but he was always the one that scared you the most. The others merely existed within a space, the lake, the wood but the green man *was* those places. He was the soul of the place, the ghost in a machine fashioned from blood and sweat and dirt. He was inescapable. Inevitable.

Perhaps that is why you feel unsettled, why you can feel the sweet itch of adrenaline warm the muscles of your limbs for action.

'Hello?' you call and as soon as the word leaves your lips you feel foolish. You dont expect a reply but you get an answer in kind. The wood seems to breath, it expands, swells, like lungs before a scream. You see movement at the edge of your vision, a flash of colour, there but not, like the after image of light when you stare at a naked bulb. You are not alone.

His face is first in the scarred bark of a tree, then the pareidolia of a bush's shimmering leaves. He circles you, just below the surface, skimming beneath the sheet of the world.

A shadow of fallen leaves sweeps across the ground towards you as though a cloud has passed in front of the sun. The shape scatters and reforms, a murmuration of discarded vegetation, twitching into the form of a face. The bare earth you stand upon is the blackness of a cavernous mouth and leaf lips reach up to drag you into the throat of the land.

You know you are falling by the way your hair lifts from your head and your clothes whip around you but there is no rush of sound, only the slow creak of growing roots and burrowing worms.

A solid surface rises to meet you and you are rolled like a die in a cupped hand. You are weighed by a fat tongue of limestone a millenia old.

You hear the wood, the green man, smack his lips.

I recognise your flavour. Yes, I have tasted the fat of your father, licked the marrow from his bones. I have savoured the rot that bloomed across his cold skin. But I have tasted you before too. In every scraped knee and cut palm. In every molecule of blood that was spilled.

"Is this death? Am I dead?" you ask.

Perhaps. Of a kind. You have all distanced yourself from the land, from the inevitable. Your father knew the simple truth: Everything grows towards death, and from death everything grows. You and yours would do well to remember it.

"So this is the end?"

No, this is a beginning.

***

Matt Elphick is a writer of dark fantasy and horror stories that make frequent use of folklore and mythology. He is a Visiting Lecturer in Creative Writing at the University of Winchester and lives in Hampshire with his son and far too many books.

The Last Summer

Hannah Brown

Sometimes, the world makes you sit with the knowledge that you fucked up. It makes you hang there in stasis, drowning in your own mistakes, seeing the surface above you, just out of reach. The surface glitters with the hope and promise, but you can never reach it. Because you fucked up.

Big time.

Breaking into the train yard is easy if you know how. This isn't related to my fuck up, just some information for the enterprising teen. No one really checks all of the fences that carefully - no one is being paid enough to do that job properly - and there's a fence over near to the woods that kinda curls up at one corner. You can peel it up and wiggle through no problem.

So I do. The train yard has always been one of those spots to me. A place to go when the world feels so damn small and crushing. As I wriggle under the chain link on my belly, camera held out and forward in one hand, so I don't accidentally crush it, I think about drowning again.

Breathe, Fawn.

Once inside, my brain reorients itself back to neutral. I creep through the skeletons of discarded trains as everything returns to almost normal. Slightly off-kilter, but liveable. There's something so lonely about train cars with nothing inside them, something forlorn about the lone engines with nothing to pull, untethered and drifting.

I stay away from the workers and they pretend not to see me as I take photos of the loneliness. Lining up my composition, pouring something from myself into what lies here. Left behind.

When I get too close to civilization, I'm warned off by the

workers and slink away, deciding to call it a day. I make my way back to my fence and my way out, but I pause on the threshold.

The woods beyond the fence are leaning towards me, buffeted into a makeshift bow by the strength of the wind. A hum buzzes throughout their boughs and vibrates through the air like static electricity.

It touches me, that sound translated into feeling, rolling over me like a wave made of a thousand stings. It paralyses me for a moment; I am overcome with a sense of wrongness. My place in the universe as but a small insignificant spec.

I lift my camera and take the picture, the chain link in soft focus with the darkness of the trees looming in the background.

And the sound recedes, taking with it that taste of fear. I finally breath out, as if I have avoided the executioner's bullet.

"Weird," I say aloud, needing to fill the silence left behind by the absence of… that.

Then I scramble through the fence and take off at a run, heading back into town.

Later, when I'm alone down in the basement developing film, avoiding the phone call I know I should be making to check in with mum, I start with that photograph. There's something there, I'm sure of it, but when I look at it…

Nothing.

Just an overexposed brush of white where the picture should be.

*

Amber's house has a back garden that butts up against the Avon river and, just beyond that, there are the tracks leading to the train yard just down the road. As I sit on the roof of her garden shed, the dark is too dense and unforgiving for me to even begin to see them.

Jackson is sat next to me, rolling a joint without much success. I'm no joint rolling savant, but even I can tell this is probably the first time he's ever tried this. Amber's house is right on the edge of town, which is why we're all out here. Her parents are only out of town for a weekend, and it would probably make much more sense to try using my place, but I live in a terraced house and we'd immediately be in trouble with the police.

So, Amber's it is. She's playing some moody guitar heavy music, blasting it out of the open wide patio doors and into the night like she's daring anyone to make a noise complaint.

"Give it to me," I finally tell Jackson.

"No," he says, tongue pointing out of the side of his mouth, "I've got it."

All the girls in our group have been going crazy for Jackson lately. The growth spurt and the swimming have made him very shoulder-angular, which seems to be something likeable. All I can think, as his tongue pokes out, is how this is the kid who peed himself in morning assembly when we were kids.

I pull my camera up to my face, pointing it up at the sky for a moment. The moon isn't big enough to be visible, and I give up on the stars too after a moment. Light pollution.

But then I hear Amber scream and turn to snap her picture as Garett picks her up in a rugby tackle of a hug. They fall over quickly, because Garett isn't exactly sober, and she falls on his chest in the grass. As she pulls herself up I take another picture, they look good together like that. Though we all know that they definitely should not be making another go of their relationship.

Especially not now that Garett is dating… whatever her name is.

"Oi," I nudge Jackson with my ankle, "what's Garett's new girlfriend called?"

"Who?" Jackson asks, finally succeeding in making the world's most curled up joint.

"Garett's new girlfriend," I say, squinting as I try to remember, "she was at Ava's party last week, right?"

"No?" He says, lighting it and taking a hit.

"The girl with the…" I realise I can recall no details about this girl other than the fact that she was white. "Fuck, give me that."

He passes it and I inhale. No point in abstaining anymore, after all. I already lost everything; a little weed wasn't going to make anything worse. I pass it back to Jackson and lie down on the roof.

"You have such a shit memory," I tell him as he lies down beside me. "You sure weed is a good idea?"

"Shut up," he grumbles. "Do you feel anything?"

Not yet. I take the joint back and take another low drag. "I wish we could see stars."

"Normally can from Amber's," he grumbles.

"No moon either," I say, reaching up my hand as if to touch that dark veil that hangs above us.

Audio feedback rips through the night, loud and distorted, almost like a scream. We both prop ourselves up to watch a Amber starts sobbing, her precious speaker having taken a short shower from an exploded champagne bottle. Without the sound of whiny guitar music, silence rushes in to fill the spaces.

There's nothing. My brain begins to scramble, trying desperately to hold on to something, a bone-deep sense of dread taking over me.

Should we be able to hear the river from here? I try to think back to the last time we had a party at Amber's, but nothing. Memories lost to the hedonistic whirl of life. It shouldn't be this quiet though, should it?

I hate getting paranoid. I sit up properly, stretching my arms over my head. "I'm gonna bounce," I tell Jackson.

He gives me a very mellow salute and I clamber down from the shed, pausing to say goodbye to everyone on the way out and rolling my eyes when I can't say bye to Garett and Amber because they're both too busy sucking face. Poor Garett's unidentifiable girlfriend.

I pick my way back through the streets, heading for home, unable to shake that clinging feeling that it's too damn quiet.

My house is empty as always, the silence echoing back to me as I stand in the threshold. I grab the house phone, for the first time actually wanting to call my mum.

But she doesn't answer.

I can't stand to look at any of my old photos. I've torn them down from my walls and hidden my portfolio. The portfolio that should've gotten me out of here for the summer. If I wasn't such an idiot.

Anyway, my walls feel weird without any of my work on them, so I go back down into the basement and develop the rest of my train track photos.

The process is methodical and comforting, just like it used to be when dad did this with me. Sometimes, when I'm down here, I pretend that he's sat in the corner, watching and critiquing as always, smoking away on his weird old man pipe. Dad was always weird, somehow even at forty he was already ancient. Mum said she thought he was a professor when she first met him at uni.

I pull the first photo out of the solution and frown. Nothing. An overexposed blur. The next is the same. And the next and the next. Some fuckups are par for the course, but no one fucks up this much.

Was my ISO too high? The f-stop too low? Or was it my shutter speed? But that didn't make any sense, none of those things would have resulted in this mess. At worse it would have simply produced a blown-out picture, not the foggy white nothingness.

I had to know. Pulling out my party photos, I went again through the painstaking process of developing them all.

Weird.

Not as overexposed as the train yard shots, not at all, but there were still weird bright spots in all of the shots of Amber. It was as if the film hated Amber specifically and had painstakingly banished her from each photo with a bright spot eclipsing her face in every one.

I should call her.

I leave my basement, pulling my phone from my pocket as I go out into the back garden and take a seat on the wonky iron patio chair, warm from being out in the sun.

I scroll through my messages, but I can't find Amber. So I search for her name; gone. God, someone must have changed the names of my contacts at the party. Probably Jackson. Whatever.

I toss my phone onto the table and flop over onto it. The air has that strange summer stillness to it. If there are any birds, they're too far away for me to hear them, but the sun beats down on my neck and back, warming me.

I'm bored.

I shouldn't be here. I should be in London. I should be working with professional photographers. In another universe, one not as myopic and chaotic as this one, I never went to that stupid party in the woods. I was never busted with ketamine in my hands.

My mum used to be a hippy, you know? Free love and rock-n-roll or whatever. But you wouldn't have been able to tell when the police brought me home to her that night. For a moment I had been worried she'd ship me off to borstal.

But this was worse. She'd cancelled my tickets to London, taken back her money, stranded me here for the summer, while she went to visit Aunt Libby in Exeter.

The only reason I hadn't run away, was what she had said to me before she left.

"If you don't care what I think about you, Fawn, could you at least think about what your father would think if he was still here? Do you think he'd be happy?"

Fuck, right?

I sigh, swirling dust motes into movement in my still and stagnant living room.

I miss you, dad.

*

It's too quiet. As I ride my bike through the village center it feels like a ghost town. There are less people on the streets than usual, less kids running through the streets, less old people on park benches.

I pedal further out of town, down side streets, towards Amber's house. She's been ignoring me for a week, and I'm done with it.

But, as I draw closer something heavy changes in the air. I turn the corner on my bike and stop dead, almost flinging myself over the handlebars.

Because there's nothing there.

No, correction, the woods are right there, leaning over towards me, bracketed by fields of bright yellow flowers. But Amber's house, the river, the road leading up to it, the train yard, they're nowhere to be seen. As if space had contracted, bringing the forest closer to town.

Standing there, frozen and straddling my bike, the silence begins to shift around me. And a low, terrible buzzing takes its place. It rolls over me, deja vu choking me, as it stings against my flesh like a thousand tiny static kisses.

I am gripped by the need to say something, but it feels as though my jaw is wired shut, as though the buzzing I can feel in my bones has more power over me than I do. Shit.

What is this?

Move, Fawn! Move!

"Fawn?"

Garrett's voice cuts through the strange heavy, buzzing silence like water on a bonfire. It recedes, as if disappointed, and I breath out shakily, finally able to move.

"Garrett!" I say, jumping off my bike and running up to him.

"Whoa," he says, smiling at me and reaching out a hand to steady me as I grind to a halt in front of him. "What's up?"

"Where's Amber's house?"

He blinks. "Who?"

I jerk away from him, his obvious sincerity rolling through the space between us like a gong. "Amber, you guys have been on again off again for like three years?"

He shakes his head as if something has hurt him, reaching up to rub his temple. "What are you talking about?"

"She…" I trail off, reaching up to grip my own head as a lightning bolt of pain bisects my temporal lobe. "Ah!"

He grabs me by the elbows, stopping me from falling over. "Fawn?"

I try desperately to hold onto it. Onto the memories of the girl who had given me a tampon that first day in year seven when I'd been caught unawares. The memories of the time she skied into me on the French trip and broke my leg. The memories of the girl who had held me when I cried at my dad's funeral.

But I—

What was her name?

I straighten, still gripping the side of my head, and I watch Garrett look at me, concern blooming across his features.

"Fawn" he says, "you're bleeding."

Blood drips across my lip, falling from my nose, I lick it away. The metal taste painful somehow. "I…" I trail off, keeping it to myself. Things got worse when I articulated them, so I mustn't. "I have to go."

I grab my bike and pedal away, headed again for home as fast as I can go. If I stop, I don't know what will happen. I'm scared of what will happen.

I ditch the bike out the front of my house and head into my bedroom, grabbing the plastic bin with all of my old photos from inside the cupboard.

I yank it open, and pull of sheafs of photos in my hands.

Blank.

Stark white.

As if they had never held friends and family inside of them before. No photos of Mum, or my friends or the train yard or anything past Orchard Avenue.

What does my mum look like?

I choke on a sob, my hands breaking out into an unstoppable shaking as I sort through the photos. Dad was still there. Jackson too. Garrett was almost still there, the edges of his photos beginning to blur.

Garrett lives on Orchard Avenue.

I jump up, running back downstairs and picking up the house

phone. I look down at the buttons and tears begin to streak from my eyes.

Because I don't remember Mum's number.

The number she ingrained into my head as a kid so that I could always call her no matter what happened. The number I had called when I found dad dead in the garden shed.

My mum's number.

My mum.

The memories were tearing away from me, and trying to hold onto them was like trying to hold water in my hands; a futile exercise in frustration.

"Mum!" I yell out, unable to stop myself. My voice breaks, and I feel that lightning sensation lancing through my head. Please no, not her too.

Please!

I fall onto the ground, gasping for air as the pain temporarily makes me forget how to breathe. "Mum," I cry out.

My head hits the ground as my arms slip out from underneath me.

Who am I yelling for?

My brain is a blur. I am barely holding onto the here and the now of it all. Tears track down my face and splash onto the floor. Blood drips down from my nose to join them.

God I can barely remember which way is up. Who was it?

Who did I lose?

Oh god, who did I forget?

*

Jackson is rolling another joint, though he's making less on an arse of himself this time. We are sitting together on my roof, basking in the last moments of the sun as it slowly slips down from the sky and towards the horizon.

Jackson lives right across the street from me, so he's still here. I tried explaining it to him, what was happening, but the explanation hurt us both so much that for a moment I had thought that maybe my brain might actually burst.

He's forgotten everyone. But I can remember them, sort of. As long as I don't say their names aloud or try to remember too much. Trying makes it worse.

"What day is it?" he asks.

"I dunno," I shrug, laying back on the roof and looking up at the cloudless sky. In the periphery of my mind I can hear the buzzing growing slowly closer, but there's nowhere to run. Not anymore.

"Summer's like that," he says, laughing, "and then suddenly we'll be…" He trails off, squinting, a muscle in his jaw jumping.

He can't say, back in school, because the school is gone. It went last week. "Back" I say to him, my eyes filling with a new flush of tears.

He looks down at me, and I can see the panic building in his eyes. I take the blunt from his limp fingers and finish rolling it for him.

"Here," I said holding it out to him. He took it with shaking hands and I light it.

"Fawn, what's happening?"

I smile at him and interlace our fingers. "Don't," I say, "it won't change anything. Let's just enjoy this sunset."

"The last one?" he asks, taking a deep drag and looking towards the sun.

"Nah," I say, reaching for the blunt as he passes it. The buzzing sound is building all around us, pressing down on us, buffeting my bones inside of my body and setting my teeth on edge. I inhale, "It's summer," I say, "summer lasts forever."

He laughs, squeezing my hand, and I ignore how desperate his laugh sounds and he ignores how sweaty my palm is against his, and we both inhale.

The buzzing feels like it is inside of us now, like our held hands are creating a loop feeding back into each other, intensifying the feeling of helplessness. I feel as though at any moment I will pass out or vomit.

I pull my camera out and turn it around, taking a quick candid photo of us, horror writ onto both of our faces.

"What's that for?" he manages to ask, over the sound of his own teeth chattering together.

"I want to remember this summer forever."

And so, we manage to laugh as we dissolve into the infinite buzz of the summer sun.

***

Hannah grew up exploring the rocks and crags of the South Wales beaches she called home and has since graduated to living on the islands in Tokyo bay. By day she teaches writing to teenagers and by night she writes until she drops. She has written horror shorts for Room Magazine and Fly on the Wall Press's Under the Sea Anthology. You can find her on twitter @Hannah_Aimee_17.

ALSO AVAILABLE
FROM BAG OF BONES PRESS:

www.bagofbonespress.com/books

Bag of Bones 206 Word Stories – A collection of horror flash. 206 bones in the human body. 206 words. 206 stories. An official 'Number One Amazon Best Seller'.

Annus Horribilis – An anthology of horror set in the pandemic riddled shit-show that was 2022.

Well, This is Tense –Second person present horror anthology. Part one.

This is Too Tense –Second person present horror anthology. Part two.

Thank you for reading this book.

Make no bones about it, we'll be back.

www.bagofbonespress.com
bagofbonespress@gmail.com
Twitter: @BagBonesPress
Instagram: @BagofBonesPress